WAKEFIELD CRIME CLASSICS

THE SECRET OF THE GARDEN

Arthur Gask was born in England in 1869. He migrated to Australia in 1920 and settled in Adelaide, where he wrote all his thirty-four crime and mystery novels. They were mostly published in England, and enjoyed wide readership there, in Australia, and across Europe.

A well-known dentist and wicked practical joker, Gask died in 1951.

'I always enjoy your stories, particularly when the criminal escapes.'
   Bertrand Russell in a letter to Arthur Gask

Also available in

WAKEFIELD CRIME CLASSICS

THE MISPLACED CORPSE
by A. E. Martin

THE WHISPERING WALL
by Patricia Carlon

BEAT NOT THE BONES
by Charlotte Jay

LIGNY'S LAKE
by S.H. Courtier

A HANK OF HAIR
by Charlotte Jay

SINNERS NEVER DIE
by A.E. Martin

VANISHING POINT
by Pat Flower

THE SECRET OF THE GARDEN

ARTHUR GASK

WAKEFIELD CRIME CLASSICS

Series editors Michael J. Tolley and Peter Moss

Wakefield Press
Box 2266
Kent Town
South Australia 5071

First published by Herbert Jenkins Limited, London, 1924
Published in Wakefield Crime Classics February 1993

Copyright © The estate of Arthur Gask, 1951
Afterword copyright © Peter Moss and Michael J. Tolley, 1993

All rights reserved. This book is copyright. Apart from any fair dealing for the purposes of private study, research, criticism or review, as permitted under the Copyright Act, no part may be reproduced without permission. Enquiries should be addressed to the publisher.

Edited by Jane Arms
Designed by Design Bite, Melbourne
Printed and bound by Hyde Park Press, Adelaide

Cataloguing-in-publication data
Gask, Arthur
The secret of the garden
ISBN 1 86254 291 0
I. Title (Series: Wakefield Crime Classics; no.7).
A823.2

ISSN for Wakefield Crime Classics series 1039-4451

CHAPTER 1

It was the old fool of a judge himself who turned all my thoughts to bitterness. I know quite well I lost my temper, but he ought to have made allowances for that. I was under the terrible disappointment of being found guilty when I fully expected I should have got off. I was worn out with anxiety, and furious, because I didn't consider I had had a fair trial. Everything and everybody had been against me, and I don't wonder I hit out. I know I threatened, and said personal things about the judge that made the court laugh, but the judge ought to have been above petty spite and have taken no notice of my outburst at all.

Instead everyone could see he was annoyed, and he just snapped out, 'Five years!'

Five years! What a monstrous sentence! The whole court seemed to gasp, and even the beast, Drivel Jones, I saw, lifted his eyebrows in surprise.

No wonder I shouted and raved, but I only got handcuffed and dragged away roughly for my pains.

Everything had gone badly for me that morning. It was the second day of my trial, and the judge was over an hour late. I was fretting and fuming in the prisoners' room. I knew the trial was bound to be finished that day, and every minute I was kept back deepened and made more unbearable my suspense.

A good quarter of an hour before ten I had been brought

there ready, and I sat with dry mouth and shaking knees, waiting for the summons that would take me into the court.

Ten o'clock struck, and I expected every second that the door would open and I would be called out. But the minutes passed and nothing happened. The quarter hour chimed, then the half hour, and then the threequarter. It was a terribly hot day, and the prisoners' room, tucked away at the back of the building, was ill-ventilated and stifling. I felt sick with the heat and the suspense.

There was one warder in charge in the room with me, and he appeared to be feeling the heat quite as much as I was. He was a surly, ill-tempered brute and, knowing his disposition, I had not attempted to exchange a word with him since we had come in. He had brought a newspaper with him, but it was apparently to be only of service as a fan.

Soon the door opened and one of the court policemen came in. He glanced at me and then entered into conversation with my guard. For some reason he was as annoyed as I was at the unpunctuality of the judge. From his remarks I gathered he was afraid the dinner hour would be curtailed. He said no one knew why the judge was late, but they had found out he was motoring up that morning from Victor Harbor and it was thought his car must have broken down.

They had learnt he was away from home from the telephone people. They had tried to ring the judge's private residence in North Adelaide but had been told it was no good to try there because the house was shut up and everyone was away. No one had any idea how long the judge would be.

As soon as I heard this, my suspense, rather to my surprise, took on a fierce and unreasonable anger.

'A nice muddle now!' I said truculently to my astonished hearers. 'Everybody to be kept waiting and the whole business of the court held up, just because Mr Justice Cartright takes it into his head to go and sleep fifty miles away from his work. Gross mismanagement, I say, and if he had his billet with a private firm he'd lose his job.'

The policeman grinned delightedly.

'You tell him so, sir,' he said, and I saw him wink at the warder. 'He'll be interested, I'm sure, and it might make him more favourable to you when he comes to make his last little speech to the jury.'

'Well,' I went on, and ignoring his sarcasm, 'I'll take care it gets in the papers. I'll write to them this evening myself. There are several other things I want to complain about, too, since I've been on remand.'

The warder looked at me contemptuously, but the policeman, cast in a different mould, was disposed to derive any little enjoyment he could from my ill temper.

'You're quite right, sir,' he laughed encouragingly, and with his mouth stretching almost from ear to ear. 'There are a lot of things want ventilating here, *and this room is one.*'

The door opened sharply and another policeman put in his head.

'He's come,' he said laconically, and the first policeman, springing briskly to his feet, left the room.

After that, in less almost than two minutes, it seemed, I was walking up the short flight of stairs that led into the dock, and even before I was in view of anybody in the court, the cold, unctuous voice of the judge was falling on my ears. He was apologising for being late.

I stood up close to the rail and looked defiantly round the court.

The judge was telling them his car had broken down, and he was lucky to have got to the city at all. The misfortune was hardly likely to occur again, however, and, in any case, the possibility of it could be put away in a few days, for in a week exactly he was returning from the seaside and would be resuming the occupation of his city house. He smiled and bowed and all the lawyers smiled and bowed in return.

'Damned lot of hypocrites!' I swore to myself. 'All pulling together the same way. Pretending to be shocked when nobody goes astray and rejoicing when some poor devil falls into their clutches – for the law must get its criminals, or it won't be fed.'

Then my trial went on, and the vile Drivel Jones opened his final speech for the prosecution.

I have often gone back in memory over those last hours in the court and marvelled over the surprises that grim old Father Time had in store for some of the actors there.

First, there was me, John Archibald Cups, aged thirty-two, ledger clerk of ten years' standing in the Consolidated Bank of South Australia, and prosecuted for systematic embezzlement by my employers.

It was a lie. I had been honest as a clock all my life, and it was just the sudden accident of chancing to pick up a ten-pound note in the corridor of the bank that had given the brutes their opportunity.

I didn't deny that I had picked it up, and I admitted that I had hesitated for a moment to consider whom I should take it to. But it was only for a moment, and in another minute it would have got round to the cashier. But they had given me no time. They had planted it there deliberately and had pounced on me the very instant I had swallowed the bait. That was why I was in the dock.

The judge, Marcus Cartright, was a consequential, bombastic old fool. He was curled and scented and had beautiful white hands. He was a well-known fop in private life and a customer at our bank. I had often seen and smelt him when he came in. He was a great friend of our chairman of directors, old Carnworthy, Sir Joseph, and I had seen the two exchange smiles and nods across the court. The judge had a cold, even voice, and was a pillar of the church in his spare time. He was great on Sunday observance, and any sunlight and fresh air on that day were to be opposed vigorously with the rigour of the law.

Drivel Jones was the bully of the Bar, undoubtedly the most unscrupulous advocate in South Australia and a Goliath in the practice of the law. Everyone was afraid of him, and with his bitter, sneering tongue he could any time make black white, and white black. He bullied and hectored all adverse witnesses in a shameful way, and woe betide the poor wretch who testified to the truth when it didn't suit Drivel Jones's book. In his private life, racing was his great hobby, and he juggled and cheated with his horses as he juggled and cheated in the law. He was a crook of the turf, but there again everyone was afraid of him, and run his horses as he might he always seemed to manage it that he was never pulled up. He was a big coarse man with a ruddy face and large brown eyes. I hated him years before he ever heard of me.

My counsel, Pierce Moon, was a gentleman, but a fool. He had been put up to defend me because I didn't have the money for anyone else. He was no good and terribly afraid of Drivel Jones. I saw afterwards that I could have done much better if I'd defended myself.

The jury – oh Heaven! how was it possible that such a lot had ever been got together in one batch all at once – was a pack of gapefaced Methody swabs. They hung on everything Drivel Jones said, and when the blackguard flattered them, and with his tongue in his leering cheek told them he was certain they would see through my rascality as easily as he did, they looked like the set of fools they were, and seemed to purr like kittens over a drop of milk. Three of them I knew well by sight. The foreman, Pepple, was the ass who kept the vegetarian shop in Pipe Street. He was a little, sallow, wizened chap with a face like one of the dried-up raisins in his shop. He used to jaw about everything, every Sunday in the park, and his great idea was to purge your life of all pleasure, so that your mind would be clean and clear to think aright. Think aright, the poor fool! – and Drivel Jones, who was the entire opposite of everything he prayed for, just turned him round his little finger. Shucksy worked at the sewage farm and was always writing to the papers about the indecency of the one-piece bathing dress. I don't think he'd ever had a swim in the sea in his entire life. He had ginger whiskers and wore glasses, so thick they made him look like an owl. I saw him scowling at me, as if he knew I were guilty, even before the trial began. Byron James was the other juryman I knew. Another crank. He was mixed up with the anti-gambling crowd and used to play the part of an amateur detective and sneak round the parks to try and catch little boys playing cards.

A nice mob I had to face that day. It was a farce my fate should have been given into their hands, and the result was a foregone conclusion.

I have said I had no friends, but it was a mistake. I had Dick Rainton the trainer. He came up for me and gave his evidence like a man, and I could see for the moment that even the asinine jury members were wavering. He told them he was with me at Victoria Park, every moment of that afternoon when I was supposed to have been betting in ten pound notes, and he was positive I had never had more than a pound on any race any time.

I think for a minute the jury fully believed it was the truth he was giving them, but Drivel Jones wiped out the impression two minutes after by sneering at Rainton as 'another betting man of the same kidney'.

Of course, Drivel Jones, in his closing speech, came down like a sledge-hammer on my life. First he handed out a lot of flap-doodle to the jury. He held up the bank directors as extraordinary benefactors to South Australia and pictured them almost as angels of light. The commercial reputation of the whole state, he bellowed, lay in their hands. They were guardians of the public money, and in the security of their funds rested the confidence and credit of the community. The offence I was guilty of was not only an offence against private morality and the bank, but also a crime against the well-being of the people generally.

Then he pretended to describe my life. He said there was no denying from the evidence tendered that I was a racecourse gambler of a heavy type and wagered in large sums of money. Where, then, did I get the money from? he thundered. Where?

I could stand silent no longer under his vile lies and, in a burst of furious temper, shouted as loudly as he was doing, 'You're a liar – you're a damned liar!' I gesticulated wildly, and made as if to throw myself at him over the dock-rail, but the warder beside me pulled me roughly back and the judge sternly bade me keep silent or he would send me below.

I subsided, muttering, to a cold fury, and had the mortification of seeing Drivel Jones further ingratiate himself with the jury. He pretended, the hypocrite, to be only pained with my interruption, and insisted that, however unpleasant, it was his duty to speak the truth and conceal nothing.

Then he went on to make out what he said had been clearly proved. He would recapitulate the evidence, he said. I had been robbing the bank for years. On and off for a long while bank-notes had been missing but, until a few weeks ago, so clever had been my methods of theft, suspicion had not been focused on me. Then I had been watched and my movements noted, and what had happened. A note for fifty pounds had gone astray on Thursday, but its loss had not, unfortunately, been discovered until after I had left the bank premises. On the following Saturday, however, it had been paid into the racecourse totalisator at Victoria Park. I had been seen purchasing tickets on several races. The following Monday week a twenty pound note was found missing. It had been taken, undoubtedly, the previous Saturday. Later it was found it had been paid into the totalisator at Morphettville, on the afternoon of that day. I had been at the races again. Lastly, he came to the matter of the bank-note I had picked up, and he pictured everything at its blackest here. I was a rogue. I was a scoundrel. I was a systematic thief!

In conclusion, he implored the jury, as men of sense and intelligence, to allow no feeling of pity to obsess their minds, but to make sure that for a term of years, at any rate, I should not be loosed upon the community to make financial security a mockery and debauch the well-esteemed credit of the state.

Pierce Moon made a rotten sort of reply. He was not a

patch on Drivel Jones, and I could see made no impression on the jury at all. He bored them, and me as well, and I was glad when he sat down.

Then came the judge, and his summing up was as vicious and as one-sided a bit of special pleading as you could wish. He never gave me a dog's chance. I could see plainly he was damning me all through, because I had been given to racing. Every time he referred to the racing evidence, he looked significantly at the jury, and he dismissed them finally with the undoubted suggestion that they should bring in a verdict of guilty.

They were only absent about five minutes, and I could see from their faces the moment they came back what their verdict was going to be.

'Guilty!'

'John Archibald Cups,' began the old judge in even, unctuous tones, 'you have been found guilty after a fair trial, and all I can say -'

He got no further. I was mad with anger and disgust. 'Fair trial!' I shouted. 'It's been all a damned farce. I've never had a chance.'

The judge held up his hand sternly, but my temper overleapt prudence and, in the few seconds I was left free, I got in a lot of telling truths. I told him he was a scented, old fool, a narrow-minded bigot and a weakling, afraid of Drivel Jones. I said Drivel Jones had been allowed to bully my witnesses shamefully, and that the man was the most notorious crook on the racecourse side. I shouted that the jury were all imbeciles, and that vices of varying kinds were apparent on their faces. I would pay out everyone who had been my enemy that day – yes, if I had to wait twenty years, I would get my revenge. I would punish them all in my own way; I would –

But here the filthy hand of the warder descended on my mouth and, choking and struggling, I was forced to the floor. I fought savagely, but the warder snipped a pair of handcuffs on me and, exhausted at last, I was forced up to hear my sentence.

'Five years, with hard labour,' said the judge curtly, and with the assistance of two policemen I was brutally half pushed and half carried down the stairs from the dock.

A minute later and I was alone again, as I had been once before that day, with my solitary warder in the prisoners' room.

I leaned back giddily on the bench upon which I had been thrown, and strove manfully to gather in my senses.

'Fiver years' hard labour! My God – it was a life-time! I should be thirty-seven then, and a broken-down, middle-aged man. Five years – and I was innocent!'

My eyes roved desperately round the prisoners' room and came upon the warder. They fell vacantly at first, and then I realised that something was very wrong.

The man was leaning back in a strange way in the chair, his face putty-coloured and pricked out in sweat. His eyes were shut and his tongue half lolled from one side of his mouth. He was in a fit and perilously near to falling to the ground.

For a second I sneered callously at him, with no intention of going to his help. 'Let him fall, and break his neck – the swine; it will be one the less for me to punish one day. Let him hurt himself and – '

A fearful thought raced through me. The key! he had the handcuffs key in his pocket – the door of the room had not been locked – and he and I were there alone. Quickly, much quicker than I can tell it, I was kneeling by his side. With my handcuffed hands I fumbled in his pocket. Yes, there was the key. I grabbed it out and with lightning speed I thrust it hard between my teeth. With desperate force I pressed the handcuffs up against my face. Click, the handcuffs opened, and my wrists were free. I slipped the handcuffs into my pocket, put back the key into the warder's pocket, took out a sixpence, a box of matches and a packet of cigarettes that I found there, snatched up my hat from the table, paused for a second to button up my coat, pulled down the hat low over my eyes and, opening the door quietly, walked quickly out into the hall.

Everything had happened in less than a minute, and five seconds later I was walking unconcernedly through the crowd. There were lots of people there, but they all seemed to be hurrying off to lunch. Fortunately my clothes were of an ordinary dark grey colour, and there was nothing conspicuous about me at all. Two policemen were talking just in front of me and one moved out of the way to give me room. I passed Drivel Jones within two feet and could easily have knocked the cigar out of his grinning face had I wished. Pepple, the vegetarian ass, was on the pavement buying a paper, and he actually glanced up at me as I went by.

A tram pulled out opposite, just as I got into the street, and without the faintest idea of its destination I boarded it and sat down.

The conductor immediately came round for the fares.

'All the way,' I said laconically, and I passed over the warder's sixpence. My ticket cost twopence halfpenny, and I saw I had booked to North Adelaide.

The conductor jerked at the bell, the car glided smoothly away, and my association with the Criminal Court of South Australia was left behind me for ever.

Really, as I sat there by myself in the corner of that tram, I would have given anything to have been able to have a long, good hearty laugh. Everything seemed to me so irresistibly funny. Here I was riding off free, untrammeled and all alone, and yet not five minutes ago I had been sentenced to five years' imprisonment with hard labour.

Surely it was a mighty joke. As we passed the post office clock I noticed it was twelve minutes to one; well, at seventeen minutes to one I had been hard in the meshes of the law. I had been surrounded by policemen, warders, and all sorts of court officials, and yet, here, now, a bare five minutes after, I was absolutely alone and for the moment absolutely free.

Yes, it was a joke; but, at the same time, the weight of the handcuffs in my pocket reminded me that the joke might still have its very unpleasant side.

Where on earth was I to go? I hadn't the remotest idea.

The situation was a desperate one, and I was quickly sobered down. I had threepence halfpenny, a pair of handcuffs, a box of matches, and a packet of cigarettes, and none of my possessions seemed to offer any satisfactory way out of the difficulty I was in.

In a few minutes there would be hue and cry for me everywhere, and unless I could run to earth at once my capture was certain and would not be even a matter of hours.

I had no means of disguising myself, I had no money to get away with and I knew of no place where I could hide.

It looked hopeless and I began to think I was a fool to have escaped at all.

The tram pulled up at the terminus, and I jumped off quickly while the conductor was re-adjusting the pole.

With no idea at all in my mind, I walked quickly up a side road at right angles to the main one. Anything to get away from where people were, and the road here seemed a lonely one. The houses were all big and all stood alone in their own grounds.

It was a fearfully hot day, well over a hundred in the shade and there were not many people about. No one in Australia comes out more in the heat than they are obliged to.

For about five minutes I walked on in a rising fever of desperation and then, all of a sudden, came the inspiration that was eventually to be my salvation.

I was passing two big high iron gates, securely fastened with a big padlock and chain, when, happening to glance through, I saw three huge dogs prowling on the drive that led up to the house. They were enormous, fierce-looking fellows, and their great eyes, I thought, glared balefully as they met mine.

Like a flash it came to me to whom they belonged. They were the guardian watch-dogs of the eccentric recluse, Dr Robert Carmichael.

The doctor was a well-known personality in Adelaide, well-known, however, only by repute, for very few had ever seen him in the flesh. He never left his own grounds and, living in a big house among the trees, the gates were always chained and barred to all comers.

His place was called 'The Tower', because of a strange sort of observatory that rose high up from the middle of the rambling one-storeyed building that was his home.

But it was not because I suddenly remembered all this that my heart began to throb in fierce quick beats. A far more thrilling chord of memory was quavering in my mind. I was remembering also that Judge Cartright's house was the one next to his.

I had heard the judge one day telling our chief cashier in the bank that sometimes he could not sleep on moonlight nights, because of the growling of Dr Carmichael's dogs, as they prowled around. I was remembering this, and it came back to me also what I had heard in the prisoners' room that very morning, that the judge's house was at present empty and untenanted, on account of all the family being away.

'What a place to hide in,' I gasped. 'What a refuge and what a sanctuary, if only I could get in. Of all the places in the world, no one would dream of looking for me there.'

It was about a hundred yards further on to the judge's home and I was breathing hard when I reached the gates. Inverary! ah yes, that was the name. I remembered it now in the ledger books. As I had expected, however, the gates were closed and, to my dismay, I saw they were spiked and very high. The walls, too, on either side were quite ten feet from the ground and generously cemented over at their tops with lumps of evil-looking broken glass.

What an ass I was, I snarled to myself. Of course, the judge wouldn't have been such a soft as to leave his grounds open for anyone to get in. They would be locked up as securely as the prison stockade.

With an oath of disappointment I went to shake one of the big gates and, to my astonishment, it yielded instantly to my touch. It was unlocked.

I looked up and down the road. The quivering heat hung like a pall on everything around. There was not a soul in sight. I slipped quickly into the grounds and very gently pushed the gate behind me. Was it to be sanctuary after all?

My guardian angel must surely have been watching over me that afternoon.

I didn't walk straight up the gravel drive but, for some reason, I don't know why, tiptoed very softly over a narrow stretch of turf that ran along the flower-bed by the side.

It was well I did so, for I should have walked to certain detection else. As it was it was only by a hair's breadth that I escaped coming to my Sedan.

I was just turning round the bend in the drive that hid the house from the entrance gates when suddenly I heard the clink-clink sound of metal striking against stone.

I pulled myself up with a jerk so sharp that it hurt me almost like a spasm of pain.

A man was bending down behind a bush just in front of me; he was hoeing among the carnations. Another step and I should have been right on him.

Very softly, and almost holding my breath, I tiptoed back along part of the way I had come. They I turned off among the bushes and, making a long detour, worked my way gradually all round the house until I had the gardener right in front of me, about fifty yards away. I knew it was vital to me that I should keep him in view, so as to know exactly where he was. He was still hoeing among the carnations.

I lay down under a thick bush and thought carefully exactly what I should do.

My spirits had risen considerably since I had entered the judge's grounds, and I quite thought now that, with any luck, I had found at least a temporary refuge from my enemies.

I had cocked my eye over the house, as I had crept round, and had imagined two or three places where I could easily break in. I had picked up a small length of iron on my travels through the garden and was thinking, Woe betide the gardener if he should happen to catch sight of me now. Indeed, so quickly had I fitted myself to the role of an escaped convict, I was half inclined, as it was, to creep round and bash him on the head for the sake of his clothes. But he was a much stouter man than I, and saner thoughts soon convinced me that nothing he was wearing would be any good to me. So I just lay and watched him, hoping for the time when he would go.

But he was a very long while on those carnations, much longer than in my impatience I imagined they were worth. Then he went round to the back, to the vegetable part of the garden, and I spent a very tedious hour watching him tie up and water the tomatoes. Then the melon plants engrossed his attention and the cucumbers wanted seeing to.

It was nearly five o'clock, I guessed, before he began to gather up his tools and get ready to go.

All the time I was just dying for a drink of water. The heat was terrific and my throat seemed almost to be closing up, it was so dry, but I dared not leave the gardener out of my sight for a moment, not knowing where he might go.

At last he locked up his belongings in the tool-shed in a corner under the high wall and, hiding the key under a big plant-pot close by, proceeded very slowing down the drive towards the gates.

I followed him stealthily to make sure and see the last of him. He produced a big key from his pocket and, once outside, was very careful, I noticed, to make sure the gates were properly shut behind him. He shook them vigorously two or three times before going away.

Alone, at last, by myself, I ran back quickly and had a good long drink from the first tap I came upon. The water tasted like nectar, and I felt refreshed at once for the further prosecution of my adventures.

But if I had thought it was gong to turn out an easy job to get into the house, I soon found I was very much mistaken.

The place was a perfect castle and, behind the fly-proof wire windows, there were bars and shutters everywhere.

It didn't suit my book to break in forcibly anywhere. I had no particular plans in my mind, but I was determining at any rate to accept the judge's hospitality for a few days, and it would never do, I told myself rightly, to leave any outward and visible sign of having gained an entrance.

It would be quite possible, I thought, that in the course of the next few days the police might search round all untenanted houses for my humble self.

I tried to get in where it wouldn't be noticed, but I was balked every time. Round and round the house I walked, but nowhere were things favourable to my design.

At last a sort of inspiration seized me and I thought I would try the roof. Standing a little way away from the house, I noticed that one part of the roof in the middle seemed to be to be flat, and I imagined I could just see over the summit of the sloping eaves, the top of a wicker-work garden chair.

Abstracting the key from under the plant-pot where I had seen the gardener place it, I opened the tool-shed door and found, as I had half expected, a garden ladder.

Quickly placing it against the side of the house, just by the back kitchen door, I scrambled up on to the roof. It was an easy matter then to crawl up the sloping corrugated-iron and, gaining the highest point in a few seconds, I was delighted with what I saw.

There was quite a spacious flat platform on the top of the roof, and it was evidently used for sleeping out. There were two wicker camp-beds there, a small wicker table and a couple of chairs. In one corner there was a trap-door that obviously led down into the interior of the house. With my heart beating wildly, I stepped over and pulled on the iron ring that I saw there.

It yielded at once to my touch and disclosed a flight of narrow stairs. In ten seconds at most I had tiptoed down and was standing breathlessly in the kitchen of the judge's house. I glowed with delight at my good fortune, but I didn't for one moment lose my head.

I at once opened the kitchen door and, going again into the garden, removed the tell-tale ladder from the side of the house and locked it in the shed. The shed key I also returned to its hiding place under the pot. Then I shut myself quietly in the house made a rapid survey of my future home.

It was very dark inside, but I had no difficulty in finding my way about. My word, but wasn't it a gorgeous home! Beautiful and costly furniture everywhere, carpets into which you seemed to sink ankle-deep with your feet, pictures and statuary just as if one was in an art salon and everything suggesting of the utmost money could buy.

As I opened door after door and the richness of everything was revealed, I wondered what indeed could be the judge's condition of mind when he was committing some poor devils like me to long terms of imprisonment in the awful prison stockade.

But interesting as were the art treasures of the house, the possible kitchen resources pressed forcibly on my mind. I had had nothing to eat practically all day, and a horrid feeling of faintness began to remind me unpleasantly of it.

I proceeded, therefore, to forage anxiously for something to satisfy the inner man. Of course, I found nothing lying about, the judge's domestic arrangements were much too methodical for that, but I soon discovered where the storeroom was. It was, of course, locked, but with the assistance of a handy fire-iron, I soon forced the door and at once saw I was going to be amply rewarded for my pains.

There was plenty of tinned stuff there – milk, sardines, salmon and corned beef – and, to my relief, some large tins of dry biscuits. Better still, on the floor there was a good assortment of bottles of wine.

I had quite a pleasant little meal in the kitchen that evening, and after a bottle of excellent claret, life took on quite a hopeful and roseate hue. I would shake off my enemies after all.

From what the judge had said in court that morning, he would not be returning home with his family until the following Monday. Well and good, I had exactly five days. I could rest and recuperate, think out carefully all my future plans and finally leave the house on the Sunday in some good sort of disguise. There would be plenty of clothes in the house, I was sure, and I should have no difficulty at all in making myself look very different from the man who had been so recently sentenced to five years.

My hunger and thirst satisfied, I felt very tired. I smoked a couple of the warder's cigarettes, had a very delightful bath in the elaborately tiled bathroom of the house and, finally, attired in a beautiful pair of the judge's silk sky-blue pyjamas, threw myself restfully, in the best bedroom, upon what I thought was most probably the judge's own feather bed.

I fell asleep almost at once and so satisfied must I have been with all my surroundings, that I slept unbrokenly all night long. I don't remember even dreaming at all.

The sun had been up some hours when I woke up next morning. It was my friend, the gardener, who awoke me. He was raking over the gravel, just under my bedroom window. For a few seconds I couldn't take in where I was, and then, I remember, I grinned delightedly to myself. Judge Cartright had sentenced me to five years' imprisonment and the first night of those years I had slept in his own bed, in his sky-blue coloured silk pyjamas.

It was really too funny for words, and my great regret was that I had no one with me to share the joke.

I got leisurely out of bed and, after a light breakfast of tea, biscuits and sardines, helped myself to what proved to be a most excellent cigar from a box on the judge's desk.

Then, for about half an hour, I stood watching the gardener through a chink in the bedroom blind. It somehow amused me a lot to think I was so near to him and he didn't know it.

Presently, I heard a loud whistle in the direction of the gates. It was followed immediately by a shout.

The gardener stopped his working on the gravel path. 'All right,' he shouted back hoarsely. 'You can get in, they're open; but push them behind you.'

A minute later, a man came up the drive leading a horse in a small cart. The newcomer was delivering a load of manure.

He greeted the gardener affably and they went round the side of the house. They halted just in front of the kitchen window and I at once got into a position so that I could hear what they were saying.

After a minute or so's cursing at the heat we were having, as I half expected it would, the talk came round to me.

They sat down together on the wheelbarrow, but, unfortunately, with their backs to me. Scraps of their conversation, however, came up plainly to my ears.

The manure-man was evidently of an opinion that things were worth a good laugh. 'Called him a scented old fool,' I heard between a lot of huge guffaws. 'Threatened to break his damned neck the first day he got out – cursed at the jury like hell too . . . all awfully frightened . . . the vegetarian chap's not going to open his shop till the bloke's caught anyhow . . . got clean away, clean as a whistle . . . the damned police poking round everywhere . . . beating the hills even . . . sure to be caught soon, however . . . recognised anywhere by his nose . . . big as a donkey's, with a konk in it like a damned Jew's.'

They moved off after a minute or two, and I must confess a certain misgiving had risen unpleasantly in my mind. I knew I had a peculiar nose, but was my appearance really so unusual, I asked myself, that I should be recognised anywhere?

I went back into the bedroom and examined myself critically in the cheval glass. Not at all a bad face, I told myself, but certainly looking older than thirty-two. Just ordinary eyes and complexion, brown curly hair and a sharply closed firm mouth. But the nose – ah, the nose! There was no doubt about it, it was dangerously conspicuous. A well-developed Roman nose of a most pronounced type! The great bridge in it was a conspicuous feature. I had been called Julius Caesar in my schooldays, and at the Bank had been known as 'The Duke' to my intimates, because of my supposed resemblance to the large-nosed Duke of Wellington.

I sighed deeply as I regarded myself in the glass, but there, it couldn't be helped, and I comforted myself a few minutes later. So great hitherto had been my good fortune that I was hopeful it would go on again.

I spent four days altogether in the judge's house and, on the whole, except for the monotony of continual tinned food, it was quite a happy time.

I followed almost exactly the same routine every day. Each morning, it was the gardener who woke me up. I always heard him come in, and his first care was always the carnations just under my bedroom window. He used to turn the hose on them before the sun came round.

About an hour later, I used to get up, have a nice cold bath and then spend the day either in reading, playing chess with myself or going through the judge's private papers.

At five o'clock, the moment the gardener had taken himself off, I used to go into the garden and have a good fill of the judge's fruit. His apricots, especially, I found most delicious, and I have never tasted better, before or since.

The rest of the evening, until I took myself off to bed, I used to spend in a delightful little summer-house at the extreme end of the garden. It was so beautifully peaceful and quiet there and I would sometimes lie for hours on the comfortably padded seat, listening drowsily to the faint and humming sounds of the city, so near and yet so far away.

Sometimes I varied part of the day slightly by going up on to the flat part of the roof for an hour or so. There was an awning attached to each of the wicker couches and I used to roll them out and lie there until the sun made it too hot and I had to come in.

The outdoor parts of my stay were most enjoyable but, even still, there was a little fly in the ointment there.

I could never get rid of the idea that I was being watched by someone from the tower of the house next door.

The tower dominated every yard of the judge's garden. It commanded such a clear view of everything, and when I was lying on the judge's roof it seemed to my imagination to be peopled and haunted with hundreds of pairs of eyes. Mind you, the whole time I never caught sight of a soul and never once saw any movement behind the rail of the tower but, still, as I say, there was always the uncanny feeling that I was being watched, and it got on my nerves.

The judge had quite an extensive library and was evidently a man of taste and education. I read a lot of Shelley while I was there and went twice very carefully through *Prometheus Unbound*. My games of chess with myself were rather slow, but I worked out a fine variation in the King's Gambit that on several occasions I found most effective in later years.

About the judge's private papers. It was vital for me that I should find some money somewhere and in pursuit of this object I broke into his big roll-top desk. I found he had many interests besides those of the law. He was, for instance, treasurer for some local church funds. There was one drawer, with a neat little gummed label on it. 'New Wing for St Snook's Church' it read. There was seven pounds ten in the drawer. Most appropriate, I thought. Instead of one new wing for St Snook's, it would provide two new wings for me. It would greatly assist me in my flight.

In the desk there was a cheque-book also, with plenty of unused cheques, and from his pass-book in another pigeon-hole I noticed he had quite a tidy balance lying at one bank.

On Saturday morning, the fourth day of my stay, the gardener pushed half-a-dozen letters into the letterbox of the front door. Significant of the shortly impending return of the family, I thought, with a bit of a gasp; but having nothing better to do, I went through them.

One was from a man, Henry Tuppins by name, evidently a tenant of the judge. He wrote from somewhere in North

Unley, asking if he might cut down the large gum tree in his front garden as it was obstructing the light in the house. He wished to know if the judge could possibly see his way to rebuilding the wall at the back, as it was in a state of great dilapidation and cows and horses were continually breaking through.

There was an excellent little typewriter in the study, and I thought it would be only nice to reply to the letter at once.

So I wrote back to Mr Tuppins; yes, certainly, he could cut down the tree, it had become a regular nuisance and it would be doing me a favour if he would. As for the wall, well, I couldn't decide for certain, off-hand, but the best thing would be for him to come up one evening to dinner and we could talk it over afterwards at our ease. I suggested the evening of Monday week and hoped he would be able to come because I had an excellent brand of cigars that I would like his opinion on. I begged he would make no reply if the arrangement suited him, and I signed the letter with a good flourish in the judge's best style.

I had no difficulty at all in forging the judge's signature. There were heaps of examples to copy from in his private letter-book, and for the last ten years and more, as ledger clerk, my chief work at the bank had been to do with people's signatures and the varying ways in which they signed their names.

My imagination excited by this little correspondence adventure with Mr Tuppins, I thought I could well spend a profitable half hour in composing a letter, also in the judge's name, for publication in the press, upon the evil of narrow-minded views on Sunday Observance. So I wrote a chatty letter to two leading daily papers in Adelaide, the *Advertiser* and the *Register*, giving effect to these views.

I wrote, it was open to every man to change his opinions, and I had changed mine. I pleaded for a real day of rest, a day of sunshine and fresh air, a day away from the vitiated atmosphere of stuffy churches and chapels and halls. A day out in the open, whereby the refreshed and purified body would give home and shelter to a clean and purified soul. I said the arduous toil and worry of the working week had in many cases really physically unfitted young growing people for the sectarian discipline of the seventh day. They wanted some recreation on Sundays, I insisted, not a further piling up of the worries, doubts and perplexities of their working-day lives.

I concluded by remarking that in the course of many years' experience on the bench, I had always invariably noticed that the worst offenders brought before me were recruited from among those who had been most strictly brought up in their early lives, and I pointed out that among civilised people it had long since passed into a proverb that clergymen's children invariably showed themselves in later life to be the worst of all.

I felt quite pleased with myself after writing these two letters. It was very small-minded, I know, but they seemed to put quite an artistic crown on my efforts to spite the judge. Anything to make him look ridiculous, for there, I knew, I could punish him most. I put the letters in the house 'post-box' in the hall, trusting to chance that their presence would not be detected and that in due time they would be posted along with the other letters that the family would certainly put there.

By the Saturday afternoon, I had thought out all my plans, and was all prepared to leave on Sunday. I had selected certain articles of clothing from the judge's wardrobe and, with these, I thought I could present a sufficiently altered appearance to pass muster in the dark.

I determined to leave the house about eight on Sunday evening and go down boldly to the railway station on North Terrace. I would mingle with the usual crowd of holiday-makers and book to some station in the hills; once there, I should be able to lie low indefinitely, I thought, and later on, pick up the Melbourne express at night from some township far away from the city.

I guessed, so short are people's memories, that in a week or two at most, all description of my personal appearance would have been forgotten by everyone except the police.

In the evening, about five o'clock, I went out into the garden and after a good fill of fruit retired as usual to the summer-house to smoke and read and while away the hours until I was ready to go to bed.

I settled myself comfortably in a corner and for about ten minutes, I think, lay back and went carefully over all the plans in my mind.

Then suddenly, with a terror so great that it is vivid to me even now, I heard footfalls on the gravel path outside, and before I could move hand or foot in my paralysed surprise, a shadow fell across the entrance to the summer-house, and a second later a man stepped quietly inside.

'Good evening to you, Mr Cups,' he said very quietly. 'No, don't be frightened. I'm a friend. I'm Doctor Carmichael from next door, and I've come to warn you that the judge's servants are coming home tonight.

CHAPTER 2

I stared at him in horrified and amazed surprise. The shock of his appearance, and of his addressing me by name, had completely taken away all my powers of speech, and all I could do for the moment was gape, and wonder what was going to happen next. My tongue seemed to be cleaving to the roof of my mouth and there was a horrid feeling of sickness about me that made me feel limp.

He was a good-looking man, about forty-five, with a fine intellectual face, and dark, thoughtful eyes. There were hard stern lines about his mouth, but his expression was softened just now by an amused, if rather grim, smile.

'Surprised, are you, Mr Cups?' he went on quite genially. 'Oh, no, you needn't shake your head. I know all about you. We've been close neighbours for four days, and I must tell you that to me, at all events, your little excursion here has been quite an incident in an otherwise monotonous life.'

'What do you mean?' I asked savagely, finding my speech at last. 'I'm sure I don't know what you're talking about.'

The smile left his face instantly, and he closed his teeth with a snap.

'Don't be foolish, Mr Cups,' he said sternly, 'and don't be frightened either. I tell you, man, I'm your friend. I saw you come in here on Tuesday dinner-time, and when the evening paper arrived I knew at once who you were. I saw you get in through the roof and, had I wanted to, could have given you away any time.' He advanced into the summer-house and sat himself down carelessly upon the seat opposite to me. Taking a silver case from his pocket, he offered me a cigarette, and upon my refusing complacently helped himself to one.

'Well, don't if you don't want to,' he remarked, and then he went on slyly, 'but perhaps your stay here has given you a partiality to cigars.' He laughed in great amusement and nodded towards his own house. 'Yes, I've got a pair of excellent binoculars over there, and I've seen a lot that's been going on.' He sat silent for a long moment, but the whole time he was watching me intently. 'Look here, Cups,' he said at last, 'I'll put all the cards upon the table and explain exactly what I'm prepared to do.' He puffed thoughtfully at his cigarette. 'I expect you've heard something about me, and know that, like you, I've got a grievance against the world too.' His voice became very hard and bitter. 'I hate what they call society, and there's no justice in any court of law. I read what you told them all the other day, and it's quite true. I agree the dice were loaded against you, and that the evidence on which you were convicted was weak in the extreme. I admired the way in which you spoke out, and I admired the damned impudence with which you got away. I tell you, the newspapers have been most entertaining reading since Tuesday, and several times I've almost been inclined to throw you one over. But we'll talk of that later on. The thing is now, what were you proposing to do. Mind you' – and he smiled very gravely at me –'you can trust me. I'm quite prepared to help you and be your friend.'

All the time he had been speaking my eyes had been fixed intently on his. There was no deceit or trickery about him, I felt sure, and a contemptuous mocking at convention was quite in accordance with the strength and courage of his face. I realised that he was being, as he said, quite open with me, and that it was in every way to my advantage to make of him a friend. Commonsense, too, told me that already, as he said, I was in his power, and had everything to gain and nothing to lose.

'Well,' I said slowly, and I smiled for the first time, 'I had thought of getting away tomorrow night. I've found some money in the house and with some of the judge's clothes I thought of going to North Road Station and booking to somewhere in the hills.'

He shook his head ominously in a disapproving frown. 'Ah, the very thing they were expecting,' he said. 'They're reckoning you've been hiding somewhere close to the city for four days without food, and will be bound to come out some time today or tomorrow. Through the newspapers, the police have especially warned everyone to be on the look-out now, and your description is posted up in leaded type everywhere.'

I felt myself go cold in fright again and the awful sickly feeling came back to the pit of my stomach. The man in front of me stood up and looked at his watch.

'Well, I don't think we'd better stop talking here, at any rate. Come over to my place and we'll talk over what had best be done. At any rate, I'll give shelter for tonight.' He walked out of the summer-house but, when outside, turned back suddenly. 'Look here, my friend,' he said eyeing me very sternly, 'no tricks, mind. I'm trusting you and, besides, I tell you straight I'm a dangerous man to mishandle at any time. I'm just helping you because everyone's against you and because I liked the look of your face.'

For the moment he glared at me dark and menacing, but almost instantly he broke again into a smile.

I felt myself grow hot in annoyance at his distrust, but I answered him meekly enough. 'I'm not quite a fool, sir,' I said quickly, 'and you've told me enough to make me understand how hopeless things are. My only chance now is to take what you give me, and I swear to you I'll be grateful, whatever you do.'

He nodded and led the way towards a corner of his own wall.

'One second, Doctor,' I exclaimed, 'Mayn't I go into the house and fetch some things? I came out into the garden tonight, you see, quite unprepared.'

He thought for a moment and then nodded again. 'Yes, but be quick,' he said curtly, 'we may have wasted valuable time already. Close the door after you, when you come out.' He smiled grimly. 'It will make them more puzzled than ever to know how you got in.'

In less than a minute I was out in the garden again. I had brought a hat and light overcoat of the judge's, and some small odds and ends that I thought would prove useful.

Dr Carmichael was waiting for me at the foot of a light ladder propped up against the wall. He smiled when he saw the look of surprise in my eyes. 'How did you think I got over?' he asked. 'The wall's much too high to climb, and the judge is too devilish fond of broken glass.'

He mounted first and I followed. On the top of the wall there were some thick sacks over the glass. I pulled the ladder up after me and, as he had done, dropped to the ground on the other side. Taking the sacks with us, we crossed through the garden and went up to the house.

'You go inside there and wait for me,' he said pointing to the back door. 'I'm just going to unloose my dogs again. They're fierce with strangers, although they wouldn't hurt you if I were with you.'

He rejoined me in a minute or so and led the way into a very large room that at one time had evidently been used as some sort of servants' hall.

'This is where I live,' he said. 'I spend most of my time in this room.' He put his hand on my arm and led me up to the window. 'Now let me have a good look at you, in front of the light, if you please, Mr Cups.'

For quite a minute, and a very long minute it seemed to me, he took me all in. His eyes were deep and thoughtful, and his face was the face of a man with whom other people's opinion would count very little and who would always determine all things for himself.

'Hum,' he said presently, but very softly and more to himself. 'Plenty of courage, almost reckless in fact. Rather self-indulgent but not vicious. A good hater, but perhaps a good lover too. Trustworthy, I should think.' He raised his voice and smiled pleasantly. 'Yes, I'll trust you, Mr Cups, and I don't think I shall be going far wrong, although, of course' – and he made a pretension of some fear – 'by so doing I'm bringing myself under the displeasure of the law. Yes, I'll help you to get away.'

A wave of some deep feeling touched me, and I felt an embarrassing mist before my eyes.

'Tut, tut, man,' he went on quickly, 'we are both outcasts, you and I, and it will be most amusing to see those who would catch you, at their wits' ends. But come, you're the only visitor I've had for a very long time now, and you're in luck's way. I'm cooking a leg of lamb tonight, and it'll be better than the tucker you've had at the judge's, I'm sure. Sit over there and I'll have things ready for you in five minutes.'

In silence, I watched his preparation for the meal and meditatively called to my memory all that I had heard about this strange man.

Half a dozen years ago Robert Carmichael had been perhaps the best known surgeon in the Commonwealth. He had been the doyen of his profession in Sydney and the most brilliant and daring operator in the state. His income had run well into five figures. Just when he was in the zenith of his fame, a woman, a patient and the wife of a patient, had crossed his path. The woman's husband had been well known as a brute and a blackguard. Openly defying convention, the woman had left her husband and gone to live under Dr Carmichael's protection. The whole business had caused a dreadful scandal, and the husband had sought for and obtained a divorce. The suit had been undefended and the judge, hearing only one side, had referred in scathing terms to the conduct of Dr Carmichael. He had strongly urged the matter upon the consideration of the General Medical Council and the doctor having many enemies, the council had taken it up. They found that Robert Carmichael in the pursuit of his professional duties had led astray one of his patients, and had been guilty of infamous conduct in a professional way. They accordingly at once erased his name from the medical register.

It meant the end of everything for Carmichael and sounded the death-knell to all his hopes, ambitions and fame. Professionally speaking, he was to be henceforth a dead man and the fruits of his mighty talents were to be no longer gathered for the world.

In an hour, so to speak, his professional life was closed. But a worse tragedy was in store for him. The woman for whom he had sacrificed so much committed suicide. She dared not live to share the sorrow she had brought upon her lover.

The shock of it all had almost broken Carmichael but, shaking off the dust of Sydney from his feet, he had come to Adelaide and for five years, surrounded by these high, enclosing walls, he had lived alone.

Report had it that, a rich man, he was devoting his life to literature and chemical research. But no one knew much about his present life, and there were hardly half a dozen people in the whole city who had even seen his face.

Such, then, was the life story of the man who was now preparing my meal for me.

Soon, seeing that I was watching him, his handsome face broke into a bitter smile.

'You know all about me, as I say, Cups? No, don't pretend you don't. It's a good thing, and at all events, will save me from referring to the matter myself.'

In a few minutes we sat down to our dinner. My host produced a bottle of good white wine and under its genial influence our sorrows receded to the background for a while.

He chatted humorously of the details of my escape from the court and I was naturally exceedingly interested in all that had taken place afterwards in the city during the last few days. It appeared that the authorities had been thunderstruck at my disappearance, and for a long while would not believe it was possible I could have left the court building. Finding the key of the handcuffs still in the warder's pocket, and no handcuffs in the room, they had jumped to the conclusion at once, as I had intended they should, that the handcuffs were still on me. Therefore, for the first hours after my escape, they had concentrated on searching every crack and cranny of the buildings of the court, holding it impossible that a handcuffed man could go out for half a dozen yards in the public street without being noticed and pounced upon. When it had begun to dawn on them that I must have got rid of the handcuffs somehow, and they began to look farther afield for my humble self, evidence began to pour in that I had at least got as far as the street. Pepple, the vegetarian, had come forward and said he had seen me when he was buying a paper in the street. Pressed to explain why he hadn't given the alarm, he'd said he hadn't remembered who I was, until he was having his tea. The police had been furious with the man, and the following day Pepple had written indignantly to the *Advertiser*, giving in detail the abuse he said he had received.

Then, Drivel Jones had rather incautiously admitted that a man, uncommonly like me, had passed him in the hall and a considerable amount of ridicule had in consequence descended upon his head. To get a poor devil five years and then to unprotestingly allow him to escape before he had served five minutes, seemed to the public incomprehensible, and the blustering advocate had come in for a good deal of chaff.

On the whole, Dr Carmichael said, the people were treating my escape as a sort of joke and the general hope seemed to be that I should get away. That was why the police had been sent on so many fool's errands and put on so many false scents.

My nose, as I had heard from the conversation in the garden, had figured largely in all my descriptions, and it appeared that considerable annoyance had been passed on to certain respectable members of the community because of their nasal appendages. One of the city aldermen had been twice stopped and asked to give an account of himself in the street, and an over-zealous policemen had actually arrested the Reverend Pumpkin Tosh just as he was setting out to preside at a leg-of-mutton supper in aid of the chapel funds.

The good people of Adelaide were making quite a game of anyone with a big nose, and with small boys it was now the custom to follow excitedly after anyone so endowed.

But if the public were laughing, the police were in deadly earnest. I had made them the laughing-stock of the city, and from the youngest to the oldest they were working their hardest to get hold of me again.

After our meal, Dr Carmichael took me round the house. Only four rooms were furnished at all.

'Nothing like Judge Cartright's,' he remarked smiling, 'and you won't sleep in a feather bed tonight. But you can sleep soundly all the same, for the dogs wouldn't allow a rat to cross the garden when they're about.'

We went into the library and from floor to ceiling, the walls were lined with books.

'The great souls of the world to commune with,' commented the doctor solemnly. 'One can never be quite alone, with all the mighty spirits here.'

He asked me whether I played chess and when I told him my analysis of the King's Gambit in the judge's house, he seemed very pleased.

'We'll have a game tonight then,' he said enthusiastically, 'but I warn you beforehand that I'm pretty strong.'

We climbed up into the tower and he whispered to be very quiet.

'Sound carries wonderfully in these gardens,' he muttered, 'the walls are so high. I nearly always heard you when you opened the kitchen door and always knew when you turned on your bath at night.'

There was a splendid view from the top of the tower and, when I looked over, I could quite understand the uneasy feeling I had so often experienced in the judge's place.

Every yard of the judge's garden was plainly visible, and I almost seemed to be looking into the windows of the house.

Dusk had just fallen as we went up the tower and, for a long while, we both stood silent watching the lights of the far-flung city beneath us.

'Look,' he whispered presently. 'See those two policemen up the road there under the lamp. They've always been in couples at night since you escaped. The impression seems to be that you're a desperate man.'

Before I could make any reply, we heard the clang of a gate and the sound of high laughing voices from the direction of the judge's garden.

'Look out,' whispered the doctor, and he pulled me sharply down on to the floor of the tower. 'Don't show up above the rail whatever you do, there's the afterlight of the sunset behind us.' Then he began to laugh very softly. 'Now for some fun. They're the judge's servants who've just come back. The first act of the play begins.'

Breathlessly, we lay and watched through the rails. There were four of them – three girls and a man – and they all came very slowly up the drive towards the house. In the half light of the new moon, we could see they were all well laden with parcels. They bundled them down unceremoniously outside the kitchen door, and the three girls with shrieks of merriment raced for the apricot trees in the back garden. We heard them pulling down the branches and the sounds of breaking twigs as they greedily plucked at the fruit.

'Pigs,' called out the man. 'I'll tell the judge tomorrow, and won't old Cartright give it to you. You'll all get six months.' Then he moved very leisurely to unlock the door and, a few seconds later, up went the lights.

For a long while, it seemed nothing happened, only loud giggles from the vicinity of the apricot trees. Then the man pushed open the door and called out sharply. 'Hi, come here, you girls. Stop your fooling, I want you at once. Come along now, quick.'

By way of reply one of the girls threw an apricot and we heard it ping against the wire of the fly-proof door.

'Damn,' shouted the man. 'Come at once. Someone's been and broken in.'

A minute later, one of the girls gave a shriek and the telephone bell began to whirr violently inside the house. We heard a lot of shouting in the receiver and several times we caught the word 'police'.

'Now for it,' whispered the doctor, rubbing his hands. 'In ten minutes, your friends will be up here.'

But the police were up in five, it seemed to me. First came two, running breathlessly up the drive, then another one, who was evidently a superior, and finally, a big motor-car discharged half a dozen more through the gates.

'It's him right enough,' called out one of the first policemen to the newcomers as they reached the house. 'He's been here. We've found the handcuffs. He's not been gone long either, for the soap in the bathroom's still wet.'

The doctor gripped hard on my arm to attract attention and turning round I saw his face looked rather anxious.

'Hush,' he whispered with his finger to his lips. 'We must go down at once. They'll want to search this place. I never thought of that.'

Very softly we crept down the stairs and then Dr Carmichael pulled me into the darkness of the hall.

'Look here, Cups,' he said quickly. 'Of course, the police will want to come over here. They're bound to search my place. It's quiet and lonely and if you've only just got away from next door it's just where they would think you'd try and hide. I can refuse them for the moment and make them get a search warrant, it is true, but that will only mean greater trouble in the end. They'll be suspicious then and the search will be hotter than either you or I will like. So I am bound to let them come if they ask, you understand.'

'Yes,' I replied numbly and with a great sinking in my heart. 'Then do you want me to cut and run?'

He scowled angrily at me. 'Thank you, Cups,' he said icily, 'but I'm not that sort. I promised I'd help you, and I was never a liar in all my life. I'll hide you somewhere, man.' He eyed me hard for a few seconds and then rapped out harshly, 'You're not a coward, are you? I take you to be a brave man.'

I could feel my face draw up almost into a sneer. 'Try me,' I replied curtly. 'Nothing frightens me over much.'

He seemed to hesitate for a moment, and then, opening the door leading into the garden, he whistled very softly into the night. 'You shall hide in the kennels then,' he said grimly. 'No one will dream of looking for you there.'

Hide in the kennels. I gasped in horror to myself. What does he mean? My blood might well run cold. I thought of those dreadful beasts I had seen through the gates, with their horrid jowls and fierce bloodshot eyes. Hide in the kennels – surely not when they were there?

My uneasy contemplations were cut short by swift rustling sounds outside. The noise of padded footfalls on the gravel and the deep breathing of big beasts scurrying along.

'Stand close to me,' muttered Dr Carmichael, 'and don't let them for a moment think you are afraid.'

We had drawn back into a corner of the hall and he had switched on one of the lights. A moment later and three huge creatures padded in stealthily and came noiselessly towards their master. I say, noiselessly, but once they saw me they emitted low deep growls and, with paws uplifted, halted menacingly in their approach. If they had been unpleasant to look at when I had gazed on them at a distance the other day, they looked terrible when seen now close at hand. They were large as young calves but with beautiful long sinuous bodies that had all the grace and elegance of deer. They had huge heads and terrible-looking jaws, and their eyes were wild and fierce like beasts of prey.

'Livonian wolf-hounds,' whispered the doctor, 'the fiercest and most dangerous dogs in the world, but loyal and obedient to those they love. Come here, Pilate, here Herod, here Diana.'

Very slowly and very reluctantly, it seemed, the huge beasts approached their master, with their eyes, however, the whole time fixed on me.

'Now, Cups,' said the doctor quickly, 'stand still and let them get your smell. They'll never touch you when I'm here and when I'm not here either, once they understand. They're very intelligent.'

I stood quite still as he directed and gradually they stopped their growling. Then they let me stroke them and although they certainly evinced no signs of friendship, they at least stopped glaring at me with their awful eyes.

Suddenly the telephone bell whirred and with a grim nod to me the doctor made to pick up the receiver.

'Just in time,' he whispered. 'I was sure it would come.' I held my breath almost, lest I should make a sound.'

'Hello,' called out the doctor. 'Yes, I'm Dr Carmichael. What do you want? . . . what? . . . who? . . . No possibility at all. I've three big dogs always loose in the garden. They wouldn't let a rat cross over . . . He couldn't have possibly, I tell you . . . Do you think it really necessary . . . Who are you, do you say? Inspector Benton . . . Well, I suppose I must, but I tell you I think it great nonsense . . . All right, wait till I've called in the dogs, and when I've shut them up, I'll come and open the gate . . . But it's most annoying.' He hung up the receiver and turned back to me.

'They believe you were actually in the house when the servants came in and they're dead sure you got over here. We must be quick as lightning. Oh, one moment, wait. Lie down, Diana. Down, Pilate, down.'

He ran out of the room, but was back again in less than half a minute. He was carrying a small bottle and a dagger-shaped open knife.

'Here, take these,' he said quickly, 'although I'm sure you'll not need them. They'll give you confidence. The bottle contains strong ammonia. If the dogs threaten you, just pull out the stopper. Diana's the only one I'm afraid of. She's the least certain of them all. Look out if she makes for you, crouching very low. Now, come on quick, and whatever you do, don't speak. Keep close to me in the dark. Come on, Diana, come on, Pilate, come on, Herod.'

He switched off the lights and, followed ghost-like by the three huge hounds, we passed from the utter darkness of the house into the faint moonlight of the night.

My feelings were not pleasant to consider. It was no good pretending I wasn't afraid. My teeth were chattering in fear. Half an hour in the darkness with three ferocious dogs. Anything might happen. Still, I tried to console myself, all things were preferable to five years in the Stockade.

We had not far to go. The kennels were only a few yards away and just round the side of the house. Dr Carmichael flashed a little electric torch, and I saw for the first time that he was carrying a short whip.

'Tread very softly,' he whispered, 'and follow me close as I go inside.'

We passed by a small narrow door into a high-railed sort of caged enclosure, about twelve feet square. It was cement-floored. At the back, there was another portion roofed over and partly protected from the wind and rain by a length of abutting wall. There was no door between the two parts.

'In you go,' whispered the doctor, 'right inside. Lie close up to the wall, for they may flash their torches round. I'll try and make the dogs keep close to the rails, here outside, but as you value your life, don't move and don't make a sound.' He raised his voice sharply to a menacing tone. 'Lie down, Diana, lie down,' and he cracked angrily with his whip. 'Down, Pilate, damn you,' and there was a startled yelp.

The three huge beasts crouched sullenly by the rails and for quite a long minute it seemed their master stood threateningly over them with the whip uplifted. Then he stepped back through the door and, closing it with a bang, strode quickly down the carriage drive towards the entrance gates.

A tense deep silence followed and by the faint moonlight I

could see the three dogs crouching motionless, and staring like graven images into the shadow in which their master had just gone.

Presently, in the distance, there was the rattling of a chain, the clang of opening gates and the murmur of gruff voices. Then came quick footsteps over the gravel, and the murmur and voices grew louder. The dogs pricked up their ears and, all getting simultaneously to their feet, they emitted low, deep growls.

Dr Carmichael came up the drive with a tall fine-looking man in an inspector's uniform. Behind, followed four ordinary policemen. Almost at once they came within earshot of where I lay.

'I'm, of course, sorry, sir,' I heard the inspector say, 'but everything points to the man getting over here.'

'Everything but my dogs,' said Dr Carmichael. 'I tell you they've got a keener scent than bloodhounds on a short trail, and a cat couldn't have come here without their knowing it and giving tongue.'

'Well, sir,' replied the inspector, 'we'll soon see. We'll run through this place in five minutes and be satisfied one way or another.'

Arriving opposite the kennels, the party at once stopped, as I expected it would. At the sight of so many strangers the dogs bristled with rage, and their angry growls fell most unpleasantly on my ears. One of the policemen started to flash his torch on their faces, but the doctor seized his hand quickly and turned it down.

'Don't do that, please,' he said sternly. 'If you anger the beasts, there'll be no peace for any of us here tonight. They'll be growling and disturbing everyone the whole night through.'

'Yes, drop that, Simpson,' the Inspector said sharply. 'He's not likely to be hiding in there although, on second thoughts, from his impudence, it'd be the very place he'd go to,' and the inspector, who was himself nearer than any of them to the rails in his turn flashed a torch right on to the angry dogs.

The effect was startling. With a fierce snarl Diana sprang forward and hurled herself savagely against the bars. The whole railing seemed to quiver under the shock, and the badly frightened Inspector jumped back so hurriedly that he fell over and dropped his torch.

'By James,' he swore disgustedly, as he picked himself up, 'if the beggar's in there he deserves to escape. What dreadful brutes to have on the premises. Aren't you sometimes in danger yourself, Doctor?'

But Carmichael gave him no answer. He was far too busy with Diana. He had wrenched open the kennel gate and, long before the inspector had picked himself up, he was in among the dogs and driving them savagely back into the corner with his whip. He lashed at them without mercy and in a few seconds they were crouching down cowed, and only the bitch now making any sound at all. She was still growling faintly. For quite a long while their master stood over them with the whip, and then slowly, very slowly, he retreated backwards out of the cage.

'Look here, Inspector,' he said sharply, and noticed his face was very white. 'Take your men away from these kennels quick. So many strangers enrage the dogs, and candidly I'm not at all confident about the railings here. They want re-cementing. Did you see how they moved when the bitch sprang just now? I quite thought they were coming down.'

'All right, sir,' said the inspector in an uneasy tone. 'Move off, you fellows. Spread out and go over every yard of the garden, although from what I've seen just now,' and he looked significantly at the big beasts in the cage, 'I think, after all, it's a waste of time.'

The four policemen with evident relief disappeared into the garden, and I saw their torches immediately flashing all over the place.

The inspector and Dr Carmichael, however, remained close to the kennels and stood thoughtfully regarding the dogs. The latter were quite silent again, at last.

'Gave me quite a shock, sir, that,' remarked the inspector mopping his face. 'I had not idea the brutes could look so awful.'

'They're very dangerous animals,' replied the doctor seriously, 'and I'm afraid their bout of rage is not over yet.' He raised his voice. 'One wants a bottle of strong ammonia when they're like this. It would keep them well at a distance. Just open a bottle and let some of it dribble on the ground.'

'Oh?' asked the inspector, 'would that keep them away?'

'Just for a while it would; at any rate, until help was forthcoming.

'Yours is a very lonely life here, Doctor, isn't it?'

'Yes,' Carmichael said drily, 'but I like it so. I have my books and my studies.'

The inspector shrugged his shoulders. 'Well, give me the city, Doctor, for preference; the lights, the pictures and the bars. These brutes would soon get on my nerves, and I'd expect to be torn to pieces one day.'

They moved off a little way and their voices sank so that I could no longer catch their words, but Carmichael, I noticed, still kept looking my way. He never, as far as possible, for one moment took his eyes off the kennels.

And all this time I was bathed in a sweat of horrible anticipation. I could not exactly say I was afraid, but I was without hope and numb in my despair. I was sure that evil was coming to me in one way or another. Either I would be discovered by the police, or I would be torn to pieces by the bitch, Diana. But I don't think I worried about it particularly. I was cool and collected in a way and quite prepared to defend myself to the end. I held my dagger softly, loosened the stopper in the ammonia bottle. As far as possible I was prepared.

For the moment, however, it seemed the danger had passed. As Carmichael and the inspector moved away, a deathly silence fell over the place. The great dogs crouched in the corner by the rails, and I, only a few feet away, crouched in the shadows cast by the abutting wall.

About fifty yards down the drive I could see a solitary

policemen keeping watch, and I could just notice that he was smoking. A sudden and familiar aroma came up to me through the night. He had taken one of the judge's cigars.

It must have been quite five minutes before anything stirred. Then I saw the four policemen return and with Dr Carmichael and the inspector a consultation was held in front of the house door. The lights had been switched on in the hall and they were all in full view.

'Well, sir,' I heard the inspector say, 'what about inside the house?'

'Just as you please,' Carmichael said. 'You can go where you like.'

'Well,' said the inspector after a pause, 'I'm quite satisfied, but I'm thinking of what headquarters will say. We'll just run through the place and, as you tell me only a few rooms are furnished, it won't take us long. At any rate, it will satisfy everyone, and you won't be bothered again.'

They all immediately went inside the house but, as the lights in the rooms only went up slowly, one by one, I guessed the search, in spite of the casual tone of Inspector Benton, was the thorough one he doubtless intended it should be.

At last, however, they all appeared again, and the inspector and Carmichael chatting pleasantly together, they set off leisurely to leave the place.

Unfortunately, however, the direction of their steps brought them near to the kennels again, and one of the wretched policemen, the one behind all the rest, had to flash his torch, in pure bravado, as he passed.

In a second the fat was in the fire again. Diana was hurling herself in fury against the bars, and this time Pilate and Herod joined in the uproar.

Dr Carmichael turned like a madman and, racing back, lashed furiously at them with his whip. Herod crouched back obediently at once, but it was a minute before Pilate and Diana could be driven from the rails and it was safe for the doctor to get inside the cage.

'Don't move,' he shouted to the policemen. 'If they see you moving it will only make things worse.'

I guessed what was in his mind: he wanted to be quite sure when all of them had left the place. He was taking no chances that one of them might hide somewhere and remain behind to play the spy.

Diana gave a lot of trouble again. Not content with growling this time, she snarled and showed her teeth and once I was almost sure she was on the point of throwing herself on her master. She subsided at last, however, and the three of them crouched sullenly in the corner to where they had been driven by the whip.

'Only two minutes now, Cups,' whispered the doctor as he pulled the gate behind him. 'I shall be back before that, I hope, and then it'll be all over.'

'All right,' I whispered back, 'I'll hold on until then.' A moment after and I cursed that I had answered at all. It was damnably foolish of me to have spoken, and I realised it before Carmichael had gone even five yards.

My voice had attracted the attention of Diana. It was like a change of scene in a theatre and the sudden shifting of interest from one set of actors to another. A moment back and the huge bitch had been all eyes and ears and fangs only for the men outside her cage. Nothing had been of interest to her except the strange intruders she could see beyond the bars that held her back. They were the cause of her anger and it was upon them she desired to vent her wrath. Now all was changed. In a second they were forgotten and another set of obsessions gripped her mind. Inside the cage was now the focus of the storm.

She raised herself up stealthily upon her feet and like a statue carved in stone stood peering in my direction. A low deep growl – another – and her right paw was uplifted ominously from the ground. Then followed a long tense silence and softly, very softly, I tipped up my bottle of ammonia and allowed a thin small stream to trickle to the ground.

Not a sound was breaking on the silence of the night and

not a movement anywhere, not even the rustling of a leaf or the quivering of a tree. Scarce daring to breath, I watched the bitch.

Suddenly, after a long while it seemed, I heard the clanging of a gate, but it brought no meaning to my mind. I was numb and hypnotised and had my being in another world. All my thoughts were centred on Diana. Nothing else mattered.

The bitch was puzzled. She put down her paw and growled again. Then she walked round to get nearer to me in another way and finally she stood still with her great head thrust sharply forward, her tail behind her stretched out stiffly like a rod of steel. And all the time, neither of us took our eyes off each other for one second. There was no movement near me, only the trickle, trickle, of the ammonia on to the floor of the cage.

Suddenly Diana crouched, and I knew the extreme moment had arrived. I held my knife up ready and prepared myself for the struggle that I thought was about to come.

But nothing came in the way I expected. As I drew the one long deep breath that in tense expectant moments one always takes, there came up to me a choking blast of the strong ammonia I had been pouring away.

For eyes, nose, and throat it was horrible, and heedless of all consequences, I gasped out loudly with the pain. I was dimly conscious of what was evidently the beginning of a roar from Diana, but its tone was changed abruptly to one in which surprise and, as with me, pain, had the greater part. The huge beast choked and spluttered and jumped back precipitately to the corner of the cage furthest from where I lay. Her two companions started to snarl angrily, but they could evidently now smell the ammonia too, and they made no attempt at all for a nearer acquaintanceship with me.

Just as I was beginning to realise that, at any rate, I was now safe for the moment, I heard the voice of Dr Carmichael and the cracking of his whip. 'All right, Cups? Thank goodness the police have gone at last.'

Two minutes later and I was lying faint and sick upon a bed in the house. The doctor had carried me in.

CHAPTER 3

I felt very ill and it was not until I had had two injections of morphia that I dropped to sleep. The reaction following upon my release from the kennels had been too much for me, and my harassed nerves were almost on the point of breaking down.

The next day the doctor would not allow me to get out of bed and refused resolutely to discuss any details of what had happened the previous evening. He kept dosing me with some filthy tasting concoction and once used the hypodermic syringe again.

'Make your mind a blank, Cups,' he kept on saying, 'and forget everything of the past week. Your nerves are worn out. That's all it is, and you'll be right as rain tomorrow when you've had some rest.'

But it was three days before I could trust myself to think of the dogs without shaking and nearly a week before I felt well and calm again.

The doctor was kindness itself to me the whole time. 'You see you've had a rotten spell, man,' he remarked to me one day when I was getting better. 'That business at the Court was quite sufficient of itself to shake anyone to his foundations, and what happened after nearly put the finishing touch. I quite thought you were in for brain fever.'

Then he went on very seriously. 'But do you know, friend Cups, we had a much nearer escape that evening than either of us thought. That nosy inspector pretended to be only going over the house in a casual sort of way, just, as he put it, to satisfy them up at headquarters. But, in reality, he was more than suspicious about me. You know how sound carries when rooms are empty. Well, I heard him distinctly tell his men, when I was standing outside, after they had all gone in to make the search, to make jolly sure and not leave a spot unturned anywhere. He said I was just the very kind of man to help a beggar like you to get off. Now what do you think of that?'

I remember I laughed, in spite of the uncomfortable feeling I had.

'Now, doctor,' I replied, 'he wasn't altogether a bad judge of character, was he?'

'Well,' said the doctor grimly, 'he came a cropper afterwards at any rate, for he went on to suggest to his men that the mad-dog affair, as he called it, was only perhaps, after all, a put-up stunt on my part to blind them. He was a fool there at any rate.'

At last I was allowed to see the newspapers and most interesting reading they were.

For many, many days my affair was the chief topic of interest and discussion. To judge from the general tone of the various articles that appeared, I had become in the public eye almost doubly a hero of romance.

If they had smiled at the way I had escaped from the court in the first instance, they had just rocked with laughter when they learnt of my sojourn in the judge's house.

Not knowing what a great part pure chance had played in the matter, they imagined that I had come purposely up to Judge Cartright's residence to make it my temporary home, and the sheer impudence of the idea tickled them immensely.

The 'Cups of Mirth', as one of the papers referred to me and, broadly speaking, that was the general impression in the public mind.

When in due course the judge's supposed letter on 'Sunday Observance' appeared in the public press, and in spite of all attempts at secrecy, through the indiscretion of one of the judge's own servants, the true source of the letter leaked out, the hilarity was redoubled.

Writers in the newspapers opined that one day it would come to be regarded as a classic joke, the music halls took it up and on all sides people were asking each other, 'What the devil is that Cups going to do next?'

Dr Carmichael smiled grimly as he read out these references to me and several times remarked cynically that he was sure it would be always the lasting sorrow of my life that I was not out among my friends to enjoy the applause.

But people's memories are very short, and interest in anything soon dies down. In a few weeks the inevitable happened, everything about me was forgotten, and my name was mentioned in the papers no more.

Then started a long period of quiet and happy association with Dr Carmichael.

After the events of the first night of my coming over to his house, the doctor had always insisted that at least it would have to be a matter of weeks before I could stand any chance of slipping safely away. So I was to make my home, he said, with him, and together we should get some mutual pleasure out of each other's society.

I soon fell into the routine of the house and very quickly took on my part in the everyday life we lived. In the mornings I did the house-work and worked in the garden, leaving the doctor free for his literary studies and chemical research. In the afternoons, I did more gardening, and in the evenings only were we together for any length of time.

So high were the walls and so well wooded was the garden, that practically nowhere were we overlooked. But to make things doubly sure, in case of any chance observer, I wore a suit of the doctor's and one of his old hats. We were not unlike in size and build and with my hat low down over my eyes, I could be mistaken any time for the doctor himself.

The dogs had soon got accustomed to me. For the first few days they had been kept shut up, but as it was I who now always took them their food, we had soon become good friends. Funnily enough, Diana took a particular fancy to me and when I was in the garden, she was nearly always by my side. I rather think she remembered the thrashing the doctor had given her.

Everything in the house was always carried out with regularity and precision. At ten every morning the one and only tradesman called. He brought everything wanted for the house and rang a bell down by the drive-gates to announce his arrival. There was a small wooden window in the wall, of which he had the key. It was his custom to unlock it and put, on the shelf inside, all that had been ordered the previous day. There he found, always ready, the order for the next day. The doctor very rarely saw him and sometimes, he told me, months passed without their exchanging a word.

Every morning and evening the newspapers were thrown over the wall.

The postman was the only other person to have dealings with the house, but even then, he rarely had a letter to deliver.

Occasionally, contrary to the general belief, the doctor went out, but it was nearly always a Friday evening that he chose for these excursions, when the shops were open until late. A short walk and a ten-minute tram ride would then bring him into the city, where no one knew who he was.

He banked at the Bank of All Australia and most of his business was done through the post. When he wanted money, he would draw an open cheque to 'bearer', and present it himself, but here again, the cashiers were never aware that it was Dr Carmichael himself who was confronting them.

All these things I learnt very quickly, and I marvelled how the doctor could have borne his silent lonely life for so long.

'I was just getting tired of it, Cups,' he said to me one day, 'and if you hadn't come, I might any time have gone outside for a few days to a hotel, just to see what it would be like again. I expect, however, I would have come back soon.'

As I have said, it was the evenings only that we spent together, and our games of chess were what we enjoyed most. Dr Carmichael had told me he was a strong player and he found that I was one too. There was not the tenth part of a pawn to choose between us, and many were the Homeric struggles that we had over the board. Sometimes I won, sometimes he did, but there was never any certainty about the matter, and in that lay the great charm.

The doctor was also a man of very wide and varied knowledge, and many were the discussions and arguments we had together. I was not by any means an ill-educated man myself and had thought over many of the problems of life with the same interest that he had.

'I can't understand you, Cups,' he said meditatively one evening. 'You've read a lot and you've thought a lot and yet at thirty-two you were just content to be a poor ambitionless bank clerk, with nothing to look forward to at all.'

'Oh, I don't know,' I replied evasively. 'I used to have my dreams like everyone else, I suppose. I was always hoping for some great explosion to come into my life, but I was too lazy to lay the train myself. I thought one day I'd write a book and put all the people in that I hated, under thinly veiled names.'

'Well, but why did you hate people, Cups?' asked the doctor curiously.

I shrugged my shoulders. 'Chiefly, I suppose, because they had more money than I had,' I said candidly. I went on bitterly. 'But, no, I didn't really hate them for that. I hated them for the arrogance their money gave them. Anyone with money is a god, anywhere. Here, you may be the biggest, vilest, ugliest, most diseased blackguard in the state, but if there's cash behind you, you're respected. Respected, mind you. People will bow and scrape and try to catch your eye. They'll have a toadying smile always ready in case you should look their way. They'll be so pleased if you take any notice of them and if you're rich enough you can spit on them and they won't mind. I tell you, I've seen it every day in our bank. Look at the racing world. It's the same there. If you're rich, you're respected and you can do any damned thing you like. You can run your horses to suit yourself. They can be 'on the ice' one day and the next day you can win as brazenly as you like. You can have the brute's head pulled off early one week with the jockey lugging him back, and the next week he can go out and win by half a street. But no one will say anything to you if you're rich and respected. The committees of the racing clubs will invite you to lunch (probably you'll be on the committees yourself), you can nod rudely to the paid officials and they'll be only too pleased that you're taking any notice of them at all. In fact, you can do anything and you'll still be respected. They only drop on the little people and the poor.'

'Well, Cups,' laughed the doctor when I had finished my outburst, 'don't you think you rather give yourself away? It's envy that's galling you now, because they're rich and you're poor. You make yourself out rather a fool too.'

'What do you mean?' I asked irritably.

'Why,' he said grimly, 'from what I've seen of life, it's only the fools that are poor.'

I looked at him without replying.

'Yes,' he went on frowning, 'if a man's got any grit in him, he never remains poor. He gets money somehow.'

'Then what do you advise?' I asked sarcastically. 'Should I take up a life of crime?'

'Not with that nose, Cups. Your remarkable nasal appendage must bind you to a life of respectability. There can be no dual personalities with you. But seriously what can you do for a living in another state, if you get away?'

'I'd go on the land,' I said sullenly, 'or get a job with horses. I understand something about them.'

'What does a bank clerk know about horses?'

'My father was a breeder and till he died I worked with

him. All my life, until I was twenty, I spent out in the bush and then, like an ass, I came into the city to live.'

'Very foolish, Cups. If I had my time over again, I'd live my life in lonely places. There's peace and happiness there and not the fevered rush for pleasure that kills you in the end.' He was silent for quite a long while.

'Well, well,' he said at last. 'We must think later on what we'll do with you, but just now, we'll have a game of chess.'

I had been with Dr Carmichael about six weeks, when, one day, in the middle of the morning, he called to me to come into the house.

Rather to my surprise, he took me into the library and, moving a chair forward, bade me sit down in front of the window.

'Look here, Cups,' he said, I thought rather hesitatingly, 'I've been thinking a lot about you lately, and how I can manage to get you away. You see, you can't remain here for ever, man. I like your company very much but, to be quite frank with you, your coming here has upset my ideas. You've brought back to me the longing to go into the world again. I rather think now I've been a fool to shut myself up here at all. I've been like a sulking child. I'm only middle-aged, I've plenty of money saved and I'm beginning to realise that one day, I shall be a long while dead.' He laughed happily. 'So, you see, Cups, I'm like a boy who wants a spree and I've got a proposition to make to you to show you where you come in. Now let's have a look at you very carefully.'

I wondered what on earth he was driving at, but my easily apparent perplexity seemed only to amuse him. He pulled another chair close up and sat down right in front of me.

'You see, Cups,' he said in a cold professional manner, 'whenever I think of you – getting you away – I am always faced with the same one difficulty – your nose. No, you needn't laugh, man.' He shook his head warningly. 'You won't do so in a minute.'

'I only laughed, Doctor,' I said apologetically, 'because you look so serious.'

'And I am serious, Cups.' He looked at me gravely. 'What's your life going to be, if wherever you are you're always to be haunted by the idea that someone may recognise you suddenly and give you away to the police. The world's a very small place, you know and, even if I get you away safely from here, there can be no security or lasting peace for you like this.'

I shrugged my shoulders. 'Well, it can't be helped. I must put up with it.'

'I'm not so sure,' he replied quickly, 'and that's what I've called you in for. Now let's make a good examination of your precious nose and I'll tell you what I can do.'

For quite five minutes he pinched and pulled me about. His next words startled me.

'Yes, Cups,' he said decisively, 'if you're willing to risk it, I can cut all that bridge away and give you a nose no different from anyone else's.'

'Risk it?' I said enthusiastically, when I had got over my surprise, 'I'd be delighted if you'd do it. At any rate, you can't make it look more conspicuous than it does now.'

'That's not the risk I mean,' he said gravely. 'The operation's safe enough, but it's the danger of my having to operate and give you the anaesthetic as well. You see, it's a very delicate operation at any time, cutting away bone and cartilage so as to leave only the slightest trace of scar. I shall have to take away a good flap of flesh too, and the whole time I shall have to have you deeply under the chloroform so that you don't make a movement any way. It won't be a short operation either, and single-handed it will take me a very long time.'

'Well, I'm willing anyhow,' I said, still delighted with the idea, 'and if I do peg out, well, I shan't know anything about it, anyhow.'

'That'd be all very nice for you, no doubt,' the doctor said grimly, 'but what about me, saddled with a nice fresh corpse in the house in this hot weather?'

'I never thought of that,' I replied laughing, 'but at any rate we could have a good deep grave ready so as to be prepared for anything. I'll dig it myself under the big fig tree. It'd never be discovered there.'

'Well,' said Dr Carmichael, 'I'll think it over, but now you can go back to your work.'

For three days the doctor made no further reference to the matter at all and, although I was bursting with expectation, a certain delicacy of feeling forbade me to mention it.

As I thought over it seriously, I realised it was by no means a small matter for him to take on gratuitously to take on so great a risk. Of course, it would be a splendid thing for me, and the very idea of it opened up wonderful vistas of a new life, free from all worry and distrust. I should be able to move freely everywhere again, I thought, and face my enemies with all the security of a man in a mask.

On the fourth day, a Thursday, I remember it was, Dr Carmichael announced at breakfast that he was going out for the day, but he vouchsafed no reason for his excursion and in accordance with my usual custom I made no enquiry about the why or wherefore of anything.

The whole day I worked diligently in the garden, but, many times, my eyes turned to the big fig tree and I wondered interestedly if I was destined to lie under there. I felt exactly like a gambler who wanted to stake everything on a single throw.

About five o'clock, the doctor returned, and I could see at once by his face that he had some unusual news to impart.

'Here you are, Mr Archibald Cups,' he said grimly, 'I've got a little present for you.' He took a small packet out of his pocket and handed it to me. 'Have a good look at it, man, but don't drop it whatever you do. There are six ounces of chloroform there, and it's your passport to the open road. You can start digging your grave tomorrow.'

I know I beamed with delight, and I started thanking him in a rather confused way.

'Tut, Tut, man,' he exclaimed, brushing me away. 'Wait till it's over until you thank me. I'm looking forward to it, quite as much as you. It's an adventure, Cups, and we're getting even with the humbugs who would hound us both down.'

That evening at supper he seemed brighter and happier than I had ever known.

'Yes,' he said gaily. 'I've quite made up my mind now to give up this place here. When your little affair's over, we'll both go out again into the world and have a good time. We'll travel together, but at first we'll play round Adelaide and see some of your old pals. It will be a tremendous pleasure to me to take you about where you're likely to meet those you know and see how they'll all fail to recognise you. I shall make an excellent job of your nose, and really I think the first person we ought to go and see must be the judge.'

I smiled rather uneasily and shook my head.

'Nonsense, man,' he went on, 'we can easily think of some excuse. You can make out you travel in cigars or else have a new line of sky-blue silk pyjamas to propose.'

He laughed in great enjoyment, but I must confess I felt no little shaking in my shoes. I had certainy no hankering to run unnecessary risks, and the judge was the last person I wanted to see. I was remembering unpleasantly that Judge Cartright was supposed to have a most remarkable memory for faces and it was his boast that he never once forgot a man he had sentenced to punishment, no matter how the long the interval of years might be. But there was no chilling the gaiety of Dr Carmichael and for the moment I let it go.

'Oh, by the by,' he said presently. 'I met your friend Drivel Jones at lunch today, or rather I sat near him in the Australasian Hotel. I learnt it was he from a friend accosting him by name. He talked a lot about racing and certainly does think he's a big pot. He's brought a chaser called Babylon over from New Zealand, and when the winter comes, over the fences, he says he's going to scoop the pool. He's a big coarse bully, just as you described, and we must try to take him down somehow. I went round afterwards to have a look at the vegetarian chap. I may, of course, have been mistaken, but I quite thought he gave everyone a very searching look as they came into his shop. He's got a most beefy-looking assistant there too, who was never, I'll swear, brought up on nuts. An observant chap, that vegetarian, and when he sees you, it'll be a fine test whether I have been successful or not in altering your appearance.'

I said nothing, but I squirmed at the very idea of this last suggestion and privately made up my mind that whenever I went out, I'd give Pepple's shop a very wide berth.

It was that arranged the operation should take place on Sunday, and the next day, in preparation, I started digging the grave. I have never quite made up my mind whether the doctor was really serious about that grave or whether he only regarded it as a joke. I really think now that he intentionally made me get it ready to bring home to me the seriousness of the whole affair.

I had ample time for meditation while I was digging it. The ground was terribly hard. We had had no rain for over two months, and every square inch of earth had to be broken with a pick. Two hard days' work it gave me and when, on the Friday evening, it was finished to the doctor's satisfaction, my hands were horribly sore and blistered.

'Quite a nice little resting place, Cups,' said Dr Carmichael looking down, 'and what better could anyone want?' He stood musingly by the graveside. 'Yes, after all it's peace and rest. If we only think and reason, everything tells us that death is rest. Do we die, like Diana, like a dog? Why not? Man is such a vain creature, Cups. He thinks he's really so important that death can't possibly be the end of all for him. All his life he's an animal here. He eats, drinks, sleeps and makes love, just as all animals do, and yet, when death comes and he's had his fill, he's quite certain he's going to start off on some new forms of excitement, all over again, somewhere else. His obsession is that he's not an animal, and yet every moment of his life should tell him that nature regards him simply as an aminal. Same laws, Cups, for men and dogs. Nature makes no distinction here – then why after death!'

'Really, Doctor,' I replied laughing, 'just now, a long glass of cool beer would be far more to my liking than any discussion about death. If I snuff it on Sunday, I shall know all about it then, and I'm quite content to wait now.'

'You're a gross materialist, Cups,' the doctor said, turning to go in, 'and such men as you are the despair of pious individuals like myself.'

On the Sunday morning early, I lay down on a narrow table in one of the empty rooms. Dr Carmichael had made me thoroughly spring-clean it the previous day, and the strong odour of disinfectants hung heavy all over the place.

'Delightful, Cups,' said the doctor, imbibing deep sniffs, 'Reminds me of old times. But it's a pity there's not a bigger audience here, for I feel in good form today. I'm going to do you justice, man. Now settle yourself comfortably, breathe naturally and let yourself go. Think of the new life before you, in this world – or the next. Fold your hands and close your eyes. Yes, that's it, you're doing it very nicely.'

Softly, it seemed, the sickly vapour crept into my lungs, slowly the silence gripped me and then dim, dimmer waned the lights before my eyes. Swiftly the shadows met me – the long dark valley opened – and oblivion came.

It might have been many hours before I awoke, but the doctor told me later it was barely two. I felt terribly knocked about and bruised and with difficulty could breathe through the bandages about my face. I could see nothing and the slightest twitch hurt horribly. My head felt full of lead.

I groaned and immediately the doctor glided up.

'All right, old man,' he said very quietly, 'everything's over and it's all gone off A1. I think I've made a thoroughly good job of it, but you mustn't move or open your eyes. I've done more than I intended and put in half a dozen little fancy stitches that will quite alter your face. The skin will feel very tight and drawn at first, but I'll give you a touch of morphia if the pain's too bad.'

Oh, how I cursed everybody in the next few days. Dr Carmichael, Judge Cartright, Drivel Jones, Pepple the vegetarian, everyone I had known came under my ban. Myself, perhaps, I anathematised more than anyone else. Why had I been such a fool to allow myself to be cut about like this? Why had I been such an ass to let this mad enthusiast mess about with me? Anything, the Stockade even, would have been preferable to misery like this. I was in the depths of depression. But things were not bad for very long, and in a very few days my spirits and hopes began to revive. At the end of a week I felt almost well, and, when at last the plaster and bandages were removed, I realised most gratefully that the change in my appearance was fully worth the suffering I had undergone.

I remember so well my astonishment when I looked in the mirror. It seemed quite a different person that looked at me back. The great nose was entirely gone and instead there was one, small, that promised to be almost graceful in outline. The shape of my eyes was altered and my eyebrows were straighter and had lost the outward curve.

'You see, Cups,' said the doctor proudly, 'I've made quite a nice job of you as I promised. It's a little bit early to tell what the final result will be, but everything looks very promising. You will be different not only in profile, but also full-face. Taking part of the muscle, as I have done, at the corner of both eyes will make you look quite different when anybody stares you straight in the face. Mind you, when you meet people you've known before, you may often find them staring curiously at you, but it will be only the subconscious part of them that will be finding a vague likeness in you, and I am sure that feeling will pass immediately away.'

I thanked him most gratefully, but he only laughed and said I really deserved something for the risks I'd run. Then he went on in a graver tone.

'There are two things you must always be careful of, Cups. You needn't worry about the scars, for they will hardly show at all, unless you get very hot, and then they will only appear as little white lines. It is not they that will ever give you away. It's your walk and your voice. You must set at once about decisively altering both. The walk will be easily done. You must cut the heels of your shoes right off or else reduce them to a minimum. That will throw the style of your walking back and alter your gait. The voice, however, will be a different matter, and you'll have to train yourself a lot there. I should have liked to have had a snip at your vocal chords when you were under the chloroform, but that's more than I could manage here. What you must do is to habitually alter the poise of your head. Keep you chin low down and nearer to your chest – that will change the pitch of your voice and give it a deeper tone. Now start on it right away.'

Dr Carmichael was nothing if not thorough, and from that time forward he continually drilled into me the urgency of disguising my voice. He would no longer allow me to speak in the ordinary way and every evening made me read out loud in the new voice I had assumed.

Just a fortnight and a day after the operation, on a Monday morning it was, he announced his intention of going, the following Saturday, to the Port Adelaide races at Cheltenham.

'Drivel Jones,' he said looking up from his paper, 'is running his great chaser Babylon in the hurdles there, and I'm interested to see what the animal is like. He spoke so cocksure about him the other day when he sat near me at lunch, and the sporting correspondent of the paper here seems inclined to share his confidence. This man says that just now probably only one horse in the Commonwealth could lower his colours at level weights, and that's Death Arrow from Perth.'

'Death Arrow's a five-year-old mare,' I commented, 'by Long Bow out of Poisoned Berry. She's only a hurdler, not a chaser.'

'Well, a good hurdler makes a good chaser, doesn't he?' asked the doctor.

'Not always,' I said, 'and conversely many a good steeple-chase horse is often no good over the sticks.'

'Well,' he said, smiling, 'I'll go and see for myself next Saturday if this great Babylon bears out what you say. At any rate he's the champion chaser of New Zealand. But come out into the garden now. I've got a little job for you.'

He led the way to the big fig tree where I had dug the grave.

'Now, my boy,' he said laughing, 'If you don't mind, I'll just get you to fill this in at once. I'm perhaps one of the last men in the world to be superstitious, but twice lately I've dreamt of this darned grave, and this morning I woke up just as you were about to tumble in the earth over me. You were crying, too, and the tears looked so funny running down your new face.'

'Rightoh, Doctor,' I said cheerfully, 'but I guess I would shed a tear or two if I was burying you. I'm quite a grateful sort. Oddly enough I was going to suggest myself filling in this hole today, before the rains came. As an old bushman, I'm sure there's a change about and the weather's going to break. I smell it in the air.'

'I don't think so myself,' said the doctor, shaking his head, 'but as you mention it I'll go up and see what the glass says,' and he turned off to go up into the tower where the barometer was hanging.

I got the spade out of the tool-shed and tucking my trousers into the tops of my socks was prepared for an unpleasant morning of dusty work.

Suddenly, and just as I was preparing to shovel in the first spadeful of earth, I heard a faint cry from the direction of the tower followed by several loud crashes and the sound of one final heavy fall.

I stood stock-still with the spade uplifted in my hand and my heart seemed to stop beating in my chest. There was something so ominous about the silence that ensued.

For a moment I waited and then a dreadful apprehension of terror seized me. Throwing down the spade, I ran swiftly into the house. In the hall, at the foot of the stairs leading up into the tower, I found Dr Carmichael lying huddled on the floor. His neck was twisted at a horrible angle, his face was ghastly pale, and his eyes were staring with a dreadful, frightened look. He was conscious, but he couldn't breathe properly. He turned his eyes towards me as soon as I came up. I threw myself down on my knees beside him.

'Don't touch me,' he gasped faintly, 'leave me alone.'

'Oh, I'll go and get a doctor at once,' I wailed.

'No good,' he panted. 'Cervical vertebrae – neck broken. I'm finished,' and he closed his eyes.

'Oh, doctor,' I exclaimed, 'I must get you help.'

He opened his eyes again and smiled very faintly at me.

'Good chap, Cups,' he whispered. 'I give everything to you . . . don't be afraid . . . have courage, man.'

His voice trailed away to silence, and in a sweat of terror I thought the end had come. Suddenly, however, some new strength seemed to touch him and, staring hard, his eyes caught mine in warning.

'Look out, man' he whispered. 'Look out . . . tell Angas Forbes.'

A dreadful spasm crossed his face. He tried to breathe. His head fell sideways, and his eyes closed very slowly. Then he was quite still.

Dr Robert Carmichael was dead.

CHAPTER 4

The hours following upon the death of Dr Carmichael were the most dreadful ones I can ever remember. I was literally bowed with woe.

I sat on the stairs there, stunned and paralysed with grief. Only a few feet away the body lay stretched out quiet and still and so close to me I could have touched the dead white face by the simple stretching of my hand.

I thought of the awful tragedy of it all. The great strong man struck down without warning in the prime and pride of life; the giant dwarfed to nothing in a few seconds by the harsh touch of death. The fine keen intellect bereft of power; the mind, a ghost to wander in the shades; and all the knowledge he had garnered, dry and withered and of no further service to his kind.

Then I thought of my own position and my tears dried instantly in the very fever of my fears. I had lost my protector. I had lost the only man who could save me, and I was alone again against the world. I sat with my head in my hands and stared vacantly and with despairing eyes across the hall.

The house was dark and still. The blinds were all down on account of the heat, and only the slits here and there told of the burning sun outside.

I roused myself with an effort. I must do something. I must get away. No one in an Australian summer could remain in a house with a dead man longer than a day. But I must get some money.

I tiptoed into the study and tried the dead man's desk. It was unlocked. Lifting it up, I went swiftly through the drawers, but there was no money there, only receipted bills and stacks of memoranda about chemical affairs. There was a big safe let into the wall, and I looked around for the key.

Then it struck me horribly that I should have to search to body for it. I believed the doctor carried the safe-key in his belt.

For quite a long while I hesitated, and then at last overcoming my repugnance I returned into the hall.

I knelt by the dead man. How white and waxen the face was, and yet it seemed now he was sleeping, and I fancied almost that I could trace a smile.

I unloosened his belt and pulled it away and, from his breast pocket, I took out his case. I tiptoed back into the study. I could feel a bunch of keys in the belt, but the pocket-case I examined first.

The first thing I came across was a cheque he had made out only that same morning. It was an open bearer cheque for fifty pounds. Breathlessly I held it in my hand. My heart began to beat wildly and I started to think hard. I could cash it over the counter myself. After all, it was mine! Often Dr Carmichael had told me he had no relations, and his last words to me had been, 'I give everything to you.' What a godsend it would be. I could get anywhere with fifty pounds. But dare I? Dare I go out and cash it myself! I stepped hurriedly to the mirror over the mantelpiece.

No, it was madness; my face was not yet properly healed. Anywhere I should attract attention with my face like that.

Suddenly a wild idea seized me. Dr Carmichael had said the next fortnight would make all the difference to my wounds, and by then it would be quite safe for me to go out. Why should I not wait? What was there to prevent me? Then my knees began to rock and tremble under me. My mind was in a whirl and my thoughts came up like sparks of fire. There was only the dead body between me and safety, I told myself, only that cold white figure in the hall. I could hide it – ah! I could bury it. There was the grave out yonder ready there. It was fate – it was ordained.

I sat down on the couch to get my breath and feverishly asked myself what the dead man would have me do.

'Courage!' he had whispered to me in his dying breath; and courage undeniably had only one course to urge.

I would be an arrant coward to bolt – it would be relinquishing all in a panic of fear. Everything in the place was morally mine. He had made me his heir. I must wait, then, and collect my heritage. A little courage and a little patience and I should return into the world as he had wished me to return. I musn't be an ingrate and a fool. I must be worthy of the friendship he had extended to me and the risks he had undoubtedly run on my behalf.

In a few minutes I had become quite cool, and once my mind was made up I quickly and methodically set about the carrying out of my plans.

First, I went out and shut up the dogs. It gave me quite an eerie feeling to find them, all three, sniffing curiously just outside the hall door. I had never known them there before, and I wondered uneasily what mysterious forces of intuition I should be up against next.

The dogs locked away, I went back into the house and, taking a sheet from the dead man's room, I rolled it round the body and tied it up at both ends.

I made my mind a complete blank as I was doing this, and also when I was lowering the body into the grave. With the first shovelling in of the earth, however, my numbed brain took on some feeling again, and suddenly I remembered the dead man's dream. A dreadful fit of sobbing seized me and, even as he had seen, the tears streamed down my face as I stood by the grave-side.

What a friend I had lost, and what a good man he had been. Not good, perhaps, as the world held it, but good in his kindness and in the disdainful courage with which, in the hour of need, he had helped a fugitive-stricken wretch like myself.

What a broken life his was! Once, courted and flattered; once, popular and with a host of friends. Now lowered furtively and with hurry into a nameless grave, almost within an hour of his last breath, no pomp of ritual, no pride of ceremony, and no mourners, save one man, and he a convict under sentence of five years. My sobs were all his requiem as I filled in the grave.

I was nervous and frightened that night and, with the doors all closed, sat huddled in a corner of the room. The house was full of shadows, and many times I heard the noise of ghostly footfalls in the hall. I had pulled in a mattress to sleep where I had had my meals and had brought Diana in to be with me for company. The great bitch was uneasy too, and with mournful eyes stared restlessly round the room. Every now and then she kept standing up to listen, and to my terror it was always at the door leading into the hall that she went. She cocked her ears in warning, and several times she growled as if something told her someone were hiding there. Towards midnight, however, she came and lay down at my side, and together, at last, we dropped into fitful slumber until dawn.

With the sunrise I felt much better, and with my courage back I set about getting the situation well in hand. There were lots of things for me to do.

First I had to make out the daily list for the man who would call at the window by the gates. There were several old lists of the doctor's lying about, and I had no difficulty at all, first go off, in making a very fair imitation of his handwriting. Indeed, so easily was it to imitate that the possibilities I saw before me raised my heat beats again to dreadful excitement.

I knew all about signatures, and for ten years it had been my life work to examine and verify the signatures on the cheques at the bank. I knew exactly what points were always looked for, and how one judged – almost automatically as it were – as to whether signatures were genuine or not.

I say my heart began to beat in excitement; but it was not the thought of successfully forging any paltry grocery lists that stirred me. I was thinking of the doctor's banking account and of the large number of securities he had told me he held. What if I could come to handle those?

The very idea for the moment took my breath away, and then the sweat stood on my forehead in big black beads. Hurriedly I possessed myself of the key from the dead man's belt and, opening the big safe in the wall, breathlessly went through the contents.

The doctor's pass book was the first thing I came upon, and I saw there was eight hundred and fouteen pounds lying to his credit. Nearly all his withdrawals, I noticed, had been made as he had told me, by open bearer cheques. There was a deposit account book, and he had lying at short notice at four per cent. Then there was a huge stack of government bonds, bonds to bearer for the most part I saw, with my eyes almost starting from my head. I started to total them up until a small memorandum book on a shelf attracted my attention. It was labelled 'Investments', and in a few seconds it told me all I wanted to know.

In securities and investments the estate of the dead man was worth nearly sixty thousand pounds and a good proportion of it was in a liquid and easily negotiable form.

I lay back in the armchair and for a long while gave myself up to my reflections.

What was I going to do – what had I the courage and the nerve to do? It was the parting of the ways.

I became cold and collected and reviewed everything from every angle I could conceive.

To begin with all that the dead man had left was mine, morally. He had given it me as he died, and in justice it was all mine. But in law? In law – I sneered bitterly to myself – not one penny piece was mine. He had died apparently intestate. I laughed mockingly. What did I care about law? I asked myself. I snapped my fingers contemptuously and let my thoughts run on.

Well, if it were all mine, how could I lay hands on it? The bonds to bearer would be easy enough; but for the other monies, Dr Carmichael's signature would be continually required. Could I manage it? Could I have the nerve to remain here in this house, week after week, month after month, take on the role of the dead man, forge his signature repeatedly, and gradually, bit by bit, realise the securities and draw in the deposits, until eventually all and everything were secure in my hands. Could I do it? Why not?

I knew all about the dead man's mode of life. I knew his habits, his inclinations, and his tastes. I knew exactly what he was accustomed to do, to whom he was accustomed to speak, and the few people – the very few people – he was known to by sight. The manager of the bank knew him; but he had not seen him for two years. The postman knew him; but he was old and stupid. The daily tradesman knew him; but for a year he had only seen him very occasionally, and then through the little window by the gate.

For a full hour by the clock I lay back and considered everything carefully, and the more I considered it the easier I thought the whole business would be.

I only had to sit tight, I told myself, be careful, and no one would find me out.

But the signature! I was forgetting that, and yet that was decidedly the most important point of all. Could I forge it successfully? Dr Carmichael had always used his typewriter for correspondence, and so, fortunately, only a signature wwould ever be required.

I took out the already filled-in cheque from the pocket-book and very carefully, as a bank official, analysed the signing of the name.

Yes, it would be easy, I told myself. With a little practice I should have no difficulty at all.

Dr Carmichael had not been dead many days before I realised to the full what strength of character must have been his.

To have lived for five long years alone in that house, nursing the sorrow of his broken life, with not a soul to speak to and thrown back on his own resources, I knew must have been a searching trial for any cowardly weakness that was in him.

The loneliness must have been terrible. I found it so before even a week had passed.

To wander about the gloomy house, to lie watching the distant city from the tower, to sit in silence in the garden all, in turn, brought home to me the utter dreariness of such a life.

And yet I, unlike Dr Carmichael, had so many things to look forward to.

I had mapped out my future actions in a calm deliberate way, and resolutely had put out of my mind all fear of any untoward happenings.

Three weeks exactly after the doctor's death, and five weeks after the operation, I was to make my first excursion into the city to cash the fifty pound cheques he had drawn. I was dreading it, and yet, at the same time, I was looking forward to it. I had never been a coward or one to be afraid of taking risks, and yet I knew it would entail every scrap of my resolution to walk calmly along the city and pass unruffled through the doors of the All Australian Bank. But I meant to go through with it boldly, and in the few moments of misgiving that I had I was not a little cheered and buoyed up by thinking how amused and pleased Dr Carmichael would have been with the course of action I was pursuing. The whole idea of the impersonation would have appealed to his cynical sense of humour, and I could picture the grim smile he would have worn had he been there to see me marching into the bank.

The fateful morning arrived at last and, just before ten, with a quickly beating heart, I let myself out of the gate. I was wearing an almost new lounge suit of the doctor's and it fitted me very well. If anything, I was a trifle broader in the chest than he had been, and perhaps half an inch longer in the legs. I had got on a light Trilby hat, and was comforted not a little by a pair of the slightly smoked glasses that the doctor had generally made use of when reading in the garden.

Making sure to secure the gates behind me, I walked briskly down the road towards the trams. I met several people but was relieved – they either didn't notice me at all, or else they gave me only a very passing and uninterested glance.

In less than a quarter of an hour I was in the heart of the city and walking nonchalantly through the crowded streets. With every minute my confidence was increasing and, long before I had reached the bank, I was delighted. I had passed several people I knew without turning a hair.

Pausing before a long mirror in an outfitter's shop window, it struck me how well dressed I looked. The doctor's suit was certainly beautifully cut and, as I say, it fitted me very nicely. My hat, however, didn't quite please me. It looked rather too big, so I went in at once and bought another, paying for it – remembered with a smile – with two of the notes originally intended for the new wing of St Snook's Church.

Funnily enough, my conscience pricked me here, and I determined in due course to forward a donation so that St Snook's should not in any case be a sufferer.

At last I passed into the bank and with, I flattered myself, a very calm face tendered my bearer cheque for endorsement to the ledger clerk in the window under the letters A to D. At the same time I handed in Dr Carmichael's pass book to be made up to date; I wanted to know exactly how the account stood.

The clerk took the cheque casually and then, glancing at the name on the pass book, at once gave me a beaming smile.

'Should we send it on to you, sir?' he asked pleasantly, 'or will you take it next time you come in?'

I felt a sudden pang of uneasiness. Of course, I ought to have posted the pass book. Handing it in, without cover as I had done, the clerk had jumped at once to the conclusion that I was Dr Carmichael himself. I had to let it go at that.

'Oh, post it on, please,' I said casually, 'but let me have it in a few days, please.'

'All right, sir,' he replied. 'You shall have it tomorrow,' and he proceeded to initial the cheque.

Crossing to one of the cashiers I handed over the cheque, and at my request he returned me ten five pound notes.

I was just putting them in my pocket-book, preparatory to leaving the bank, when a rather elderly looking man came up and, not a little to my trepidation, addressed me.

'Dr Carmichael?' he asked deferentially with a grave bow.

I bowed haughtily in return. There was a nasty catch in my breath for the moment, I couldn't have answered him if I had tried.

'I'm the assistant manager,' he said. 'I'm sorry, Mr Bultitude is very ill and will be away for some weeks. He mentioned to me about your deposit account; and I understand you telephoned you would be withdrawing half of it – three thousand pounds – at the end of the month. The ledger clerk told me you were here, and I just wanted to verify the matter. It's your wish it should be transferred to the current account?'

My mind jumped with a great bound of relief. What a stroke of good fortune that old Bultitude was away ill! Not that he would probably have remembered Dr Carmichael very well after two years; but still, it took away the uncertainty of everything, and for the present, at any rate, I felt I was safe.

I pretended to hesitate before replying. 'Oh, well,' I said after a moment. 'Yes, let the arrangement hold good. Transfer it to my current account, please. I shall be using it, I expect, within the next few weeks.

I left the bank with my head very high in the air. Really, how easy everything was going to be. Chance was certainly coming my way now. All in a moment, and quite by accident, I was established as the dead man at the bank now, and with prudence and without too much haste I should surely be able to carry my plans through.

I was so pleased with myself that I thought I would have lunch at the Grand Australasian Hotel. I regretted my decision, however, ten minutes afterwards for, to my horror,

Judge Cartright walked in. For the moment I thought he was actually going to seat himself at my table, but the obsequious head waiter bowed him on, and I heard him sit down just behind me.

I didn't dare to look around, but all through lunch I could hear the calm, polished voice, as he talked with a companion, and several times the smell of the scent he used came up offensively to my nose.

The lunch was not by any means, however, an unhappy one for me. I was moving in a new world and, added to the novelty of my surroundings, there was the thrill that peril and risk always give to the man who ventures and is not afraid.

That night before I got into bed I took stock of everything and carefully reviewed my prospects of success. I reckoned that in six months at the latest I could realise all Dr Carmichael's estate and get quit of the Commonwealth for once and all. Only one thing troubled me, and that only a little. What had the dead man meant when he told me to look out for Angas Forbes?

Who was this Forbes? And when was he likely to appear?

CHAPTER 5

In a very few days after my first visit to the bank, my confidence in myself was firmly established; and one morning when I took careful stock of my appearance in the looking-glass, I was quite sure no one would ever recognise me again.

It was not only that my wounds had healed beautifully, and that they were now only really discernible when you were actually looking for them; but also that my wild expression seemed to have altered. Whether it was the mental torture I had undergone, or whether it was the lonely silent life I was leading, there was undoubtedly a great change in me. My face was far firmer and far harder than that of the old Archibald Cups, the ledger clerk of the All Australian Bank. My eyes were sterner, and in repose there was a cold, bitter expression about my mouth. There was also something of the quiet confidence of power about me, I thought – the arrogance perhaps of knowing I was a rich man.

I was not in any way superstitious, but many times it came over me that in assuming, as I had done, the role of Dr Carmichael, something of the mental characteristics of the dead man had descended upon me at the same time.

I had no fear of anyone or anything now. Good opinions or bad opinions would be henceforward of no moment to me. I was absolutely cynical in my views of life and in the main I regarded the outside world as being entirely made up of people who either always bullied or always cringed.

I had only to go into the bank now and there was concrete evidence of the respect in which I was held. Be my past bad and reprobate as it was supposed to be, I was bowed in and bowed out with deference that could not have been greater had I been a haloed saint.

I had money – that was all.

There was no doubt a great deal of good luck was coming my way – for two out of the three people I most feared were suddenly removed from my path.

Bultitude, the manager of the All Australian Bank, died; and Usher, the assistant manager, reigned in his stead. Trotter, the postman, was put on superannuation pay.

One fine Saturday morning I let myself out of the gates in a very pleasurable frame of mind. I was going to the race meeting at Victoria Park, the first meeting I had attended since my arrest for embezzlement at the Bank.

It was a glorious autumn morning and there was a crisp champagne feeling in the air. I was looking forward with great interest to the racing and to seeing many old acquaintances there.

Almost the very first person I saw on the racecourse was my one real friend of former days, Dick Rainton, the trainer. Greatly to my dismay he looked worried, seedy, and anything but prosperous. He was pale and thin, much thinner I imagined than he used to be. And although I only saw him for a few seconds it struck me he looked shabby. It came quite as grief to me, for I remembered how loyally he had spoken up for me at the trial, although in so doing he would certainly not have been applauded by the big-wigs in the city who controlled the racing world.

I went up and sat in the grandstand and for a while watched the racing without mingling among the crowds. Two men came and sat down just behind me and began discussing the people who moved thickly before us. I was amused with the racy way in which they discussed the notabilities of the gathering.

'There's Blogger, the stipendiary,' said one. 'Conceited ass, thinks he owns the racecourse, he does, although he's only a paid servant of the club, just like the gatekeeper there, but he doesn't do his work half so well. Boorish, uneducated chap, real bully, too; drops on the little jockeys like a load of bricks but takes jolly good care to leave the important ones alone.'

'Damned sight too pally with some of the trainers for me,' said the other. 'How the blazes is he going to pull up his own friends? Look at the last meeting here. Bullock runs those two horses of his in the welter. Everybody's on Moorish Bride. Carries more than half of the tote. Well, as you saw, Antidollar wins, pays seventeen pounds. Splendid scoop for the stable, but the blinking public let down thud. What happens – nothing! No fuss, no enquiry, just considered the natural thing; and next night, what do you think? Blogger and Bullock dining together at the Australian Hotel. Gee-whiz – aren't we all mugs?'

I heard the other man laugh. 'It's all in the game, old man,' he said. 'They're all in the same clique. But, hello, there's Rainton, there by the rails. A lot of tabs going about him now. They say he's in queer street and has got a bill of sale on the furniture in his house. I'm sorry if it's true, because he's a straight sort, that chap, and that's why I expect he's not got on.'

They went on talking of other people, but I didn't hear any more of what they said. My thoughts were far away, and there was a choking lump in my throat. Poor old Rainton, and his nice little wife, too! I had had many a happy time with him and had often dropped in for a chat at their home. Well, I could help him now, and I could do it quickly, too. I must think of the best way.

The racing was quite good that afternoon, but the hurdles and the steeplechase interested me most, no doubt because in my youthful days I had often schooled horses over the jumps.

In the hurdles a very pretty light chestnut mare, Moonlight Maid, took my eye. She had rather short legs, but was beautifully symmetrical in form and just the very animal I thought to give a good account of herself over fences. I didn't like the stable she was in, however. The redoubtable Bullock was training her, and he was the gentleman so uncomplimentarily referred to by my neighbours on the grandstand a few minutes back. One could never be at all certain what he was really up to, and whether he was out to win or not.

I chanced it anyhow and had a tenner on her in the tote. She got off beautifully; but she hadn't jumped two hurdles before I knew my money was lost. The lad riding her, Macarthy, was supposed to be pretty good; but this time, at any rate, he was riding a bad race. He had the mare too much on the bridle all the time and steadied her far too much, I thought, as she approached the jumps. At the hurdle in the front of the stands, just what I was expecting happened. She jumped short and came a jarring purler, giving her rider a nasty fall. Another animal seemed to jump right on top of her, and yet a third horse was involved in the mishap and brought down. There was a dreadful gasp from the crowds, but to the great relief of everyone it was soon seen no one was much hurt. Moonlight Maid herself got quickly to her feet and bolted half round the course before she was caught.

'Wretched brute,' said a man in front of me. 'Animals like that ought not to be allowed in hurdle races. She's never been properly schooled as yet, or she can't jump for nuts.'

I went round into the paddock and had a look at her when she went back in her stall. She had got a nasty gash in one of her forelegs, and Bullock was cursing loudly. He had got the stable veterinary surgeon with him and from their remarks as they were examining the mare I guessed they had both backed her this time. Apparently they were putting all the blame on the poor horse, and none, as in my opinion they should have done, on the jockey. Had she won, she would, I noticed, have paid just over eleven pounds in the tote.

I didn't catch sight of Rainton again that afternoon, but I saw Drivel Jones marching about the place like the great 'I

Am' he evidently thought he was. One of his horses, The Rooster, was made a hot favourite in the welter and started at less than two to one. It came in a bad fourth, however, and the public looked rather glum. The general opinion seemed to be that it was one of The Rooster's 'stiff' days.

All the next day I was thinking a good bit about Rainton and in what way I could put him on his feet again. At first I had been for sending him a good sum, anonymously, in bank notes, but after a little cogitation I soon dismissed that idea. To be of any service to him, I told myself, I must find out exactly what his present position was, so that any help I gave him would be adequate and of permanent good.

Besides, my visit to the racecourse, I found, had fanned an old flame, and it was now starting my mind upon a very interesting chain of suggestions and ideas.

One thing, I determined to go and see Rainton himself without delay.

On the Monday evening, just as it was getting dark, I called at Rainton's house. His wife, the pretty Nellie Rainton of old days, answered the door. If Rainton had looked bad the other day, his wife looked positively ill, I thought, and her eyes were swollen as if she had been crying. I asked in a deep voice if I could speak to Mr Rainton.

She looked frightened. 'No-o,' she replied hesitatingly. 'I'm sorry, but he's not in.'

An instinct told me she thought I had come about money and I hastened instantly to remove the idea.

'I'm a stranger to him,' I said quickly. 'My name is Wells. I've come about putting some horses under his care,' and I handed her a card.

Her face cleared at once and the frightened look, I was glad to see, dropped away, but she still hesitated again.

'He's not in just now. He's' – she broke off short and then stood silent as if she were thinking – 'well, will you come in and wait. I don't suppose he'll be very long.'

I was shown into the drawing-room that in old times I had

known so well. There was a girl in there, sewing. She was about twenty-two or twenty-three, I noticed, and she was pretty, with big dark eyes. I had not seen her before, but from her likeness to Mrs Rainton I knew at once who she was. She was Nellie's sister from Victoria. I had heard about her.

She left the room at once, and for about a quarter of an hour I was left in there alone, to ponder over the many changes that had taken place since my last visit to the house.

Presently I heard the front door open, the quick pattering of light footsteps into the hall, the sound of a lot of whispering, and finally a heavy tread towards the room that I was in.

In a few brief seconds Dick Rainton stood before me.

Dear old Rainton, how I longed to take his hand! How I longed to seize hold of him and tell him who I was. His face, I knew, would have broken instantly to beaming smiles, and his old honest eyes would have looked into mine with all the trust and pleasure that only true friendship feels.

But I didn't dare to do it. Mine was too big a secret to give to any man, and the very possession of it would only have thrown another worry on Dick Rainton's mind. It were best that I should be a stranger – if, indeed, it were only for a while.

So I stood up and faced him coldly. He was holding the card I had given Mrs Rainton in his hand.

'Mr Rainton?' I asked.

He bowed, without replying.

He looked, I thought, very white and ill. 'I've come to see you about some horses I want to put under your care.'

His face seemed to brighten a little. 'Will you sit down, sir?' he said. 'You have some horses you want me to take?'

'Yes,' I said, 'or, rather,' I went on with a smile, 'I want you to buy these horses for me, and then take on their training.'

'Are they Adelaide horses?' he asked curiously.

'Yes. One's Moonlight Maid, now in Bullock's stable, and the other, I see, comes up for sale at Fentum's yard on Wednesday. It's the gelding Pirate King.'

He pursed his lips dubiously. 'They'll want a lot for Moonlight Maid, sir, even if they will sell her at all.'

'I don't think so,' I replied confidently. It's Bullock's opinion she ran a bad race on Saturday, and he's just the very man to fire her without giving her another chance if someone offers him a good price now.'

Dick Rainton smiled a quiet smile. 'You may be right there, sir, but what do you expect to have to give?'

'Oh, anything up to three-fifty or four hundred,' I said, 'but I think you'll get her for much less than that. Two hundred guineas is what I figure they ought to take. I want you to do the deal.'

He looked down to the carpet without replying then looked up quickly as if about to speak but instead was silent for quite a long time. Then he blurted out, 'Look here, sir, I'm sure it's very good of you to want me to take your horses, but to be frank with you I'm thinking of giving up training.'

'Giving up training!' I said, and I am sure the surprise I felt was readily apparent in my voice. 'Why – what do you mean?'

He seemed rather confused. 'I've not made a success of it,' said rather falteringly. 'I've not done well lately; I've – '

I interrupted him roughly. 'Nonsense! You trained Alice Beauty, who won the Adelaide Cup; you had Monsoon, who won the Great Eastern Steeple at Oakbank; you won the Derby with Hard Lines, and the Ledger with Blue Spot, and you've had lots of other winners too. Why – what do you expect? You can't always be winning. Everyone has bad and good times.'

He just opened his mouth in astonishment. I had reeled off his best successes as pat and readily as if they had been my own. He didn't know what to make of me.

'Come, Mr Rainton,' I went on. 'You'll train for me. I'm only starting with two; but I may be racing extensively later and perhaps I'll give you a string.'

He found his voice at last, but he spoke reluctantly, as if his words hurt him and he was ashamed.

'I'm sorry, sir,' he said, slowly, 'but I can't train for you. To be quite honest, I'm in financial difficulties and can't carry on.'

'You've a bill of sale on your furniture?' I asked bluntly.

He started and his face got very red. 'Everyone, I suppose, knows it now,' he said bitterly. 'The bad news always gets around.'

'And so will the good news,' I interrupted heartily. 'It'll be all over the place in two days that you're buying horses and quite free from debt.'

'What do you mean, sir?' he asked, quickly.

'I mean,' I replied, now slowly and emphatically in my turn, 'that I'm here to make you promise to take my horses, and I'm going to set you on your feet for that reason. Now – how much is this precious bill of sale?'

'Two hundred pounds,' he said, slowly, but with no expression in his voice.

'It's nothing,' I said briskly. 'You'll soon work that off.' I took out my pocket-book and extracted a number of notes.

'Look here – to begin with, I'll lend you five hundred pounds. You can pay me back when you're prosperous again. Then there's another five hundred for buying these horses; but they won't cost you that. Go up to two-fifty for Pirate King. There's a thousand pounds here,' and I pushed the notes across the table to him.

He made no attempt to pick them up. Instead, he leaned towards me and stared hard into my eyes. For the moment I felt uneasy, but the light was bad and I had my back to the lamp.

'Who are you?' he asked, hoarsely. 'And what do you know about me?'

'You've got my name there,' I replied coolly, and nodding towards my card, 'and I know you for an honest man.' I stood up and picked up my hat, as if to go.

Poor old Rainton looked dreadfully perplexed. He took out his handkerchief and mopped his face. Suddenly he seemed to make up his mind. He opened the door and, to my embarrassment, called out to his wife. 'Nellie – Nellie! I want you a moment.'

Mrs Rainton had evidently not been far away, for she appeared from round the corner almost before he had finished speaking. She looked white and scared. He held out the notes for her to see. They were all fifties.

'This gentleman here, dear,' began Rainton with a catch in his voice, 'wants me to train for him, and he's lending me five hundred to set me on my feet. Do you think I ought to take it from him?'

'Oh, sir,' said Nellie, turning to me and looking as if she were going to cry. 'It's a perfect god-send to us, and I know he'll pay you back. He's a good man, my husband, but everything's gone against us lately. Our old hurdler, Antioch – the breadwinner, we used to call him – was killed at Victoria Park. Then Mr Doughty died, and all his string was taken from us and sold up. Then my husband got into trouble with some important racing people here, because he spoke up for a friend of ours who was falsely accused. They got some other horses taken away from us – and then I fell ill. We've had awful expenses, and – '

'Hush, hush, dear!' broke in her husband. 'This won't interest Mr Wells here.'

'But it does,' I said, with rather a catch in my own voice now, and I turned sympathetically to Mrs Rainton.

'You were referring to that man Cups, weren't you? I remember reading that Mr Rainton gave evidence at the trial.'

'He was a falsely accused man, sir,' said the trainer, solemnly, 'and never robbed the bank. I knew him intimately – and he was not that kind.'

'Where do you think he escaped to?' I asked.

'I could never hazard a guess, sir, but I'm afraid, now, my poor friend is dead!'

We chatted for a few minutes about the happenings of my trial, and it warmed my heart to know in what esteem they still held me. Then Mrs Rainton asked me, rather nervously, if I would like a cup of tea.

'Or a glass of beer?' suggested Rainton. 'I've got a nice cool bottle in the cellar now.'

I sniffed up appreciatively. Someone was frying bacon in the house. Mrs Rainton saw me.

'I suppose – I suppose,' she asked rather timidly, 'you wouldn't care to stop to our meal? We haven't much to offer you,' she went on lamely, 'but I make my own butter, and my sister fries bacon like no one else.'

Greatly to Rainton's astonishment, I thought, I accepted at once. I was quite reckless now about the chance of being recognised, and fully believed I was quite safe. But, still, I wanted to put it to the test. If the Raintons didn't discover me, I argued to myself, no one ever would.

In a few minutes we were all sitting down to tea, and I had Nellie's pretty dark-eyed sister just opposite to me. Now I always flatter myself I made that meal a great success. There was a natural feeling of restraint among us at first, but I resolutely laid myself out to put them at their ease. I pitched them a good yarn about my life. I told them I was rich man and fond of the turf, but that all my relations were against racing, and that was why I was lying low. I could never do things openly, I said, in my own name.

We spent quite a happy hour at the meal, and it was pure delight to me to see the relief in Nellie Rainton's eyes. She looked like a reprieved prisoner.

Going home that night I thought a lot about the Raintons; but strangely, it was only the face of Nellie Rainton's sister, Margaret Price, that came to me in my dreams.

Rainton bought Moonlight Maid for two hundred and twenty guineas, and the next day Pirate King was knocked down to him for a hundred and eighty-five.

According to my instructions he had bought them both absolutely in his own name, and in the case of the gelding it was most amusing to hear the buzz of surprise that went round the saleyard when he started to bid. It was supposed all over the city that he was in great financial straits, and when he started confidently to go up tenners and fivers there was a tremendous lot of whispering and much nodding of heads.

I was standing just behind Bullock, who trained usually for Drivel Jones, and the stout trainer's muttered comments to a friend gave me great pleasure to overhear.

'What the devil's up with Rainton now,' he whispered, 'and from where in heaven's name is he getting the cash?'

'Don't know at all,' replied his friend, 'but I hear he paid off Lazarus yesterday!'

'The devil!' said Bullock. 'And he downed me yesterday, too, with a most dirty trick. He sent an old hay-seed looking fellow over to my place to buy Moonlight Maid, and like a fool I let her go for two-thirty-one quid. If I'd known it was for him – he shouldn't have had her at any price!'

'Why don't you make out, then, that there was a mistake?' said the other. 'Say you meant three-thirty-one.'

'But it's too late. He paid cash and took her away. It was only this morning I heard she'd gone into Rainton's yard.'

'Well, there's something up, it's sure, and we'll know later what it is.'

Bullock and his friend were not, however, the only curious ones. Rainton told me lots of people tried to pump him, but I knew he was a close man, and I had no fear.

I went down to his place the next day and had a leg up on both Moonlight Maid and Pirate King. The mare was a beautiful mover, and I put her at a couple of hurdles at the end of the paddock. As I expected, leaving her to herself, she cleared them like a bird, but she jumped both of them very high, I thought.

I pulled up where Rainton was standing. He was watching me with a rather puzzled look.

'Not the first jump you've taken, Mr Wells,' he said quietly, 'and your riding reminds me of someone I used to know.'

I brushed his remark aside. 'The mare jumps like a cat,' I said, 'but it's fences she ought to be over not sticks. I want you to get her ready for the big steeple, and I'll ride her myself, that is, if I can get down to the weight.'

He stared at me in a sort of amazed surprise, but my next words made him stare harder still.

'Now, look here, Rainton,' I said, 'I'm going to get some fun out of this. For the next three or four months at any rate I shall be at a loose end, and I'll do a bit of riding for a living. You must get me a licence to ride.'

At first he thought I was joking, but I soon convinced him I was in deadly earnest. I explained my plans to him. 'Now for the future,' I insisted. 'I'm going to be one of your lads. No one must know me here as Mr Wells. I'll be Huggins from New Zealand, or anybody you like. For the future I'll come down here in quite different clothes, and you must put me wise in just the ordinary way. I've done a lot of hunting, and can ride, as you can see, but I've never ridden in a race as yet, and I expect I've got a bit to learn.'

Rainton didn't say much, but I am sure he thought a great deal.

A week later I got my licence and then started as extraordinary a life as it will ever be my lot to experience.

I had no less than four distinct personalities. I was John Archibald Cups to myself, a convict, who ought to have been doing five years' penal servitude in the stockade. I was Robert Carmichael to the postman at North Adelaide and to the people of the All Australian Bank. I was Arnold Wells to Rainton and his family and, to the racing public, I was Harry Huggins, a most capable jockey over the jumps.

Rainton believed I was living at the Australasian Hotel. At any rate, he never questioned me and, if he wanted ever to write to me, I had told him to address my letters there. I came down to his place on a motor bicycle that I housed in a private garage at North Adelaide. I leased the place from the owner, and because I paid six months' rent in advance the latter probably never gave me another thought.

I used to slip out very early from my lonely home, the motor bicycle was not a quarter of a mile away, and dawn was often only just rising when I was on the training grounds and beginning my work.

I had always been a very capable horseman, and I soon found there was not much anyone could teach me. I seemed to have a natural aptitude for handling horses, and the most nervous of them would become quiet and tractable when under my hands.

Rainton, after a couple of weeks, said I was a born steeple-chase jockey and, without boasting, I don't think he was far from wrong.

I had a limpet-like seat in the saddle, and I was absolutely without fear. Even after some really bad falls, I continued to approach every obstacle with the calm, unruffled confidence of a man who had never had a spill.

I remember well my first race in the metropolitan area. It was at Victoria Park. But it was not my first appearance in public. I had had a losing mount at Balaclava and also one at Gawler, but I had so far not appeared in the Adelaide district.

Rainton came up to me that morning as soon as he saw me and asked me with a grim smile if I would take a mount that afternoon.

'It's Vixen Lady they've got no jockey for,' he said, 'and Benson's just phoned up to ask if I can give him any help.'

I smiled back at Rainton. I knew quite well what he meant by his smile. Vixen Lady was a dreadful beast to handle and was certainly one of the most risky mounts in the state. As far as the jockeys were concerned, she already had one fatal accident to her credit and had been responsible for a good many minor injuries as well. She was a well-bred animal and when it pleased her could go like the wind, but she was very uncertain in her jumping, and in some of her moods would rush every obstacle she was put to, whether it was a hurdle or stone-wall.

It was a wonder to everyone she had not been killed half a dozen times already but, so far, as far as she was concerned, she had borne quite a charmed life. With my own eyes I had seen her once laid out at Morphettville – stunned, for the best part of an hour; and then, when they were just thinking of putting the friendly bullet into her, she had got up and allowed herself to be led meekly away.

She was only kept in training because in her good moods she was really brilliant, and so little was she generally supported in the totalisator that whenever she was successful her owner invariably got a very good win.

No one was ever very anxious to ride her, and even some of the most hardened jockeys would refuse to take the mount.

Rainton regarded me curiously, waiting for my reply.

'Of course I'll ride her,' I told him. 'It will be interesting to see what I can do.'

Benson, the owner-trainer, had a good stare at me when I was brought up to him just before the race that afternoon.

'Ride her boldly,' he said gruffly, 'and don't for a moment let her think you're afraid. If you're in any doubt keep her back till after the stone wall, because it's there she's twice come to grief.'

I touched my cap respectfully and muttered, 'All right, sir.' She was carrying eleven stone two, and as I could weigh in at ten stone eight I was well able to do the weight. I stroked and patted her for a moment or two before I got into the saddle. She was certainly not an animal for a nervous man to ride. She kept looking round and showing the whites of her eyes. She was quiet as a sheep, however, in the preliminary canter, and went down to the starting post as if she were one of the best mannered beasts in the world.

I heard afterwards that everyone was most interested in us. People asked Benson from where I'd been dug out, and there was mild speculation about the odds of my being killed.

The starter gave us all a beautiful send off and, making up my mind quickly what I would do, I bustled the mare forward to get her well out in front. I was full of courage, but my experience of racing had been so very meagre that I knew I would feel more confident if I were free from the other horses for the first jump.

Vixen Lady responded like the high-bred dame she was, and we were soon leading by some three or four lengths. Approaching the first obstacle I let her take it at her pace, and she skimmed over it like a bird. The second she also took beautifully, and then came the stone wall bang in front of the stands. Here, I thought, she seemed about to falter, but giving her a hard sharp cut with the whip I wouldn't let her slacken, and almost before I knew it we were over and danger was passed.

I heard a great cheer as I went by, and I remember even now the intoxicating feeling that it gave me. It was like some strong heady wine that made me absolutely reckless of danger, and determined me, at any risk, to try and get the mare home first.

But after the stone wall all else seemed to come easy, and at every further obstacle I drove the mare forward with a confidence so absolute that I really astonished myself. I never gave her a chance to scamp, and like a beautiful and precise machine she cleared everything in her way. Coming down the straight I eased her ever so little, and almost effortlessly she ran home a winner by five lengths.

The crowd gave me a rousing cheer for my success, and Benson was most enthusiastic about the way I had ridden his mare.

'That's the way to handle her, my boy,' he cried. 'No one's ever ridden her before like that. All she wants is a bit of courage with the lad on top, and she'll jump sweet and clean as a deer.'

Rainton met me a beaming smile, too. 'You certainly have brought me luck, Mr Wells,' he whispered. 'I simply had to have a fiver on her as you were riding, and she's paid seventeen pounds ten at the tote. Eighty-seven pounds ten's a glorious win for me just now, and won't they be pleased at home.'

My success on Vixen Lady brought my name at once before the public, and by pure good luck at the very next race-meeting on the following Saturday I received another unexpected win.

In a way, perhaps, this second success was as pleasant a one as I can ever remember, mainly, I think, because it helped a little unimportant one-horse man as against some of the most fashionable racing stables in the state.

I had just run a very respectable third on a rotten beast in the hurdles (it would have paid eighty-one pounds in the tote had it won), when the trainer of Vixen Lady came up and asked me if I would like a mount in the steeple.

'It's not much of an animal, and it's got no chance at all, but it belongs to a pal of mine from up-country, and I'd like him to have a run for his money. It's Farmer's Boy I want you to ride.

I had just heard of the animal and that was all, but Benson told me all about him. His owner, it appeared, was a little shop-keeper somewhere in the country up Balaclava way, and he had brought him down to the city more, it was believed, for the sake of swank than anything else. Years ago, however, the horse had been a pretty good third-rater and had won a few little races up somewhere in the bush, but it was fourteen years old now and not up to much. He had no chance at all among metropolitan horses, and yet for some reason the handicapper had given him ten stone. I should have to declare about eight pounds over-weight.

Agreeing at once to take the mount, I was duly introduced to the owner, Mr Tommy Pucker. He was a common, vulgar little chap, but very affable and friendly. He was as impressive in his riding instructions as if the race were the Melbourne Cup.

'Keep him going the whole time,' he implored. 'He's safe as a house at the jumps, and he'll warm up like anything as he goes along and will be fresh as a daisy when he's done about a couple of miles. Give him plenty of stick.'

He offered me a vile-looking cigar and introduced me to his wife and daughter. The two ladies both shook hands. Mrs Pucker was very red and stout and the daughter fat and big like her ma, but with a good-natured smiling face. Not at all bad-looking in her way.

'I'm sure you'll win, Mr Huggins,' the mother said. 'Trainer Benson thinks we've got quite a chance, and my husband's putting twenty on in the tote. All our friends are on it, too.'

I cursed Benson for a liar, and really felt genuinely sorry for the simple folk. Celerity, the top weight with twelve stone seven, would just walk round Farmer's Boy, I knew.

I cantered slowly before the stands on my way up to the starting post, and some of the remarks I couldn't help hearing were quite the reverse of complimentary.

'This is not a ploughing competition,' called out one. 'Take him home.'

'Hurry up, old Noah,' called out another, 'or you'll be too late for the ark.'

But Farmer's Boy wasn't at all a bad mover, I found, and as soon as the starter sent us off I was agreeably surprised with my mount. He wasn't a slug by any means, and he certainly took the jumps as if he were an old hand at the game. He jumped desperately slowly, it was true, and always almost stopped after landing but, as his owner had told me, he wasn't given to falling.

It was a very small field and there were only six runners. A couple of hundred yards from the start and I was, as I expected, a good many lengths behind but, after the first obstacle, with a nice cut from the whip, the old boy put on pace and seemed, I thought, to be quite respectably holding his own.

At the fence opposite the grandstand two of the horses in front of me fell and, bustling up Farmer's Boy, I was greeted with ironical cheers as I went by. We cleared the obstacle, however, in great style, but at that point I calculated we were a good fifty yards behind.

Then suddenly I began to think there might be something in the old beast after all. I thumped him heartily with the butt-end of the whip, and responding gamely he began actually to gain on the leaders. It was very gradual, but when we were on the other side of the course opposite the stands there was not a foot more than ten lengths between us and The Seagull, who was then leading.

Farmer's Boy battled on bravely, but when The Seagull at length approached the last obstacle – and the distance between us was about the same – I naturally thought the whole thing was up.

Still, I determined at any rate to give the Pucker family a good run for their money, and with hands and whip I continued to urge my solid conveyance on. It was well I did so, for suddenly and unexpectedly my opportunity came.

At the last obstacle, a simple brush-fence, The Seagull fell and so close were the three horses together that he brought down Celerity and Bonjour as well.

Now was my chance, I realised, and well wide of the floundering animals I drove my mount over the bush-fence into the straight.

But the straight was a long way from home and, even as we passed the fallen leaders I got a flashing glance of Bennett, the jockey of Celerity, up on his feet and stretching for his whip.

I gave one fierce cut at Farmer's Boy and was delighted that he bucked up at once to quite a respectable pace. But we had gone very few yards before a great rousing cheer boomed up from the stands, and I knew instantly what had happened. Celerity had been remounted, and he was now no doubt following hot foot in pursuit.

Now I always flatter myself I didn't then for a moment lose my head. My riding experience in races up to then had been, as I have told, very little, and I might quite reasonably have been excused if I had just thoughtlessly flogged on my mount until he had died away to nothing.

But I did nothing of the kind. Instead I just thought and reasoned the whole matter out. I looked up towards the winning post and calculated how far we had yet to go. Then I cocked my eye back and saw how far Celerity was behind and exactly what his jockey was doing. Bennett was working his whip like a flail, and from the resounding noise of the whacks I could hear, his blows were evidently in deadly and desperate earnest.

But punishment like that, I argued, couldn't be of much good for long, and on top of the shaking Celerity had probably just received, the effect might soon peter out.

So I took things quite calmly on Farmer's Boy, and finding he was rattling along now in first-rate style I held back my whip and rode him only with my hands.

Nearer and nearer came the winning post, and louder and louder sounded the whacks on poor Celerity behind, but I just held my breath and waited for the supreme moment to come.

The crowd were wildly excited, and roared strenuously for the favourite to cut us down.

Suddenly, when only about ten yards from home, the fine head of Celerity loomed up upon my side. Now or never, I called to myself, and in a lightning flash my whip was up. One fierce hard cut and Farmer's Boy sprang forward. The favourite was shaken off as if he were standing still, and with a good two lengths to spare we passed the post in front.

Instantly, and as if by magic, all the shouting ceased. Being only a six-horse race, only one dividend would be declared, and Farmer's Boy, the wretched and despised outsider, would scoop the pool. The crowd were badly hit. Then their better feelings got possession of them. A thin clapping of hands, a few isolated 'Bravos', and then a long big rousing cheer as I came up to weigh in. 'Well ridden, sir; a fine judged race,' called out some man by the rails, and the cheers grew and grew in volume until I finally disappeared into the weighing- room.

It certainly panned out a good thing for those who had had the courage to back Farmer's Boy.

Just over two-thousand-five-hundred pounds had been invested in the tote, but only fifty-four pounds ten had gone on my mount, and it paid forty pounds five for each one pound invested.

My employer in the race might have been a vulgar little chap, but he was undoubtedly a good sport. He searched me out in the paddock later, and was most grateful to me in his thanks. In fact, he almost had tears in his eyes. He insisted upon my taking another of his vile cigars, and then, in saying goodbye, he unobtrusively pressed a many times folded banknote into my hand. As soon as he had gone, I unfolded it. It was a fifty.

Rather to my discomfiture I met the whole party again about half an hour later, just by the bandstand. They all looked in the seventh heaven of pride and happiness, and when they caught sight of me I had to endure all the thanks over again. Mama Pucker held my had for an uncomfortably long time, and the girl took a flower out of her dress and insisted it should be mine. With everyone looking on, I was glad to get away.

From that day a most successful riding career began for me, and almost at once I sprang to the very forefront of cross-country jockeys. Without boasting, there was no one could better me at the game, and over the jumps my services were soon continually in demand.

In a few weeks very rarely was I without a mount, both over the fences and over the sticks.

I soon became a great favourite with the public, and with 'Huggins up' people at once rushed to support any horse I was riding in the tote.

I was proud, too, when they looked upon me as a 'straight' jockey, and in their minds there was never any question whether the horse was out to win or not when I was riding.

To my great amusement Drivel Jones came up one day and asked me to ride his chaser, Babylon, at Morphettville. The regular jockey of the stable was ill.

I was on the point of refusing, when Drivel Jones suddenly winked his eye.

'Don't knock him about,' he said, looking me hard in the face. 'It's not one of his good days, and if we win there'll be a seven pound penalty at Oakbank to put up. Take it easy, you understand. Myself, I think Robin Adair will win,' and with a measuring nod he walked away.

But if he thought Robin Adair would win, the public certainly thought otherwise, and with me in the saddle Babylon was at once backed down to a very short price in the machine.

The race needs no description because I made the great black gelding win, right from beginning to end. He got badly balked, it is true, at the last fence, by a horse falling just in front of him, but I brought him around smartly and won a good race by a length.

He paid only two pounds eleven.

Drivel Jones's face was a study when I came into the enclosure after the race. He gave me a vile black look, and I could see he was cursing me under his breath. He never said a word to me, but Rainton told me afterwards he went about telling everyone I had knocked his horse about. People, however, had a shrewd idea why he was angry, and there was a lot of quiet amusement about the seven pounds penalty Babylon would now have to put up.

One racing paper quite openly 'guessed' Harry Huggins would not be asked to ride for Drivel Jones, esquire, again; but it left it to its readers to wonder why. It made the significant comment, however, that it would be a good thing for racing in Australia if there were more jockeys like me.

The great majority of the people in the Commonwealth are interested in racing, and it may be wondered why I was never afraid some or other of the officials of the All Australian Bank would not one day recognise, in the capable jockey Harry Huggins, their eccentric customer, Dr Robert Carmichael.

But I really never had any fear on that score. At the bank no one had ever seen me without my smoked glasses, and these I knew made a vital difference to how I looked. Besides,

I argued, if it ever did dawn on anyone for a second that there was some likeness between the two, they would contemptuously dismiss the idea in the next second. On the bare face of it, the whole thing would seem too absurd.

So, as I say, I never worried about that matter at all.

CHAPTER 6

The weeks rolled quickly on, and with the middle of June the brief sharp winter of South Australia set in. By then, however, many things had happened to me and in many ways I had completely altered my mode of life.

I had got rid of the hounds. I had sold them to a dog fancier up in the bush. It had gone to my heart to part with them, and over Diana especially had I almost shed tears.

But I had to get rid of them. I was away now so much and they were being neglected. Besides, to me now their use was gone, and the hour was getting nearer and nearer when, as Dr Carmichael, I should be known no more. Any time now I must be prepared to slip suddenly away. My arrangements were nearly all compete, and I tarried only because my confidence and assurance were so great that I was determining to realise to the last item every penny of the doctor's estate.

With the departure of the dogs I took on a daily servant, a sort of gardener handy-man, and never perhaps was an employer more particular about the habits and character of his prospective servant than was I.

My servant would be seeing me at home, just as I was, and I had no desire there should be any chance of his recognising me on the racecourse. Unlike the people at the bank he would know me without my smoked glasses and, conversant with all my goings out and comings in, he would very quickly put two and two together if only his suspicions were once aroused.

So I advertised for a teetotaller and strict Baptist, thinking that that would about fit the bill. I guessed a gentleman of that description would never be found within many miles of a racecourse.

It was certainly dreary work interviewing the candidates and I was a long while coming to my decision. Finally I settled on a very white-faced little man who for forty years and more had slunk through life under the name of Hooker. He had brought with him a long recommendation from his minister, to the effect that he, Hooker, had never missed one of the reverend gentleman's weekly exhortations for more than seven years, and I must say that from Hooker's general appearance, I was inclined to believe the statement might be true.

So Mr Hooker was duly engaged, and in a contemplative, peaceful fashion, he set about putting the much neglected garden in some form of order.

I must say that on the whole he was rather a good servant, but all the time he was with me, I am quite sure, he never over-exerted himself once. Also, before he had been with me a week, I had grave doubts about his teetotal principles. He slept too long on the wheelbarrow after his midday meal to satisfy me, and I got to notice smells other than those of peppermints on his breath sometimes when I came near. But I thought he was as satisfactory as anyone I should be able to get and I consequently let him alone.

And all this while I had been gradually realising the securities of the dead man, and one by one I had been disposing of his interests in various undertakings. I had never, as I had foreseen, had any difficulty at all at the bank. They were courtesy itself to me the whole time.

By the beginning of July I had got together in various places just over forty-thousand pounds, a very good proportion of which was in medium-sized Commonwealth notes, and I was reckoning that in about another six weeks or two months I would safely have cleared up all there was for me to handle.

Looking back in the after years, I am sure I very much enjoyed my life at that time. There was just the very spice of risk and danger in it that made strong appeal to my restless and unsatisfied nature, and it was moreover a life that called for initiative and courage at every turn of the wheel.

I never knew exactly what was going to happen to me, and every day I rose to the call of new enterprise and new adventure. Although everything on the surface seemed to be going so easily for me, I was never sure there was not some danger threatening me from below, and that all in a flash I might not have to cut and run.

Dr Carmichael had been such a well-known man once in New South Wales it seemed impossible that, sooner or later, someone would not come enquiring after him in Adelaide.

My transactions now often took me to the bank, and there were always plenty of people about when I went in. I knew I was a person of great interest there and I wondered how long it would be before I was one day pointed out by one of the clerks as Dr Carmichael to someone who had once known the real doctor. Then the fat would be in the fire, and I would have to vanish instantly in the best manner possible.

But I had made all preparation for flight at any moment, and I flattered myself I was prepared for all eventualities.

Australia is a very wide place and an easy country to bury yourself in when once away from the big centres of civilisation. But it is a difficult country to hide in in the towns and cities, and a more difficult country still to get out of and proceed to other countries if you should happen to be wanted by the authorities.

The passport system, for example, is a very strict one, and among other things any passenger on an overseas-going steamer has always, before being allowed to set foot on the boat, to get his passport first viséd by the income tax authorities. This, of course, means double identification, and it is not an easy thing, I can tell you, at any time to steal away unnoticed from the Commonwealth.

But I had no intention of leaving suddenly for overseas. When I should see fit to drop the mantle and role of life of Dr Robert Carmichael, I intended to slip away from Adelaide, and under a different name, of course, make my home in a distant part of the Commonwealth until it would be perfectly safe for me to take passage to Europe.

Were any suspicion at any time raised against me I was not going to try and foolishly bolt away on some steamer homeward bound. It would be the very place in which they would first look for me, and with wireless installations everywhere I should be then a certain and an easy capture.

So it will be realised I had carefully thought everything out, and as a result I was reasonably confident that in any suddenly threatening emergency I could run safely to earth. I was ready to escape in any direction and had provided several good hiding places with elaborate preparation for a long stay in them if necessary.

I had a small bungalow at Port Noarlunga and another one on the marshes near St Kilda. I had a car hidden in the hills; I had a bathing hut on the beach at Henley; and last, but not least, I had a powerful little motor-boat lying in a secluded reach off Port Adelaide. And everywhere I had provisioned for either a long hide or a lengthy journey. I believe I had arranged for everything.

I say I was happy in those days, and I repeat I am quite sure I was. The greatest reason was perhaps, however, because I had at last fallen in love.

Pretty dark-eyed Margaret Price, Nellie Rainton's sister, was giving me my real first love affair in life. I had never much cared for girls and certainly none of them had ever interested me as Margaret did. I had spoken very few words to her and was uncertain even if she knew that I admired her. But she was often in my thoughts and I was always finding excuses for going up to the Rainton's house.

I think Nellie Rainton knew from the first that I admired her sister but could never determine whether she was pleased or not.

I couldn't fathom Nellie Rainton, and always had an idea that she was suspicious about me. Once when I broke into a good laugh about something, she turned round and stared at me so intently and with such startled eyes that for a long time afterwards I was uneasy.

But she was always very nice to me, was Nellie, and most grateful to me for the help I had given her husband.

There was no doubt that I had helped her husband just in the nick of time. I learnt afterwards that when I had appeared on the scene it had been only a matter of days before he would have been sold up.

Now, in a few short months, everything was different and his future seemed assured. My association had apparently brought him amazing good fortune all along. Several of the horses he was training came into form and even the very moderate Pirate King turned out to be almost a little gold-mine. Three times in succession the gelding paid a dividend, two firsts and one second, and as the two first dividends were both over ten to one, Rainton had certainly no cause for complaint.

My popularity was also an excellent advertisement for him, and several owners, to be in a better position to secure my services, transferred their horses to him, so that he soon had almost as many animals as he could manage to train.

So far we had not raced Moonlight Maid in public since we had bought her, but we had been putting her to good work over the fences with a view to the Grand South Australian Steeplechase in August. She was under my special care and I had great hopes of her success. Properly handled, she would jump like a cat, and of her speed and staying powers I never had the slightest doubt.

I had long ago lost all fear of being recognised anywhere as the once John Archibald Cups, and I moved about freely in the city just where my fancy took me.

One day, being quite by chance in the neighbourhood of Pepple's grass and nut shop in Pipe Street, I walked boldly in and asked for a shilling's worth of almonds. The assistant served me. He was a brawny chap and looked, I thought, very much like a prizefighter. Pepple himself came in when the almonds were being wrapped up. He gave me one quick hard stare and then passed back into the inner part of the shop. I hadn't seen him for over six months and he looked more skinny and dried up than ever. A few days later just for amusement I went in again. Pepple and the assistant were both there, but this time Pepple served me and the whole time he never once took his eyes of my face. He stared so hard that with all my assurance I was glad to get away.

Damn the little fool, I thought, but I expect it's only his way.

Two days later, however, a letter from him appeared in the *Advertiser*. It was headed 'Occult Waves', and just typical of Pepple's state of mind.

One day last week, he wrote, he had been quietly reading in the back part of his store, when suddenly and without any warning he had sensed the presence of occult waves and his own astral being had at once moved in harmony to them. He had felt all in a twitter and he couldn't make it out. He had gone quickly into his shop and had there found his assistant serving almonds to a strange man. He had noticed nothing particular about the stranger then and the latter, completing his purchase, he had gone straight away.

Immediately the occult waves had died off. The incident had certainly seemed strange to him, but in the course of a few days he had quite forgotten it. Then suddenly two days ago, the day before yesterday, to be exact, the same thing had occurred again. Suddenly he had felt the same waves stirring and suddenly he had experienced the same twitter down his back. Then the shop door had pushed quickly open and a customer had walked in. It was the same man who had caused the vibrations a week ago.

Then Pepple went on with a long rigmarole that only his fellow lunatics would understand, but the whole gist of it was, that in his shop that day Pepple's astral spook had met another astral spook that had once been his enemy in a former life. The two spooks had apparently recognised one another and at once started to give each other cheek.

Instead of making me laugh, the letter only had the effect of making me intensely angry for, as I recalled bitterly, as foreman of the jury, this ass at the trial had once practically held my fate in his hands.

I was very angry, too, with newspapers about that time, for they began to give me a very anxious and annoying time. They wanted to start the interview business with me and to know all about my parentage and where I was born.

It all began because one Saturday afternoon at Morphettville I won the double on the hurdles and the steeple. They were both hard-won races, and in the hurdles I had soundly trounced a crack Victorian horse from over the border. The Adelaidians were delighted and cheered me vociferously as I weighed in. Coming out of the weighing-room, I found a little knot of reporters waiting for me. A press-photographer snapped me at short range, and I was invited to disclose all my family history for the edification of the readers of the various Sunday papers.

I refused point-blank with a black scowl and elbowed my way angrily through the throng. I saw at once the danger I was running and suddenly cursed myself for a fool. Publicity like this was the last thing I wanted. But the reporters were not easily to be shaken off, and it was not until I had been absolutely rude to them that I could get away.

Next day, however, they had their revenge and over my scowling photograph in one of the Sunday papers I read:

HUGGINS, THE MYSTERY JOCKEY
WHO IS HE?

Then followed nearly a column and a half of curious speculations about me. There was nothing much they could say with certainty, but it seemed as if it had only just dawned on them that they knew really nothing about me. Where did I come from, they asked, and what country was the land of my birth? What had I been doing before I became a jockey and was I doing it now only just as a hobby? Was I a rich man? Where did I live? What was the other part of my life? I used to ride backwards and forwards on a motor-bicycle, they said, and no one had ever met me away from the training ground or the racecourse. I never mixed with the other jockeys. I was taciturn and short of speech. I must be an educated man, for one day a pocket edition of Shelley had dropped from my coat. And so on, and so on. A nice tale they made of it, and I was furious.

Rainton said nothing about it when he met me on the Monday, but Nellie Rainton, who happened to be with him, stared at me, I thought, harder than ever.

Passing down Pipe Street that evening just before six, I happened to catch sight of Pepple's pugilistic assistant slipping through the side door of a public house. He was evidently getting 'a spot' before the places closed.

All of a sudden it struck me that I might catch Pepple alone, and in a spirit of devilry I made for the vegetarian shop.

Yes, Pepple was there all by himself and he was bending down behind the counter, doing something to some shelves. He didn't see me until I was right upon him. The newspapers had put me in a furious rage all day and I was delighted to have someone to vent it on.

I leant over the counter, and as Pepple turned round to gape at me I gave him a good box on the ears.

His eyes stared and for the second he was too astonished to cry out. Then before he could recover himself I picked up a large bag of flour off the counter and jammed it over his head. He spluttered like a vicious cat to get the flour out of his mouth and nose, but I knocked him sideways with a handy sack of nuts and, calling out something, I don't quite remember what, pulled open the door and expeditiously left the shop.

It had all happened in a few seconds and all down the street I was laughing to myself. I had not hurt Pepple, but I had no doubt given him a good fright and provided more material for further flap-doodle about his precious astral self.

During all that week I fondly anticipated reading in the newspapers a highly coloured account of my visit to the vegetarian shop, but to my disappointment nothing appeared; and then something happened of a far more interesting nature that for the moment drove all thoughts of the grass-feeding Pepple entirely out of my mind.

A man was arrested on the Cheltenham racecourse for stealing a lady's hand-bag. It appeared she dropped it without noticing its loss, and a man behind her was seen to snatch it up and endeavour to get away unseen.

But he was pounced upon by another man who had watched the whole episode, and promptly given over to the police. At first he had refused resolutely to give his name or any account of himself whatever but, yielding at length, he had turned out to be David Fielders, one of the assistant cashiers at the Consolidated Bank.

Appearing next day before the city magistrate, the evidence had been so conclusive that Fielders had had no course but to admit his theft, but he had asked through the lawyer he had engaged that he should be dealt with summarily and not sent up for trial.

But the magistrate had hesitated and was very curious about two twenty-pound notes that had been found upon the prisoner, and pressed him about where he had obtained them.

At first Fielders had sworn he had won them at the races that same afternoon but, it being pointed out that he had been taken into custody before any monies had been distributed by the totalizator, he had started prevaricating and giving different stories to account for their possession.

Sternly pulled up by the magistrate, he had finally broken down and burst into tears, admitting at last that the notes belonged to the bank.

According to the newspapers there had been silence after this for a long moment in the court, and then Pierce Moon, who by a strange coincidence had been watching the case in the interest of the lady from whom the bag had been stolen, had realised the significance of the admission.

He had remembered, it appeared, as it were all in a flash, that this man David Fielders had been the principal witness against me, when he, Pierce Moon, had been the defending counsel in what was now known as the notorious 'J.A. Cups case'. Upon this man's evidence principally had my conviction been secured.

Up had got Pierce Moon then at once and urged strongly that the case should be sent for trial. He had briefly explained to the magistrate his reasons and had insisted that the whole matter must be probed to the bottom.

The magistrate had thereupon committed Fielders and had refused bail. A fine hubbub there was then in the city and the management of the Consolidated Bank was very adversely criticised. A desperate attempt was made by the bank authorities to prevent anything further from leaking out, but they were quite unsuccessful in their efforts, and a nice tale was soon unfolded.

A smart reporter from the *Register* got hold of one of their clerks, and from him, on the quiet, gathered in a lot of information that the public were most interested to obtain.

It appeared that for many months now all the employees of the Consolidated Bank had been under a cloud. Continual thefts were occurring in the bank, but so artfully were they perpetrated, and in so many different ways had they taken place, that nothing ever pointed conclusively to any one single man.

So far from my conviction having stopped the thefts, they had been worse than ever since I had gone away, and no one in the bank now believed that I had been a guilty party. A lot more evidence had also been unearthed, to prove conclusively that all along David Fielders must have been the man.

The facts disclosed by the *Register* caused a sensation, and in a few hours almost, let loose a flood of correspondence in the newspapers.

Interest in the Cups case was revived at once, and the evidence brought forward at my trial was reviewed and discussed by scores of different writers during the next few days.

Finally the *Times of Adelaide* itself took up the cudgels on my behalf, and in a leading article under the heading of 'Grave Miscarriage of Justice', referred scathingly to the evidence brought forward at my trial.

It condemned Judge Cartright, himself, unsparingly, and, quoting extracts from his final speech asked bitterly, 'How, then, would it have been possible for any jury not to have recorded a conviction after so pointed a summing-up?'

It went on to recall my vehement and heated protests at the conclusion of the trial, and expressed the impassioned hope that at whatsoever cost, justice and retribution should now as far as possible be done.

But finally it suggested to its readers that perhaps as far as human recompense was concerned it might be too late now.

'Where is this wretched man?' it asked in conclusion. 'Where is this John Archibald Cups, who in the supreme moment of his agony was lifted like a spirit out of the hands of the law? Does some lonely unnamed grave hide him, or must we wait to find him until the sea gives up its dead? Dead or alive, we grieve it was his misfortune to be so misjudged. Happily we take comfort to ourselves that such cases as his are rare, but to his friends and his relations we tender now our most heartfelt sympathy and regret.'

The next day came an angry, vicious letter from Pepple. 'Have no mistaken grief,' he wrote, 'J.A. Cups is not dead. He came into my shop last week and threw a bag full of flour over my head. He hit me with a sack of nuts and slapped my face. I did not recognise him until he shouted out that I was an herbivorous ass, and then, although he looked quite different to the Cups of the trial last year, I knew him at once. He had certainly altered strangely in appearance, but there was no mistaking the man. He swore at me just like he did at everyone in the court. He was quite mad with rage.'

My tardy vindication was a sort of bitter pleasure to me, but I did not enjoy the correspondence half so much as I ought to have done, because in the middle of it I was laid up for a few days with a painful spill from a fall in the hurdles. I was not much hurt, it is true, but I was quite unconscious for a few minutes, and the annoying part of it was that the Jockey Club doctor was most interested in me when I came to.

'How did you get those scars, man?' he asked gently touching my nose.

'I fell down and hurt myself some years ago,' I grunted.

'No, no,' he said sternly. 'That's not true.' He shrugged his shoulders indifferently. 'It's your own secret, of course, and if you don't want to tell me, well, hold your tongue. But you can't deceive me, all the same. Those scars are of quite recent date. Mind you, I'm not curious; but I take of my hat, anyhow, to the man who patched you up. He was an artist, if ever there was one.'

I felt uneasy when he turned away.

CHAPTER 7

Towards the end of July everything still appeared to be running smoothly for me. The day of the Great Steeplechase was near at hand and we had got Moonlight Maid well up to racing pitch. With some good experience now of cross-country races, I thought that I had never had a more promising animal under my charge.

She was an almost perfect jumper, was game as a pebble, and had plenty of pace. She would stay every inch of the three miles easily; my only fear was that she had a very nervous temperament and was liable to get easily upset, especially in the early part of the journey. She disliked crowds immensely, and she invariably pricked her beautiful little ears whenever there were many strangers about.

We had given her one run in public and she had come through the trial with complete success. In a field of eight horses at the Port and carrying eleven stone two she had won easily. The public had been quick to recognise her as the good thing she undoubtedly was, and with me up she had paid less than two to one in the tote.

Her success had incurred a seven pound penalty for the Great Steeplchase, but that was really what we had arranged for. Her weight there was ten stone two, and with the penalty bringing it up to ten stone nine I should be able to ride with the declaration of only a few pounds overweight.

After her win at the Port the best price on offer against

her for the big race was ten to one, but that did not matter in the least to us. Rainton had got forties about her as soon as the weights were out and was content with the good wager of two thousand to fifty for an outright win.

The public interest in me had by no means died down, and there were whisperings everywhere whenever I appeared, but the newspapers had stopped asking about my private life, and except referring to me occasionally as 'Mystery Huggins' they left me alone.

I often used to wonder what Rainton thought of me. He never said a word, however, and the only member of the family who referred to anything in any way was pretty Margaret Price.

She and I had got very friendly together, and when we were alone, which sometimes happened in the mornings when she was giving me a cup of tea after I had come back to the stable with Moonlight Maid, she would refer archly to the mystery that was supposed to be surrounding me.

She had a very pretty smile and was never chary of showing her beautiful teeth.

'Good morning, Mr Wells!' she said one day. 'No, there's no letter for you!' She laughed lightly. 'Perhaps your wife doesn't know your address yet.'

I laughed in return. 'And she's not likely to either, Miss Margaret,' I said, 'for, as I've told you a good many times already, I'm not married.'

She shrugged her shoulders prettily. 'Of course you'd say that – you men always do.'

I looked at her very solemnly. 'Look here, Miss Margaret,' I said, 'do you really think I'm telling you a story when I say I'm not married?'

She hesitated for a moment and became quite grave in her turn. 'I don't believe for a moment your real name is Arnold Wells, anyhow; you're hiding something from everyone, I'm sure.'

'Dear me, Miss Clever!' I said sarcastically. 'And how, pray, did you learn that?'

'You told me yourself!' she replied, pertly. 'You've told it to me many times, too. I can tell it in your manner and the way you look about you. You feel safer now, but when you first came you watched everyone as if you were not certain they wouldn't be giving you away. I've noticed it often in you.'

I looked at her steadily for quite a long time before attempting any reply. She was certainly being decidedly frank with me, but there was not a spice of resentment in her tone. She seemed rather amused, that was all.

In spite of myself I had to smile. 'And I suppose, then, Miss Clever,' I asked, rather reproachfully however, 'you've been impressing these ideas of yours on your sister and Mr Rainton?'

A quick sparkle of anger flashed to her eyes. 'Thank you, Mr Wells,' she replied with a little bow. 'I haven't discussed you with anyone yet, I'd like you to know. I'm not quite that sort.'

She looked so pretty in her annoyance that I just longed to pick her up there and then and kiss her, but I shrugged my shoulders and said very quietly, 'Well, it's very sweet of you if you haven't, that's all I say.' I reached out and laid my hand lightly on her arm. 'Look here, Miss Margaret,' I went on, 'one day I'll tell you everything; just now I'm obliged to keep silent. I'm not married, anyhow. I can tell you that straight away' – I squeezed her arm ever so slightly – 'and lately it's begun to be a great joy to me that I'm not.'

Whether she understood my meaning or not I wasn't sure; but I believe she did, for she gave me a arch smile as she walked back into the house.

I went home that evening woefully pondering how on earth I was going to fit pretty Margaret in with my intentions for flight.

I thought a good deal about Margaret in the days that followed, and to the exclusion of all else it was she who was now continually in my mind.

I was genuinely in love with her. Of that I was certain, and it was this certainty that made me so apprehensive about linking up her life with mine. After all, I was a fugitive from the law, and however little that fact troubled me, it might be a different matter as far as she was concerned.

I must tell her everything, of course, and, even if she cared for me, was her temperament, I asked myself, one that could be content and happy under the shadow always hanging over, however distant and remote it might be, of discovery and possible arrest.

It worried me, I can tell you, to think of it all; and another thing happened that week that went to pile up my worries and fill me at the same time with intense anger.

I saw my man Hooker at the races, and the devil of it was he saw me there, too. It was immediately after the hurdle race. I had come in second and was returning to the enclosure to weigh in. For half a minute we were held up until they opened the gates. There was the usual dense crowd by the railings, and I let my glance wander carelessly round on those standing there.

Suddenly I saw someone staring at me, staring at me incredulously with bulged and startled eyes. It was Hooker, I saw at once, and with his white face and widely opened mouth he was the very picture of stupefied amazement. He was close up by the rails, not five feet away from me, and for a good half minute at least he was taking me in. I made no attempt at all to turn my head away, and tried to act as if I had never seen him before. I looked at him idly and without recognition, just as I looked at any of the others there. Then I yawned behind my whip as if I were bored and looked among the crowd again; my glance went through Hooker as if he were no more to me than any of the others there.

I saw the man pucker up his face in doubt. He screwed his eyes together and squeezed half over the rails to get as near a view of me as possible. I could feel his eyes wander over every part of me. My face, my hands, my clothes, even my very boots interested him, and I wondered angrily if he were even calculating the latter's size.

At last, however, the gate was opened, and with more relief than I would recognize even to myself, I rode in.

The incident certainly annoyed me intensely, and alone by myself that night I pondered exactly what harm might now accrue. Whichever way I regarded it, the business for the moment certainly looked ugly enough. Hooker was an inveterate gossip, I knew, and I'd had always to be very stern to keep him at his distance any time.

If he were really certain he had seen me, then he would 'yap' about it on the spot to everyone he knew, and it would be only a question of the gossip reaching the reporters before they would be up at the Towner House in a few minutes, to climb over the gates to get copy for their wretched papers.

But would he be certain that he had seen me? That was the thing. No, I told myself. Even if he were a hardened racegoer, and well in with all the news of the turf, it would surely seem too impossible for him to believe Dr Carmichael, the one-time great surgeon (and I was certain Hooker would know all about me), now a steeplechase jockey on the turf! Why, the very idea would seem preposterous to him. Whatever he might have thought when he was actually watching me, as soon as I had passed out of his sight he would be thinking for sure he had been mistaken.

I finally reasoned myself into a more or less comfortable frame of mind; but still, the happenings of the day brought home forcibly to me the possibilities of peril that were always surrounding me.

Again, as I had done so many times, I took stock of my position, and I reckoned that in about a month from then all things would be clear for me to go away.

I had settled practically everything, except a few small unimportant items and the sale of the house. Touching the latter, I was already in negotiations with a likely party, and with any luck I thought the deal should be carried through in the course of the next three weeks.

It came to me with a great pang that my racing career was nearly over. The Great South Australian Steeplechase was now only a week away, and with it passed there would be only a few very minor races in which I should be engaged.

Ah, well! I sighed to myself, whatever happens now I have had a great time. Fortune has been a good mistress to me and I would be a churl to mistrust her now.

Hooker arrived as usual at seven o'clock next morning and, meeting me in the hall, gave me a most furtive and embarrassed look. I nodded to him in my usual way, however, and proceeded casually to furnish directions for what work he was to do.

He worked well that morning, but there was something quite different about him from other days. He was much quieter and, oddly for him, offered no conversation at all. Whenever I happened to be near him, and he thought I wasn't looking, I noticed him taking me in, in a most careful and methodical way.

Just as on the racecourse, he was not satisfied with looking at my face. He took in everything about me, and my hands particularly seemed to interest him.

I could see he was very puzzled, and I quite enjoyed rubbing in the doubts he felt. If I were really the jockey Huggins, then, of course, he knew I must have noticed him by the rails, for I had looked straight at him as he had been standing there.

That being so, it was probably a torment to him to have to speculate if I could possibly be so casual, knowing that he held my secret in his hands.

Certainly, Mr Hooker, strict Baptist and teetotaller, was a very puzzled man that morning; and he was undoubtedly thinking more of me than of his prayers.

But if Hooker had worried me, and his recognition of me on the racecourse had inclined me to believe that the curtain on Dr Carmichael must soon be ringing down, the arrival of a letter two days later certainly strengthened my belief in that eventuality a thousandfold.

A new actor was about to appear upon the scene. On the Wednesday afternoon a letter for Dr Carmichael arrived from Sydney. I noticed the postmark at once, and my heart jumped almost into my mouth. It was so obviously not a business letter, and on the back there was the inscription of the Sydney Central Hotel.

With trembling hands I tore the envelope open and at once all my worst fears were confirmed. Dated two days previous, it was signed 'Angas Forbes'. It was quite short, and very quickly I had taken it in.

'Dear Robert,' it ran, 'I only got back yesterday and hoped to have been with you this weekend. But now I find I must go up to Brisbane first. Anyhow, expect me in about three weeks' time. Hoping you are fit and well and not too much in the blues, Your old friend, Angas Forbes.'

'Three weeks,' I exclaimed. 'Only three weeks and I must be hundreds of miles away. I must vanish before any suspicion touches me, and long before there will be any hue and cry.'

'Now let me see,' I went on to myself. 'If I get away before this Angas Forbes arrives, there may be never any suspicion attached to me at all. No one may ever learn I was not the real Dr Carmichael and my sudden flitting may be considered quite in accord with the eccentric temperament of the recluse. But I must go quickly. In a week at most I must leave Adelaide. All of the estate that I have not realised I must give up. I shall have to tell something to the Raintons and what about Margaret now?'

All day I thought and thought about the matter and was so worried and preoccupied that even Rainton himself noticed something was up.

'Not feeling well, Mr Wells?' he asked sympathetically. Then he smiled quietly, 'I do hope, though, you'll be all right for Saturday.'

I put him off with an excuse that I had a headache, but to Margaret, whom I was only able to get alone for half a minute, I was different.

'Look here, Margaret,' I said quickly, using her Christian name for the first time, 'I must see you alone this week for something very important. Will you meet me somewhere on Sunday? The others mustn't know. You understand?'

Dear pretty Margaret! She understood. The sweet face blushed a little, but the sunny smile faded ghost-like from her eyes.

She looked down for a moment. 'I'll think about it,' she whispered, 'and I'll tell you between now and then.'

With my heart beating fast I moved nearer to take her hand, but at that moment Mr Rainton appeared in the garden, and, with a quick, sweet glance at me, Margaret moved back into the house.

That week I made all preparations for leaving Adelaide on the following Wednesday. The matter of Margaret was still unsettled, but all else was clear in my mind.

I was not going to be greedy and everything I could not take with me I would now cheerfully let go. After all, I was leaving, comparatively speaking, very little, but I thought with regret of my two bungalows by the sea, my car in the hills, my bathing hut on the sands and my boat at the Port. They would all be wasted now.

At first I thought of a quick sale of them, but then I remembered I wasn't quite safe even yet, and I sensibly told myself that with their disposal went all chances of escape if I should have to take a sudden flight in these last hours.

So I left them alone just as they were, and under the name of Thomas Hardy booked a sleeper for the Wednesday night in the Melbourne express.

On the morning of the following Saturday, the day of the great race at Morphettville, strangely enough, I overslept. It was a very unusual thing for me to do. I was always such an early riser. Whether it was because I had sat up late the previous night or that I had been a longer time than usual in going to sleep I do not know, but I was pretty startled at suddenly waking up in the morning and finding by my watch that it was actually half-past nine.

At first I couldn't believe it. I hopped briskly out of bed and went to look at the clock in the hall. Yes, it was nine-thirty right enough, but where the devil was Hooker?

Even if I hadn't waked by myself, Hooker was due sharp at seven o'clock, and he couldn't get in the house until I had let him.

I opened the front door and went round the garden in my pyjamas, but there was no sign anywhere of the man, and the drive gates I saw were still unlocked.

I was puzzled and annoyed. What had happened? I asked myself, and was the fraudulent Hooker ill? He had been right enough the previous evening when I had paid him his wages. He had come in for his money with the usual oily and respectful smirk and had seemed then just as he always was.

It was true I had noticed he had been rather strange in his manner all the week, but I had put that down to his uncertainty about whether he had recognised me at the races the previous Saturday. He had been uneasy and nervous I had thought, but apparently most anxious to keep in my good books. Several times he had tried to interest me unusually in the affairs of the garden. Once, for instance, he had asked me to come out quickly to look at a snake he was positive he had seen near the wall by the drive gates, but, of course, as I had expected, there was no snake to be found there. He had been most apologetic afterwards for making me come.

All these things I remembered suddenly, but they afforded no clue to his non-appearance now.

Grumbling to myself I went indoors to prepare my breakfast, a breakfast that was, however, never destined to be eaten. I had just sat down when I remembered the morning newspaper that was always thrown over the wall on to the lawn. I got up irritably to get it.

Walking back slowly to the house I unfolded it as I came along and then the bottom seemed to drop out of my world.

What did I see, and could I indeed believe the evidence of my eyes?

A dreadful shiver ran down my back. My tongue clove to the roof of my mouth, and I could feel my heart pump as if it would burst through my chest.

There were two large-sized photographs side by side at the top of the middle page, and they were both photographs of me.

The first was headed 'The Jockey Huggins' and the second 'Dr Robert Carmichael, the eccentric recluse'.

The paper dropped from my nerveless hands, a horrible sick feeling came over me, and for the moment I was stifled and couldn't breathe.

What did it mean? I asked myself. Oh, it couldn't be that I was found out?

Feverishly I seized on the paper again, and the bold big headlines struck at me like a cruel blow.

'Romance of the Turf', they ran. 'The crack jockey Huggins and the famous Sydney surgeon, Carmichael, prove to be one and the same man. The hermit forsakes his cave for the racecourse and commands astonishing success'.

It was many minutes before I could coherently take it all in. The shock was too great for me, and my brain was numbed with the sheer amazement of it all. I had grown so confident with the passing of the months and had fancied myself so secure. It had seemed impossible I could be found out and not even Hooker's recognition the previous Saturday had flurried me over-much.

Ah, Hooker! A sudden thought surged through me. It was Hooker who had given me away. I saw it all instantly. That was why he had been so nervous all the week, and why he was now staying away.

Another thought flashed to my mind. I grabbed the paper again and looked at the photograph headed 'Dr Carmichael'. Where had it been taken? It was a dreadful effort for me to hold back my rage for everything was plain as day as I looked at it again.

The photograph of Dr Carmichael had been taken in the garden of Dr Carmichael. I had been snapped from the bushes when Hooker had called me to look at the snake.

I had to laugh then if only because I realised how softly I had been done. The dull-witted snail-brained Hooker versus the sharp intriguing John Archibald Cups, I thought, and the victory all along the line with the former.

But my laugh, however bitter, did me good, and I turned now quite calmly to consider the whole article in detail.

It was certainly well put together, and on the face of it they had carefully verified all facts before committing them to print. There were two other photographs lower down on the page that I now noticed for the first time.

One was a snap of 'Dr Carmichael leaving the All Australian Bank in his smoked glasses', and the other was quite a large photo of the garden taking in the front and part of the side of the house.

The article itself was most sensational, and the files of some old Sydney newspapers had evidently been drawn upon for details of Dr Carmichael's early life.

It told what a great surgeon he had been once and it mentioned briefly the happenings that had led to his retirement now over five years ago. Then, it said, he had come to the City of Adelaide and for four years and more had lived like a hermit in its northern suburb. Sick of the world, he had made his home in a lonely house surrounded by a dark and high-walled garden, and there night and day he had been kept from interference by the prowling of great huge beasts of the Livonian wolf-hound strain.

Then, less than six months ago, it went on, he had altered his whole mode of life. He had come out among his fellow men again, and of all strange occupations for a highly cultured professional man he had taken up that of riding as a steeple-chase jockey in public.

Then it reminded its readers how successful I had been, and how, as Huggins the jockey, I had time after time ridden the most unlikely and unpromising horses to victory.

It described how all along I had resolutely refused to give any account of myself, and how everyone had been completely baffled in their attempts to find out who I was. For a time the secret of my dual life had been a secret all my own, and no one for one moment had imagined that Dr Carmichael and Jockey Huggins were one and the same man.

Then the writer of the article himself became mysterious and denied to his readers exactly how my secret had been found out. But it was quite clear to me that he had come in contact with Hooker, for details of my homelife were disclosed with as great an accuracy as if I had written them myself.

Then, too, only with Hooker's connivance could anyone have been placed in the garden to take those photographs, and the one headed 'Dr Carmichael', as I say, actually showed me standing exactly where Hooker had posed me to get a good look at his imaginary snake.

I finished reading the article and was just on the point of putting the paper down when the photograph of the house and garden again caught my eye. With an uneasy feeling I saw that it took in the big fig tree and the ground underneath. Was it fancy, I asked myself with my heart beating a good bit faster than I cared, or could it really be that in one corner the photo showed up a patch of earth of darker colour than the rest? An oblong patch shaped like a grave, and just under the big fig tree itself?

Again my blood ran cold.

CHAPTER 8

I sank to depths of great despondency that morning before the reaction at last set in, and I became my old confident self again.

As once before in that same house, I gave way to despair, and it was only the sharp remembrance of Margaret Price that pulled me up abruptly and dragged me finally to my feet.

The moment, however, I definitely began the mapping out of my new plan of campaign the very danger of my position thrilled me, and I boldly shook off my fears and faced all my difficulties with the old spirit of courage and resource.

Cups against the world again, I grinned to myself. 'And they shall have a good run anyhow.'

At first, but for a brief second, I was inclined to give up any idea of riding in the race that afternoon, and clear off straight away by the Melbourne express, but then, I thought, how mean it would be to leave Rainton in the lurch, remembering how much he stood to gain if we won the race.

No one understood Moonlight Maid as I did, and without me I knew there would be small hope of success.

I shut my teeth with a snap. No, I would ride as arranged, and whatever happened afterwards, no one would sneer that I was a coward. After all, I told myself, tomorrow I was fairly safe, for whatever had been discovered, the significance of it would not be realised at least for a few days.

I could see at once where the danger lay. I should be unmasked the first moment the Adelaide papers reached Sydney.

As soon as my photograph as 'Dr Carmichael' was seen there, denial would follow as a matter of course, suspicion would be aroused and within a few hours at most something of the nature of the truth would be grasped.

I thought it out carefully. The Adelaide papers could not reach Sydney until Tuesday morning. Well and good. I had until then to get away unquestioned. No one would be thinking I would try to leave Adelaide and, with no suspicions aroused and no one on the look-out, a very simple disguise would enable me to escape unnoticed.

I would take the Sunday morning train to Melbourne, and once in Victoria would make my way out towards the New South Wales border. News would travel slowly in the bush, and whatever hue and cry were raised, it would soon die down everywhere, I reckoned, except in the state of South Australia itself. Besides, I thought amusedly to myself, I really didn't see how, once out of sight and away, anyone could be certain of anything about me at all.

All ideas would be in a great muddle, of course, but even the bank people would have nothing certain to go on. They would have to be careful how they acted, for with me no longer in view they would have no proof that the man they had had dealings with wasn't after all the real Dr Carmichael.

The photo of Jockey Huggins and that of the man taken in Dr Carmichael's garden might be one and the same man, but who was there to prove that the latter man had ever called himself Dr Carmichael? There was only the newspaper evidence to go on, and that all rested on the bare word of Hooker.

The snap of me taken as I was leaving the bank, with my hat and smoked glasses, would, I could see again, be in no way conclusive. It wasn't good enough.

By noon, therefore, I had reasoned myself into quite a comfortable frame of mind, and after some bread and cheese and a small bottle of champagne, I felt game enough for anything. Only one thing troubled me and that was Margaret. What was I going to do there?

The Grand Steeple was to be run at three o'clock, and I purposely arrived at Morphettville as late as possible.

I knew, as the hour drew near, poor old Rainton would be getting desperately anxious, but I couldn't help it. It was my cue now to say as little as possible, and the more I kept myself out of the way the fewer questions I would have to answer, and the more difficult it would be for anyone to get at the truth when I was no longer there.

I had hoped to slip unnoticed into the dressing-room, but I soon found that even my worst forebodings had not sufficiently realised the interest that everyone would be taking in me.

The very instant the gatekeeper saw me, he beamed all over and wanted to shake hands.

'Good luck to you, Doctor,' he shouted after me as I slipped quickly by. 'You're the pluckiest man I know.'

Everybody within ear-shot looked round, and at once a quickly increasing crowd was following me to the dressing-room.

I appeared to be recognised instantly by everyone and a buzz of excited interest hummed round.

'Dr Carmichael, the great jockey,' they said. 'Look, he was the great Sydney surgeon once.'

I almost had to force my way into the dressing-room set apart for the jockeys, and there again, I had to go through another ordeal. A silence fell over the room when I went in.

None of the lads said anything, however. They just stared and stared, as if their very eyes would drop out of their heads. I thought Astley, the jockey who was going to ride Babylon, rather curled his lips into a contemptuous sneer, but no remark was made to me, and getting quickly into my colours I left the room and went to find Rainton in the paddock.

The paddock was crowded, and my progress there was just as uncomfortable and difficult as when I had first arrived on the course, but I hardened my face like a stone and, looking neither to the right nor the left, at length arrived at Moonlight Maid's stall.

As I had expected, Dick Rainton was there; and as I had expected also, he was looking as anxious as he could possibly be.

There was a crowd of people in front of the stall, and I literally had to push my way through to get to Rainton and the mare.

Oh, the relief in Rainton's face when he caught sight of me, and when I got near he seemed too overcome to speak! But I didn't want him to speak. We had a few seconds only before us, and I wanted to all the talking.

'Look down, man,' I whispered sharply. 'Pretend to be examining the mare's feet. I'm going to tell you something and you must keep a straight face.'

We were in the stall standing close together then, and I began to pat and stroke the mare. A few feet away the crowd was watching us intently. Fortunately, they were all talking themselves, and speaking quietly I knew they would not be able to hear what I was going to say.

Rainton, I saw, was looking puzzled, but he did as I directed and turned down his head.

'Dick,' I said quickly, but deliberately. 'I'll have to tell you now. I'm not the doctor from Sydney, I'm Cups.'

I could see him start and he drew in a deep breath.

'There's a lot to explain and you'll hear it all one day,' I went on. 'I've done nothing wrong, but I shall have to cut and hide again as soon as the race is over. Now, I want a favour from you. Give this note to Margaret when I'm in the saddle. Give it to her before the race, you understand. She must have it at once.'

He nodded his head, but still without looking up.

'If I see you when it's over, Dick, don't try and stop me whatever you do. I've risked something in coming here and everything will depend upon my getting away quickly. Listen, there goes the saddling bell.'

Poor old Rainton! I knew I had given him a great shock, and like a man in a trance he led out Moonlight Maid through the interested and gaping crowd. He made no attempt at all to speak to me and, even when he finally gave me a leg up on the mare and passed a last look over us to see that everything was right, he still made no remark, but parted from me with a sad and rather wistful smile.

To whatever age I live I shall never forget the very smallest happenings of the next quarter of an hour.

It was a glorious winter afternoon, and the sun shone brightly out of a perfect high blue sky. As we went out on to the course, I thought I had never seen a greater crowd at a meeting before. Everywhere was packed, and on all sides there was a seething mass of humanity. But the Great Steeplechase, I remembered, was always a good draw, the value of the stake, two-thousand pounds, bringing the best cross-country performers together.

There were seventeen horses running. Moonlight Maid was number seven on the card, and in that order we were to parade before the Grand Stand.

For the first time in all my races I was distinctly nervous. It was impossible that the happenings of that morning should not have been without effect on even the most hardened temperament, and I could feel my face drawn hard and pale.

There was so much at stake for all of us that afternoon and my anxieties were so varied and so many.

My own security was so uncertain that I was like a man almost hemmed in by the onrush of some fierce forest fire. Margaret, too, was an anxiety, for how could I deal with her when the next few hours, I knew, would find me, once again, a fugitive before the law?

Then there was Rainton, too, to be thought of. He was hoping so much to win this race, for, if successful, he would be set up for life.

I drew in a deep breath of anxiety. My burden seemed almost too great for me to bear.

I remembered, however, that this was to be my last race, and the very sorrow of it quickened me at once into quite a new train of thought. I must ride a good race, I told myself, I must ride the best race I had ever ridden. There must be no weakening now. I must not give way to fear. I had faced difficulty before with courage and I had come out well in the end. It must be so again.

All these thoughts had flashed through me in the first few seconds after leaving the saddling enclosure, and it was well for me that I had so soon got myself in hand.

The moment Moonlight Maid and I came before the stands, if there had been any doubt before, it was patent then the interest in which I was held.

There was an instant murmur of many voices, then someone clapped his hands and finally there came up a warm and sympathetic cheer. There was no doubt for whom the cheering was intended. It followed me all down along the stands and died away when I had passed.

I pulled myself together, and now, as cold as ice, faced the barrier from where we were to be sent off. I calmed Moonlight Maid to absolute quietude and then cast my eyes thoughtfully over the other horses waiting there.

I thought, with rather a pang of doubt, what a fine-looking lot of animals they were. The very cream of the jumpers of South Australia, and three high-class performers from Victoria as well. It would be a great race, I knew, and it would not be easily won by any one.

There were only really three horses, however, that I greatly feared. Babylon, The Beauty from Quorn, and The Rake. The Rake was a top-notcher from Melbourne, and as slick as a greyhound over the jumps, but I was hoping the twelve stone four he was carrying would sober him down a lot. His jockey was Porteous, a Victorian crack, a good-looking fellow about twenty-six, as smart as paint in his profession and one who knew all there was to know about cross-country work.

The Beauty from Quorn was a lovely cream-coloured mare. She was on the small side, but she was beautifully proportioned and could leap like a cat. I doubted, however, if she would be alongside us at three miles, although at two, with her light weight of nine stone seven, she would have been a most dangerous proposition.

It was Babylon I feared most of all. Top-weight and carrying twelve stone seven, he had earned well every ounce of his big weight. Beaten only once in South Australia, and that by a bare half length when under the same weight at Onkaparinga, he was a magnificent specimen of a steeplechaser. Of a coal-black colour, well over sixteen hands, he was a quick mover and almost faultless in his jumping. The only thing, and I had studied him well, he didn't like a fast run race, and moreover was never quite at home when making his own running. I knew he would be feeling his weight at the end of the journey, and I reckoned that if we were alongside of him at the last fence, Moonlight Maid, who was a wonderful finisher, would just about chop him for speed in the run home down the straight.

The starting bell rang, and with no delay we were sent off on our momentous journey.

Instantly I dashed my mount forward. I had many times rehearsed the race in my own mind and realised that the greatest danger lay in the largeness of the field. I had no intention of being at anytime entangled in the crowd.

Fifty yards from the barrier we were well in front, and I took the first jump a good three lengths ahead. I made the pace a cracker, and crossing over to the rails, led past the stands all out on my own.

But I had no intention of making all the running, and when Wild Aster and The Beggarman loomed up I let them gradually forge ahead until, with the first mile covered, I was running only third. Here I took a swift glance back and could see that the field was already pretty extended. The Rake I could see nowhere, but The Beauty from Quorn was almost alongside me and a very little way behind the great black head of Babylon caught my eye.

We continued much in this order until nearing the stands for the second time when Wild Aster came a cropper just in front of me, and in avoiding him I had almost to pull up and in consequence lost my place.

I was passed by both The Beauty and the great Babylon himself. The Rake I now caught sight of emerging from the ruck of those behind; there was no mistaking that long head with the big white star.

I was not at all sorry that The Beauty and Babylon were in front, for it was by their actions now that I should have to regulate mine.

With a keen appreciation of the varying merits of all the performers, as I have already mentioned, I had sorted out three horses that I expected would emerge with me into the front line at the finish, and it was upon them principally that I intended to keep my eye.

The pace was still very fast, and with a pang of misgiving I noticed that Babylon, just in front of me, was shouldering his great burden as if after all it were only a featherweight for him. One after another he took his fences with the grace and precision of a bird, and there was no loss of even the fraction of a second as he landed each time on the other side. The Beauty, too, seemed quite at ease, and her jockey was riding confidently as if he had a lot in hand.

With more than two-thirds of the journey over, and on the other side of the course, and opposite the stands, Beggarman, who hitherto had gallantly retained the lead, at last showed signs of compounding and held out signals of distress.

His jockey got busy at once with his whip, but it was of no service, and the wearied son of Lazarus faded quickly out of the picture.

Six furlongs from home and with two more fences to jump, the race seemed about to work out exactly as I had anticipated.

The Rake suddenly shot up from no where, and passing me in a flash drew up almost level with Babylon on the outside. The Beauty from Quorn was still leading, however, by half a length. She was just in front of me, but a few feet further towards the centre of the course.

Approaching the last obstacle the positions were almost exactly the same. The Beauty was still leading and I was still last, but as when two hundred yards before, the proverbial blanket could easily have covered us all.

I bustled my mount up ever so little and all four we took the last fence almost in line. Now for it, I thought. We shall find the weak spots now.

Instantly his jockey shot Babylon forward, and with him avalanched The Rake, side by side and stride for stride. The Beauty made a gallant attempt to retain her position, and for fifty yards or so she still kept the lead, but the long journey had finished her and all at once she slipped back and I saw her no more.

A furlong from the winning post and I was a good length to the bad. Babylon and The Rake, both hard ridden under the whip, were locked together by themselves, and with the tenacity of bulldogs were endeavouring to determine which was the better horse. I was close upon the rails, Moonlight Maid was going like the wind, and I had got her so beautifully balanced that I was afraid to lift my whip. I could feel she was all out, and the pace was so terrific for the end of a three mile journey that I was sure some of us would crack soon. So I left the Maid alone, and with my hands clenched hard upon her withers crouched like a thing of death against the rushing air.

A hundred yards from home and the great Babylon began to falter. The weight was telling on him at last. His head slipped back to the neck of The Rake, then to the latter's girths and finally the gelding from Victoria was leading by a length.

A dreadful howl of disappointment came up from the stands. Their champions were beaten and the great prize would now be carried over the border. It seemed almost that a groan was wrung from the assembled crowds, a groan that died to silence and ended in a gasp. Then suddenly the silence broke, a murmur rose like the sighing of a wind, and in a second a fierce exultant roar burst over stands and crowds like some great hurricane let loose.

Moonlight Maid was gaining on The Rake. There was no doubt about it, I had got the gelding cold.

Twenty yards from home, I was level with his girth – ten yards, and we were neck and neck.

The Rake struggled gamely, but with each yard the mare's deadly pace was telling, and in the end I knew she would last out best. Suddenly the end came.

In a desperate spurt The Rake headed us once more, just headed us, and then fell back so abruptly that I almost thought he'd broken down.

A great mist came before my eyes, the din of myriad voices stunned me, and we'd won by half a length.

The memory of the next few minutes is very hazy. I remember cantering back past the judge's box before being led into the enclosure. I saw a perfect sea of excited people and I heard a fearful sound of cheering in which the cry of 'Carmichael' seemed to often intrude itself. I saw everywhere smiling faces in the weighing-room, and everyone almost crowded up to congratulate me.

But I either replied nothing, or answered them curtly, I know. My thoughts were quickly turned to far away, and with the race once over, all its happenings seemed insignificant and small compared to the exciting probabilities to come.

I must get away and quickly too. In a few seconds therefore I had slipped out of my colours, and almost before the race was five minutes old was hurrying out through the dressing-room door.

As I had expected and feared, however, there was a crowd assembled, and the moment they caught sight of me they began to clap their hands and cheer.

'Bravo, Doctor! Hurrah! Bravo, Carmichael!'

Frowning in annoyance I tried to push through them, but a big burly man in particular blocked my way. He had a heavy full face, with a sandy beard and very blue eyes. It struck me instinctively that he was not waiting from motives of idle curiosity but had come there for some purpose of his own.

He stared at me for a second and then clutched hold of my arm.

'You're not the doctor!' he shouted. 'You're not Robert Carmichael.' He turned round excitedly to the crowd. 'This is not the doctor here. This man's nothing like him at all.' Someone in the crowd laughed and a young man shouted. 'Get out, you old fool.' The big man got angry at once. 'I tell you, I know the doctor well,' he bawled. 'We've been friends for thirty years.' He turned back and gripped me by the arm. 'This man's an imposter here. Who are you, sir, and what do you mean?'

The crowd hushed to silence. Uneasily, I realised they had sensed a ring of truth in the fellow's voice. All at once, the interest of a mystery gripped them.

'Who are you?' the man reiterated, still gripping fiercely on my arm. 'You can't humbug me. I'm a friend of Dr Carmichael's. My name is Forbes.'

Ah, I said to myself. I might have guessed it. This is that Angas Forbes. I looked him coolly in the face.

'Take you hand off my arm, please,' I said quietly. 'Take it off at once, sir.' My temper was rising. But he only gripped me the harder. 'There's something fishy here,' he shouted, 'and I'm going to get to the bottom of it.' He turned again to the crowd. 'Get a policeman, someone, quick.'

'You fool,' I exclaimed. 'You're drunk.'

I shook violently to free my arm, but he wouldn't let go, and exasperated to a burst of temper, I stuck him a fierce blow between the eyes and he dropped like an ox.

'Make way, please,' I called out sharply, and instantly the crowd opened to let me pass. 'This fellow here's been drinking,' I said as a parting shot. 'I've never seen him before.'

I hurried quickly to where I had left my motor-bicycle in the car enclosure, and a couple of minutes later was speeding down the road to where the Raintons lived.

Whew! what an escape! I thought. But what a rotten piece of luck that the man's turned up so soon. The game's all up now. I must clear out in an hour.

But where to, I asked myself? I must rearrange all my plans.

I had no time, however, to consider this. Rainton's place was only just beyond the other side of the course and very quickly I arrived there.

I was expecting to meet Margaret. The note I had asked Rainton to give her earlier in the afternoon was to tell her to leave the course immediately the race was over and meet me at their home as quickly as possible. She would be able to make a short cut over the racecourse and be at the house sooner than would be I myself.

As I had hoped, she was in the garden when I rode up. Hearing my footsteps on the path she looked up quickly with a pretty assumption of surprise. Then she crimsoned up all over. Without a word or smile even, I took her hand and led her unresisting into a small arbour at the end of the lawn. I lifted up her face and kissed her.

'Margaret, darling,' I said, breaking silence at last. 'You know I love you and I've come to say goodbye.' She gave me a quick look out of very startled eyes.

'Who are you, then?' she asked sharply. 'And what does all this mean in the papers this morning? I don't understand.'

I had made up my mind what to tell her and very quickly and very briefly I outlined all that had taken place since I had been committed for trial.

'Now, Margaret,' I said, when I had finished my tale, 'I have honestly told you all, and you must let Dick and your sister know how I stand. I've done nothing much wrong, but I must hide away again all the same for I've broken the law.' I waited for her to speak, but she said nothing. Instead she just looked at me with heightened colour and with more than the suspicion of moisture in her eyes.

'I musn't wait now, dear,' I said quickly. 'Every moment to me now is precious, but I couldn't go without saying goodbye.'

She found her speech at last. 'A nice goodbye,' she burst out bitterly. 'You come to tell me you love me and in the same breath you say you are going away for ever.' A choke came into her voice. 'Am I never to see you again?'

In a moment she was in my arms, and it was ecstacy to me that her tears fell both on her face and mine. I comforted her in the only way I could in the few minutes left to us before I had at last to say goodbye.

I told her she should hear from me soon, and I left it to her to consider if, knowing all she did, she would ever care enough to link her life with mine.

I had meant to stay only five minutes, but it was nearly an hour before I finally tore myself away.

I parted from Margaret in a hopeful frame of mind, but it seemed almost that that afternoon the goddess of mischance was bent on shadowing me from the very moment I left the Raintons' house.

The motor-bicycle began to go wrong at once. I could get no speed out of it, and after a couple of miles or so I had reluctantly to dismount and try and put things right. It was a choked jet, I thought at first, but I soon found it was more than that, and nothing I could do would make the vile thing go. Mounting a second time, after a few yards it refused absolutely to move at all. I was plunged into another dreadful turmoil of anxiety.

It was five miles good from where I was to the Tower House in North Adelaide, and it was vital for my successful escape to get home at once.

After the struggle with Angas Forbes at Morphettville that afternoon, it was impossible to determine what would happen next. One thing was certain. All my carefully arranged plans were now upset, and I should have to think out everything anew. I must go back, however, to the house. All the money I had collected and all my securities were there, and I must get possession of them at whatever cost.

For the moment I comforted myself with the thought that no one could get near the house, and then I remembered with a horrible foreboding that the wretched Hooker had the duplicate key of the gates at the bottom of the drive.

I burst into a cold sweat at the bare idea of the possibility of the new misfortunes that might lie in front of me.

Realising now that my motor-bicycle was hopeless, I wheeled it into a field and plumped it down among the bushes. Then I set off quickly at a half walk and half run towards the city, keeping a look out, however, all the time for the chance of a lift in some passing car.

But my good fortune seemed to have quite deserted me, and I was well on to the outlying parklands before I was eventually able to pick up a taxi.

Then as quickly as possible I was driven to North Adelaide, but not knowing how things would be at the house, I dismissed the taxi at the corner of my road.

It was well that I did so, for the moment I came in sight of The Tower, I saw to my horror there was a car standing just outside the gates. There was one man in it.

For a second I was inclined to turn back, but it came to me with a thrill of fear that everything now stood poised on the razor edge, and that it might be all or nothing for me in the next five minutes. At all costs I must get my bundle of notes and securities.

I walked up coolly and turned into the gates. Quite casually I took stock of the car. It was a hired one and the driver was nonchalantly enjoying a cigarette.

I walked up the drive and, as long as I was in sight of the occupant of the car, my slow pace indicated I was in no hurry at all. The moment, however, the trees hid me from his view, I darted like a panther into the bushes and went breathlessly to reconnoitre round the house.

I heard voices almost at once and, peeping from my cover, saw four men standing on the verandah just by the front door.

Three of them I recognised on the instant. They were Hooker, Angas Forbes and Levicka, one of the cashiers from the bank. The fourth man I didn't know, but he was, I saw, a police-sergeant by his uniform. They were all trying to peer through the coloured glass of the hall door.

If I had shown any hesitation then I should have been lost. If I had waited for even ten seconds, the game would have been all up, and this history never have been written.

But I didn't hesitate and I didn't wait. Their backs were towards me and, in an instant, I sprang out of the bushes and was running like lightning along the strip of grass by the side of the path.

Far quicker than it takes to write it, I had gained the friendly cover of the side of the house, and was racing for the back door. I pulled out the key as I ran and, in a few seconds, with no sound louder than the faint clicking of the lock, I was inside the house and, with door closed behind me, was tiptoeing to the room that contained the safe.

Although never expecting it I had prepared everything ready for an emergency, and in two minutes at most I had all the bonds and notes secured safely around my waist.

Making no sound, I took down a dark overcoat and a soft felt hat. Then I got an automatic pistol out of a drawer, and also a small pair of opera glasses that happened to catch my eye. A pocket flask full of brandy I thrust in my pocket, and then I stood up ready for the next act in the play.

The whole day had been so bewildering, full of change and incident, that all along it seemed I had had to act just as the moments drove me and, standing there then as I was, I realised grimly that I had no coherent plans ahead about what I should do or to where I should go. The forces of mischance, one after another, had so avalanched themselves upon me in the last few hours that I was like a sleeper tossing fearfully in the nightmare of some dark and dreadful dream.

All I could think of for the moment was to get away from the house, I was trapped, I knew, if I remained there.

Dusk was falling rapidly outside, and as I crept stealthily again across the hall all inside the house was so dark that I had no fear at all of being seen by the watchers outside.

The need of prompt and resolute action had quite robbed me of all fears, and with a sort of bitter humour I paused by the hall door to hear what they were talking about outside.

Only a few feet away, I could hear every word they were saying, and my blood alternately boiled with fury and froze with apprehension at what I heard.

They were insistent with Hooker to know if he were sure I hadn't got back and were already in the house, and Hooker was telling them it was impossible I could have returned. To my amazement, I found the brute knew all about my motor-bicycle, and where I garaged it. He told them he had been on the watch ever since three o'clock, and it had not come back a quarter of an hour ago. He had been twice to the garage to look, and he was positive I should turn up in a minute or two.

Then it appeared Angas Forbes was urging the police-sergeant to get a search warrant at once, and he swore several times he would himself picket the house with his friends until it had been obtained. It should not be left unwatched now for one single second. He was sure there had been foul play, he kept on saying, and he shouldn't wonder if his friend Carmichael hadn't been murdered. The doctor would never have given up his dogs if he had been alive. Then the deep voice of the police-sergeant chimed in and, although it sounded as if he was considerably impressed with the views of Angas Forbes, he didn't appear as yet to be sure of his ground. Anyhow, he approved of the necessity of getting in touch with me, and promised that a couple of his men should help keep an eye on the place until I returned. He said these men were on their way up and wouldn't be long now.

I didn't wait to hear any more. I could take in the position without any doubt. It was plain to me that with each moment the danger would get worse, and if I was to get away at all I must do so at once.

Very softly I let myself out of the back door and, creeping through the trees worked my way, without a sound, round to the front of the house. Crouching behind a bush, I was within about ten yards of the four of them on the verandah. They were all sitting down now and Angas Forbes was handing round cigars. Unfortunately there was a bright moon, and a silvered patch of lawn lay between me and the path that led to the gates.

I saw Hooker's bicycle propped up against a tree and I thought interestedly how useful it might come in, if I could only get a chance.

For some minutes I lay still as death behind the bush, hoping against hope that some new idea would take the four of them to the back of the house; for as long as they remained on the verandah, it was impossible for me to cross the lawn without being seen.

But fortune was still against me and none of them showed any signs of moving.

Getting desperate at last, I returned stealthily to the back of the house. Much as I was against it, I must try now and escape over the wall and through the judge's garden. There was no help for it, but it necessitated getting the ladder out of the shed and the very slightest sound would, I was sure, be fatal.

Very gently I opened the shed door, and then suddenly a new thought struck me. My eyes fell on a large bundle of straw. Hooker had asked for it recently to protect the young plants from the night frosts.

What if I set light to it? It would blaze in a few seconds, and the flare of it would assuredly bring Forbes and his companions round the corner in a rush, to see what had happened.

I lifted the bundle of straw out on to the path and, with no delay, set light to it with a match. Then I ran back quickly to my position under the bush and waited developments.

I had not long to wait. Almost before I had regained my post of observation, the glare of the burning straw began to cast lights round the side of the house and ominous sounds of crackling came up upon the air.

The sergeant was the first to notice them. 'Hello,' he exclaimed, 'what's happening now?'

They were all on their feet in an instant and, as I had expected, in another moment they were tearing round to the back of the house.

I didn't wait even the fraction of a second. I was over the lawn and had seized Hooker's bicycle in a trice.

Tucking the tails of my coat beneath me, I had mounted and was gliding down the drive, even before they could have reached the burning straw.

I went quite slowly through the gates and, with just a casual glance over the chauffeur and the waiting car, turned into the road and pedalled quickly away.

My second and last flight had begun.

CHAPTER 9

I shall never be quite satisfied in my own mind whether I did right or wrong in going off on Hooker's bicycle. At any rate, it got me safely away, but on the debit side its acquisition undoubtedly delivered me over to another set of troubles; and by riding off on it as I did, it was destined that for many days, I would never be certain that each hour of freedom was not to be my last.

For one thing it certainly led to the almost instant discovery of my flight and, from all I learnt afterwards, if I had not taken it, it might have been hours before anyone would have known with certainty that I had gone away.

The burning of the straw undoubtedly had made Angas Forbes and his companions most suspicious but, on returning to the verandah, the discovery by Hooker that his precious bicycle had been pinched, at once made everything as clear as day.

They all then rushed pell-mell down to the gates and the chauffeur pointed out the way I had gone. He reckoned I had got about ten minutes' start.

Off they all went in pursuit, trusting apparently to chance to discover the direction I had taken. And chance served them very well.

The road in which the Tower House was situated abutted directly on to the open space of the parklands. There was the choice to anyone of three directions from there. Either they could proceed along the Great North Road towards Gawler, they could turn back right to the city, or they could go straight on over the parklands and then along the Torrens road, in the direction of Port Adelaide. The latter road was by far the most unfrequented and started, moreover, by a good run downhill. It was unlighted, after the first half mile.

The car pulled up sharply at the end of the Tower Road, for my pursuers were uncertain then which direction I had taken.

As ill luck would have it, however, and it shows yet again how black was my misfortune on that eventful day, a man and a girl were standing at a garden gate, right at the very end of the road. They had been standing there when I had passed, and exactly under the lamp-post I had noticed with uneasiness that they had a good stare at me as I went by.

'Seen a man on a bicycle?' shouted Angas Forbes.

The couple nodded their heads and pointed towards the Torrens Road, the man adding as the car moved off, 'He'd got no lights on him, but he was going very fast.'

This, then, was how it came about, that when at least three miles up the Torrens Road and pedalling at a good rate in the dark, I became aware of the hum of some distant car behind me.

The Torrens Road runs straight as an arrow for a good five miles, and after the first dip it is all the way slightly uphill.

I jumped off the bicycle and looked round. Yes, there it was right at the bottom of the rise, and for a moment I stood wondering if it had anything to do with me. I was just dismissing the idea as improbable, for with each minute I had been congratulating myself that I was safer and safer from pursuit, when something in the movements of the car's lights caught my eye.

Like nearly all Australian cars, it carried a spot-light at one corner of the top of the wind-screen. These spot-lights are little searchlights in a way, and most useful where the roads are bad, for they cast a beam, high up and a long way ahead.

Well, whoever were in the car, they were using that light now quite unnecessarily on a good road, and moreover someone was moving it, I could see, from side to side, as if to search the hedges as the car went by.

I was instantly suspicious and looked round for somewhere to hide. The moon had gone behind a cloud and it was pitch dark, except for the light of the stars. The road stretched away straight before me and the hedges on either side I could see were everywhere too thick to get through.

I threw myself desperately upon the machine and rode fiercely along, looking for some opening to escape. But none presented itself to me, and I was almost at my wits' ends, when I when that the ditch at one side of the road, just where I was, had deepened down to a shallow sort of pit, and was shadowed over by some high grass overhanging its banks.

In a second I was off the machine, and dumping it roughly down into the ditch, I dropped in myself and crouched low to the ground.

It was a poor shelter at best, but with the car coming nearer and nearer to hide in it was the only thing for me to do.

It will tell of the state of mind I was in at that moment when I relate that I deliberately took out my automatic and slipped off the safety catch. So wrought up was I by all my misfortunes that I know fully I should have shot down anyone rather than be taken.

On came the car and I took a deep breath as it drew level. Yes, they were all there, and it was Angas Forbes who was standing up next to the driver and flashing round the light. I could see the tense expression on his face, but it would, I thought, have been tenser still, had he known how near he was then to death.

Had the light come just a little lower down, and had it just flashed to where I lay, it might have set in motion a terrible train of events that would have led to sudden death perhaps for more than one.

But the light never touched me and the car passed on

quickly. I waited until it had gone about a couple of hundred yards and then sprang briskly out of the ditch and drew the bicycle up after me.

Boldness would now be the best plan I thought and, with no hesitation at all, I started to follow up the road after the car. A very little way ahead and I knew there were several small by-roads leading off right and left, any of which would in a few moments swallow me up and make capture, for the present at any rate, highly improbable.

But my evil genius was with me still. I had not gone even a quarter of a mile, when I road full into an open gully at the side of the road and was pitched violently off on to my side.

I made a great effort to save myself and partly succeeded in protecting my head, but my face came sharply in contact with the ground and my left foot was twisted under me in a dreadful way.

I was covered all over in dust, and the blood began to trickle unpleasantly from a cut on the cheek, but the dust and blood were as nothing compared to the horrible wrench to my foot.

For a minute or two the agony was so intense that I almost believed that I had broken my ankle.

I sat down by the roadside, faint and sick, and had no care nor thought for all the pursuers in the world.

But the acute anguish soon began to pass away, and I quickly began to get anxious again. The car might be returning or someone else might come along. With no lights on my bicycle and with my face all cut and bloody, I was a conspicuous person, and it would never do to be caught sitting there.

I must move on at once, but it was easier said than done, for the moment I stood up, I realised the bicycle would be of no further use. I was so shaken that it was impossible for me to mount and, apart from that, the handle-bars were all bent and twisted by the fall. I must hide somewhere at once and, leaving the bicycle where it was, in the gully, I started to limp painfully along the road.

Suddenly the moon came out and, to my relief, I recognised exactly where I was. I was just near the racecourse at Cheltenham, and close by me was the gate that opened on to the enclosure.

The gate was, of course, locked, but with feverish haste and in spite of the pain to my foot, I climbed up over the rails and in half a minute or so was resting safe, at any rate for the moment, in the shadow of the trees.

No one I was sure had seen me get over, but I was after all only just in time. The faint sounds of a car struck on my ears and slowly, quite slowly, headlights came into view.

From a gap in the palings I had a good view of the road and as the car drew level, one glance only was sufficient to tell me that it was my pursuers returning.

They appeared to be all talking together and they were evidently disagreeing about something. A little way past the racecourse gates the car pulled up and I could catch almost every word they said.

Angas Forbes wanted to search down the Torrens Road again, he was sure they must have passed me somewhere. But the sergeant was all for getting straight to headquarters without any further delay.

'He's gone, Mr Forbes,' he insisted bluntly. 'If he ever came down this road, which I doubt very much. At any rate, he'll have taken fright of our lights now, and won't be waiting for us about here. The best thing is for me to get back once to the Square, and telephone he's wanted all round. We haven't much to go on yet, it's true, but it certainly looks most suspicious his running away, and we can pull him up, at any rate, for his assault on you. That's the only charge I can see we can lay as yet. He can't get away, if we're quick about it, and long before tomorrow night I'll have him by the heels.'

The sergeant spoke most confidently, but the big Scotchman made a lot of demur, and it was quite another five minutes before, to my joy, the car was turned round again and driven away.

I started at once then to think what I must do, but the matter, as it happened, was quickly decided for itself. Attempting to regain my feet, I found I was now quite unable to stand. My foot was like a lump of lead. I could no longer put it to the ground, and at best could only crawl.

I think I really shed tears then. The utter helplessness of my position was torture to me. And the humiliation of it all too! To remember all the perils I had gone through, the difficulties I had surmounted and the awkward situations from which I had extricated myself with such coolness and finesse and now to be overwhelmed by a petty mishap, to fail just at the last moment through no fault of my own was all gall and wormwood to me. But what could I do? Everything seemed quite hopeless.

I must have lain where I was for quite an hour and then it came home to me that whatever happened I could not lie out all night on the ground. A heavy dew was beginning to fall and, miserable as my position already was, it would not be benefited by getting wet through. I looked round for some sort of shelter and the bulky shadow of the grandstand caught my eye. It would be better than nothing.

I literally crawled up those steps of the grandstand, but the first row of seats was as far as I could drag myself. Then, leaning back in a corner with my feet up on the seat, I tucked the ends of my coat round my legs and prepared myself as philosophically as I could for the night.

And what a night it was too! Starry, beautiful and still as I had ever seen it. Everything gently silvered in the moonlight and the opiate of peace and rest everywhere but in my heart. There was no sleep for me at all.

Although I was tired out to the very point of collapse, my thoughts would allow me no rest. Try as I would to prevent it, my tired eyes wandered unceasingly over the racecourse, and the memory of my triumphs there rose up in bitter wrath to chide me for my failure in the end.

Every yard of the great wide course was familiar to me, and

every turn of it and post I knew. I was mocked by every happiness I had known there.

Like ghosts, the horses I had ridden glided up out of the shadows and stared at me with big reproachful eyes. They seemed to mock that I who was their master had fallen now so low.

I remembered how The Whirlwind had jumped for me there, how Rose-bud had come away with me at the bend, how Babylon had carried me once in triumph over those fences, and how Seamada had won in the last stride before the judges' box.

That night seemed to me as if it would never end and, when morning did come at last, so dark and hopeless appeared everything, that I welcomed the day only as a change of setting to my outlook of despair.

The dawn, however, soon gave promise that it was going to be another perfect winter day and, in spite of myself, when I stretched my cramped and aching limbs to the comforting warmth of the sun, something of a very faint tinge of hope began to come back. After all, I remembered, and I had seen it too so often myself, the race is never lost until it is won.

Sitting up I carefully examined my foot. No bones were broken that I could make out, but I realised despairingly that it would be several days before I would be able to walk or even put on my boot again. My ankle was very swollen and to hang it down over the seat was perfect agony. It jumped and throbbed as if my very heart had slipped down into my foot.

I leant back again, and to quieten my nerves started a cigarette. Suddenly, to my alarm, I heard near at hand a sound of whistling, and a moment later a man appeared up on the lawn, just in front of the grandstand.

He walked leisurely to a small shed in the enclosure near the weighing-room and, unlocking the door, disappeared within.

He had passed close to me and I knew who he was at once. He was Sam Piper, the head groundsman of the racing club at

Cheltenham, and his duties were generally to look after the course. He had to see that the ground was kept well watered, and on racing days he had charge of the men who saw to the placing of the hurdles and the flagging of the course at the jumps.

I had never actually spoken to him, but I thought with a pang how often he must have seen me in my triumphs and how he would know me far better than I knew him.

In a couple of minutes or so he came out of the shed, carrying a coil of hose, and prepared for the watering of the course just in front of the judges' box.

My heart began to thump most unpleasantly. Here was a happening I had never thought of, and yet was it possible, I asked myself, suddenly, that I could make use of it in any way? But I was so weak and exhausted that I really couldn't think clearly and, for a long time, in a sort of haze, I just watched the man at his work.

Could I bribe him? I wondered, but then I thought of the terrible risk if I no longer worked alone. I would be completely at this man's mercy if I asked him for help, and was he the type of man it would be safe for me to trust?

With shaking hands I took out my opera glasses and focused them on him as he leant by the rails. I had an excellent view of his face.

He had set the sprinkler going and was now meditatively smoking and engrossed in his pipe.

Yes, his face was certainly a nice one. He had a good square jaw that spoke of determination and courage and there was a look of kindly humour about his eyes. A man about thirty, I thought, and old enough at any rate to know his own mind. I hesitated no longer.

I put down my glasses, and raising myself upright called out faintly, 'Hi! Hi!' I was shocked how weak my voice sounded.

The man took his pipe out of his mouth at once, and looked round in a most surprised sort of way. For a moment he couldn't locate the voice.

'Hi!' I called out again. 'I want you. Quick!'

He saw me this time all right, and with a second's hesitation he crossed over the lawn and stepped up to the grandstand.

'Hello,' he said, halting below the balcony and looking up inquiringly to where I sat. 'What are you doing there?'

For the moment I was too overcome to reply and he went on, 'What's up – been fighting?' Then his face broke into a grin. 'Been on the drink, have you?'

I shook my head, but I didn't wonder at his question, for I must have looked a queer sight with my face all covered with dried blood and dirt.

He came round up the steps to make a nearer inspection and I saw he was looking at me in a very puzzled way.

'Do you want to earn fifty pounds?' I said weakly.

'Depends,' he replied laconically. 'Who are you, first?'

Now from the moment I had called out to him, I had realised I should have to disclose my identity and trust the man. Indeed, I counted it almost as my best card that he should know who I was. He would be unusually interest at once.

'I'm Huggins,' I said faintly. 'I had an accident on the Torrens Road last night and had to crawl in here.'

'Huggins,' he said, coming forward. 'So you are. I thought I recognised you. Bless my soul. You do look bad. Now are you seriously hurt anywhere?'

'No, not badly,' I replied, 'but I'm crocked for a time. I fell off a bicycle and it's my foot that hurts me most. I twisted my ankle.'

In a most business-like way he proceeded to examine me.

'I'm a first-aid man, you know, and I don't think there's anything broken,' he said after a moment. And then he added shyly, 'But as a doctor yourself, of course, you would know.'

'Look here,' I said emphatically, 'I'm not a doctor at all. It's all rot and don't you believe it. That was only a newspaper stunt in the *Times*.'

He seemed rather surprised. 'Well, you want attention anyhow,' he remarked, 'and I'll get help at once.'

'No, that's just it,' I said. 'No one must know where I am. The police are after me. I knocked a man down.'

He whistled and then looked at me very straight.

'Did you kill him?' he asked quietly.

'Kill him? No,' I replied. 'A good thing if I had. The brute was after me last night and I got all this trouble in getting away. Look here,' I went on, and I could feel my voice getting stronger as hope and courage now began to come back. 'I want you to hide me. It'll be only for a few days until this damned foot is well and then I know where to go myself. I'll give you fifty pounds and more than that. Couldn't you hide me in your house now until the trouble blows over? As I say, it'll only be for a few days.'

He gave me a grim smile. 'I board with my aunt just over by the station there,' he said. 'Her son lives with her too.' He chuckled with great amusement. 'He's a policeman.'

I felt my hopes fall suddenly to zero and for a second I was sure I had betrayed myself, but with his next words I began to breathe again.

'Not that I love the police,' he said. 'I hate 'em and they're no friends of mine. Two meetings back here, they nabbed me for having a half-crown bet with a bookie on the course and got fined five quid. I'm not over-friendly with my cousin either. He's a bit of a swine.'

I took heart again at once. 'But couldn't you hide me anywhere?' I urged. 'It'll only be such a few days and, except for the risk, the money will be easily earned.'

He thought earnestly for a moment. 'It isn't the money,' he said slowly. 'I'd like to help you in any case, although with fifty quid I could do a good deal. I've got a girl over in Queensland, waiting for me.'

'I'll make it a hundred,' I said eagerly, 'and more than that. Is there no place you can think of for me to hide? I can rough it anywhere, you understand.'

He looked me curiously up and down. 'What about my little shed then? No one will be coming in there today, and there are plenty of sacks inside for me to make up some sort of bed for you.'

My heart jumped with joy at the idea. To have any hiding place for the next few days might mean eventual salvation for me after all, for, once again upon my feet, I had the several other resources of which the reader already knows.

I took hope again and in a few minutes was delighted with my ally. Mr Sam Piper showed himself a most resourceful and capable individual. He carried me down off the grandstand and, procuring some dressings from the racecourse first-aid box, he washed and bound up my wounds. My ankle he put under the hydrant tap and then swathed it well round with a compress of wet rags.

Half an hour after I had first called to him, I was lying comfortably in the hose-shed and he was off away back to his home, to get me something to eat.

'It's quite all right as it happens,' he had explained. 'I can get you plenty to eat today without anybody knowing. There's no one at home at present. The old girl's off for the day to Henley Beach and the policeman chap's on duty until dinner time.'

He was soon back and he had brought with him quite a store of provisions. He was most insistent I should make a good meal and then, when I had finished, that I should have a good sleep.

'Now I'm going to lock you in,' he said, and I shan't come near you again until late this afternoon. Have a good sleep and don't worry about anything. No one else has got a key to the shed and you're quite safe all the time,' and he went off seemingly very pleased with himself.

Oh, the delicious memory of that going to sleep! It was only a poor rough bed of sacks that I lay upon, but no bed of roses could have been more fragrant and no couch more generous with its promise of sweet gentle dreams.

Precarious as was still my position, once again, as before in my need, I had found a protector and, once again, I was safe at any rate for a time. I was like a man who had come out of hell and, as I sank gently and thankfully into slumber, through the dim mists of my consciousness shone a bright and radiant star of hope.

It was well towards dusk when I awoke and my new friend was standing over me. So sound had been my sleep that I had not even heard him unlock the door and he had had to shake me to wake me up.

'Sorry to disturb you,' he said with a pleasant smile, 'but I must be off again in a few minutes. Feel better, don't you? Well, I must put another wet compress on anyhow. I'll get that ankle down in a couple of days,' and with professional pride he began to undo the bandage on my foot.

'But you're quite right,' he went on, 'about the police. The beggars are after you right enough. All the stations have had notice and you're wanted on two charges. Assaulting that Mr Forbes and stealing someone else's bicycle. I got it out of my cousin at dinner today. There's a lot of mystery about it, he says, but everyone's on the look-out.'

An uneasy feeling ran down my spine and I answered with an assurance I did not feel.

'Pooh, it will be all over in a few days, if only I can keep out of their clutches until the thing dies down. Shall I be all right here do you think for the next few days?'

'You'll be all right every night,' he said, 'but during the daytime you'll have to go up on the grandstand again. You see, my mate will be using this shed tomorrow as well as me. He works with me during the day, but fortunately, he never comes until well after eight o'clock. What I thought I'd do is this. I'll hop round here early and carry you right up on to the top. Whoever comes you'll be safe up there.'

I thanked him as gratefully as I could for his kindness, but he would have none of it. I had not been mistaken in my estimate of the man. He was a good sport and was evidently prepared to obtain a lot of enjoyment from the difficulty and risks he now saw he ran in hiding me.

I had quite a good night's rest that night, and when morning came I felt oceans better. My leg, too, was undoubtedly slightly easier.

Piper turned up almost as soon as it was light. He had brought me some beef sandwiches and a bottle of hot tea. To my joy, he had also got the morning's newspaper.

'I've not had time to read it myself yet,' he said, 'but you can give it back tonight. That darned cousin of mine reckons they'll get you for sure today. They've found where you left the bicycle and they reckon you're hurt and can't get away far.'

'The devil they do,' I muttered, 'and if they only knew how nearly right they are too.'

Piper laughed. 'Never mind, sir, they won't look for you here. I can see this is going to mean some fun for me.'

He carried me up on to the very top of the grandstand and was most solicitous to see that I had everything as far as possible for my comfort. He had made me a nice thick bed of sacks and, lying close behind the rails, while still hidden myself, I had a glorious view of all the country around and could see all that was going on.

'Now,' were his parting words, 'I shan't come near you again until my mate Scut's gone tonight. He's a very nosy chap, is Scut, and will smell something if I give him the slightest chance. To make sure too, I shan't come for you until it's quite dark.'

For a long while I gave myself up to my own thoughts. Things really were beginning to look quite hopeful again and, if I could only lie low now for a few days until my foot was quite well again, the odds were decidedly in my favour that I should escape after all.

A dark night, and I could flit away to the bathing hut on Henley Beach. There I could remain indefinitely and ultimately escape to somewhere further afield, when the interest in me had died down. I didn't somehow reckon that after the first few days the police would be much interested in me. The two definite charges that they had against me were at their worst only trumpery ones and, on their account, they certainly wouldn't be able to work up much enthusiasm in apprehending me.

Angas Forbes would of course try and make out the blackest case he could against me but, although he'd undoubtedly got the truth of everything, he would have not a little difficulty, I thought, in bringing the authorities to his opinion.

I opened the newspaper a little nervously, wondering what more they would be having to say that morning in their continuation of the Carmichael-Huggins affair. Nothing, however, at first caught my eye, and I was congratulating myself that they had dropped the matter for good, when all at once I came across a paragraph in the column of 'General News'.

It was quite a short one, but it was ominously significant, and its very terseness made me uneasy. It was headed 'Dr Carmichael', and it just remakred that though for the present they had nothing further to add to their disclosures of Saturday, it was possible that some startling and interesting developments might unfurl themselves shortly.

I guessed what had happened at once. Angas Forbes had been round to them and pitched his tale and they were now waiting for corroboration from Sydney.

It was not by any means a dull one for me, that morning on the grandstand. After I had gone through the newspaper from beginning to end, and particularly had been interested in the sporting columns (wherein I was eulogised as much as I possibly could have wished) I amused myself by looking round through my glasses.

They were very small ones, but they were excellent as far as they went, and I could see quite a long way with them beyond the racecourse. My friend Piper and the nosey-minded Scut were, however, only about a couple of hundred yards away beneath me. They were giving the course rails a new coat of paint.

Scut was certainly a most disreputable man in appearance, and I remembered now I had often noticed him on the course on race-days. He had always looked dirty and unshaven, and was always remarkable for an intensely ragged looking coat over a jersey that, in its palmy days, had been of a most flaming red colour.

Towards midday I began to feel a bit drowsy, and I was just on the very point of dropping off to sleep, when suddenly I saw a car pull up at the racecourse gates on the other side of the course and four men get briskly out.

I was all alert again in a second, for there was no mistaking what they were. They were policemen.

Breathlessly I watched them through my glasses, and to my relief they did not turn at once in the direction of the grandstand. Instead, they walked round along the course until they came to the far corner and then I realised what they intended doing. They had come to search the bushes and the thickets on the other side. Spreading themselves out, in a most business-like manner, they went over the ground, but I wondered with a growing uneasiness what on earth they expected to find.

In a few minutes, however, they were all together again. Evidently they were discussing what they would do next. Then they all got over the rails and came straight in the direction of the enclosure and the stands.

I could feel my mouth get dry with fear. Was there never to be an end, I asked myself, of all these dreadful alarms? Was I never to escape from one peril but to fall directly into another? I wiped the sweat from my forehead with my sleeve.

The policemen came quickly nearer, and I noticed with a little gleam of hope that Piper had moved nearer too. He had left the man Scut and was now busy on the railings just in front of the grandstand.

'Hello, you there,' called out one of the policemen, directly he came within speaking distance.

'Hello,' replied Piper, 'what's up?'

'Have you seen any strangers about here,' asked the policeman, 'either today or yesterday?'

Piper put on such a fine air of stupidity that even in my dreadful anxiety I had to smile.

He scratched his head thoughtfully. 'There were two boys here yesterday,' he said slowly, 'and they'd got a white dog with them. A fox terrier, I believe.'

The policeman snorted contemptuously. 'It's a man we're after,' he said, 'not boys or white dogs.' He came close up to Piper. 'Now have you seen Huggins,' he asked sternly, 'the jockey, I mean?'

'Huggins,' replied Piper as if excited at once. 'No, do you want him? What's he done?'

'Never you mind,' said the policeman rudely, 'we want him, that's all. Now, were you at work here yesterday?'

'Yes, all the morning up to one o'clock.'

'What time did you come?'

'I had the hydrants going by eight o'clock.'

The policeman thought for a moment. 'Could anyone get in any of the buildings here?'

'No,' sneered Piper, contemptuous in his turn. 'They're all locked.'

'You've got a set of keys, haven't you?'

'Yes – I've got a set in my shed.'

'All right, then. We'll have a look round.'

They were all standing just below me and I could plainly see and hear everything that was taking place.

Piper went and fetched the keys and the policeman in charge rapped out his orders to the other men.

'Jackson, you come with me. Tweedy, you go and search round the back, and you, Pickle, go and look over the stands. Now look slippery, we're not going to be here all day.'

The separated at once and the one called Pickle was left alone with Piper.

'Come on, mate,' said the latter cheerfully, 'I'll go up with you, although it's damn rot all the same, for I was up on them less than half an hour ago, and I haven't been out of sight since. Have a fag?'

The policeman looked cautiously round and, finding his superior officer out of sight, graciously accepted the proffered cigarette. He was a short fat man, with a big round innocent looking face, and I thought, thankfully, he was certainly the least formidable of the lot. There might be even now just a chance after all.

'Damn lot of steps, aren't there,' he asked, 'right up to the top?'

'Hell of a lot,' replied Piper, 'before you get out on to the roof, but there's a fine view when you get up there. You can see all round.'

The policeman grunted in disgust and accompanied by Piper began slowly to mount the steps. He looked searchingly along each row of seats as he got level.

I was in a perfect fever of dread, but could think of absolutely nothing I could do. I just lay numb and hypnotised, waiting for the end.

The policeman came up higher.

'Hold hard a minute, old chap,' exclaimed Piper suddenly, 'I want to light my fag.' The fat policeman stopped readily enough, he seemed a bit out of breath.

'What do they want this bloke, Huggins, for?' asked Piper, pausing before he struck a match.

'Dunno,' grunted the policeman, 'he's pinched something, so I believe.'

'Damn fine jockey, anyhow,' went on Piper. 'Did you back Moonlight Maid?'

'No,' came the answer with a growl. 'I've not 'ad a winner for weeks.'

'Haven't you?' asked Piper abruptly, and with a load of sympathy in his voice, 'then I'll give you one for Saturday. It's an absolute certainty, and there are only four people in the know as yet.' He looked round cautiously and came very near to the policeman. 'Now can you keep a secret – for sure? Not tell a soul, mind.'

The fat policeman began to breathe heavily. 'Yuss,' he replied emphatically. 'I knows when to hold my tongue.'

Piper looked round in every direction, like the villain in the play – then he put his hand lightly on the fat one's shoulder.

'There was a secret trial here yesterday,' he hissed. 'A trial between The Bodger and Cask of Rum.'

'Wot,' exclaimed the policeman with his eyes doing their best to bulge from his head, 'a trial on this course, 'ere?'

'Yes,' replied Piper, 'a trial, almost before it was light.'

'Wot 'appened? come on, tell us. There's a sport.'

It was a lurid tale then that the imaginative Piper unfolded. A tale told slowly and with due dramatic emphasis. It appeared that Piper had happened to have come out extra early on the Sunday morning. He had wanted to get his work over early, he said, because a relative was coming later to spend the day with him. He had been in his shed, sorting out his tools. Suddenly he had heard voices. He had looked through the crack of the shed door. He had seen three men on three horses. He had recognised them all, at once. One was Potsworthy the trainer and the other two were the jockeys Heffel and Bert May. They were lined up just in front of the judges' box. 'Now, boys,' had said Potsworthy, 'ride just as you would in a race and see if The Bodger is good enough to beat Cask of Rum. Once round the course, a mile and a half, that's the journey, and a box of cigars whoever wins.' Then followed a wonderful account of a seemingly titanic struggle between the two horses, and of every yard almost of the race there was some happening to tell. The Bodger had taken up the running to the ten furlong post, then Cask of Rum had put in some fine work, and nine furlongs from home he was a good two lengths ahead. Then The Bodger had come again and Cask of Rum had been pegged back, then something else happened and so on and so on.

And all this while the fat policeman stood open-mouthed. He was most impressed. He never for one second took his eyes from Piper's face, and I saw with thankfulness that, for the time at any rate, he had no further interest in me.

How it would have ended goodness only knows, but suddenly the harsh voice of the sergeant was heard from below.

'Now then, Pickle,' was shouted. 'Where are you – have you gone to sleep?'

'Coming, Sergeant, coming,' called back the abruptly awakened Pickle. Then he gripped Piper's arm sharply.

'But tell me, who won?' he whispered hoarsely.

'The Bodger, by half a street,' replied Piper.

A beautiful smile beamed on the fat policeman's face. 'I'll 'ave a dollar on 'im on Saturday, and many thanks, old man,' and down the steps he trampled heavily, apparently quite oblivious that he had not been over the whole building.

I saw him say something to the sergeant, and in a few minutes they all trooped back over the course and disappeared.

Piper grinned triumphantly to me from down below and then at once rejoined his friend Scut.

At last I could breathe again, but I found I was shaking like a man in an ague. It had been a dreadfully narrow escape, but I was not grateful and I petulantly asked myself when it was all going to end. 'I am only safe for an hour or two,' I grumbled, 'something else will turn up soon and I shall be in the same old danger again.'

I felt so sick of everything that I really think I dropped asleep in sheer disgust. I must have been very tired for it was nearly dark when I awoke. Piper came up to help me to the shed. He seemed very pleased with himself as usual but as before made light of any thanks. He locked me up again for the night and went off whistling in the most happy manner possible.

Next morning my foot was undoubtedly ever so much better and to my delight I could put it to the ground. I was standing up waiting for Piper when he opened the door.

'My foot's getting on fine,' I exclaimed cheerfully. 'Nearly all the pain's gone and I can almost use it again. Now, what adventures are we going to have today?'

But for a moment the man said nothing. He had got a newspaper in his hand and I noticed suddenly that he was looking at me in a very strange, old-fashioned way.

'Look here, Mr Huggins,' he burst out at length. 'You're not playing the game with me. You're not acting on the square.'

I could feel my face get flaming hot. 'What do you mean?' I asked nervously. 'What's up?'

'That's what I want to know, exactly – what's up. Look at this now,' and he thrust the newspaper he was holding into my hand.

I looked down and instantly I saw what he meant. In great big letters, right across the middle of the page I read:

THE JOCKEY HUGGINS! £500 REWARD!

And in smaller letters underneath, 'The above sum will be paid to any person or persons furnishing such information as will lead to the discovery of the whereabouts of the same. Apply Mr Angas Forbes, The Great Australasian Hotel.

I glanced quickly over the page, but that was apparently all there was about me.

A dreadful sinking feeling came over me, and I leant against the wall for support. Once again it seemed, the bottom was falling out of all my hopes. Piper was watching me intently.

'Look here again,' he said earnestly. 'As I told you before, I don't love the police and I'm not afraid of risks. But I want to know where I stand, and no man's going to put it across me for a mug if I can help it. Now you told me,' he went on sharply, 'that they were after you just because you'd knocked a man down. You said the man wasn't hurt.' He sneered contemptuously. 'They wouldn't be offering five hundred pounds for that and I believe you killed him after all.'

I had to think rapidly. Five hundred pounds reward and the whole state would be like a pack of wolves upon my track. Whether they knew or not what I was wanted for, imaginations would everywhere be stirred and every man and woman would be hot upon the scent. I could grasp exactly how things stood. Angas Forbes was sure of everything, but he had proof of nothing until I was actually produced. He must get hold of me to show I was not the real Carmichael. Hence his masterstroke of offering a reward of five hundred pounds.

What could I do? I must tell Piper everything. What alternative had I? He had me in the hollow of his hand. I couldn't humbug him with any safety.

I pulled myself together and looked him straight in the face.

'I told you only the truth,' I said quite quietly. 'I didn't hurt the man. He's the one offering the reward.'

Piper sniffed. 'Five hundred pounds because you knocked him down. Do you want me to believe that?'

I didn't raise my voice at all. I held his eyes intently with my own.

'Do you always read the newspapers, Piper?' I asked.

He gave me a hard and calculating frown.

'Yes, always. What of that?'

'I'm going to startle you then,' I said.

'I'm startled already,' he remarked drily.

I was silent for a moment. Knowing I had no choice, I still hesitated to take the plunge. I spoke at last.

'Do you remember then last year reading about a prisoner who escaped from the courts after he'd been sentenced – a man called Cups?'

'Yes,' he replied sullenly, 'I remember, but what of him?'

'I'm Cups,' I said simply.

For quite a long minute there was silence between us. He looked at me very thoughtfully.

'You're a liar,' he said, very quietly. 'Cups had a big nose.'

I pulled him roughly by the arm. 'Look here, man,' I said angrily. 'Come into the light. See those scars there. Pass your finger over them. Feel them. I had all the bone and cartilage taken out of my nose. Dr Carmichael did it. I'm not lying. It's dead truth. When I escaped, Dr Carmichael hid me. He operated upon me and altered my face. I have to tell you everything because there's no help for it now. I've lived in his house over nine months. He died six months ago but, before he died, he gave me everything. Now his friend, this man Forbes, has come here and I can't explain anything, because if I do, they'll all know I'm Cups. I swear to you it's all solemn truth.'

It was a very quiet and thoughtful Piper that a quarter of an hour later helped me again up into the grandstand. He had been most incredulous at first, but I had convinced him at last, and in quite an enthusiastic way he had sworn to see me through. Myself I had no misgivings at all about his loyalty. I had made him understand that five hundred pounds would be a very small reward for me to give him, but quite apart from that I fully believed he would have helped me in any case. He was really delighted with the risks he was taking. It was adventure to him. He was the type of man whose energies should rightly have been expended in any direction other than the monotonous one he was then engaged upon. My coming was the scarlet patch upon an otherwise drab and uneventful life.

CHAPTER 10

It was well for me that I had been perfectly open and frank with Piper. Had I not been so, the disclosures made by the *Times of Adelaide* the following Friday would have completely destroyed all his faith in me, and in sheer disgust probably, and in spite of all risks, he would have turned his back upon me and given me up without pity to my enemies.

My foot was practically well and I was arranging to slip off that very evening, when Friday morning's issue of the *Times* exploded like a dreadful bomb among all my plans, and shattered every hope I had of getting successfully away.

Everything was found out and I was accused now openly of murder. It was no wonder the *Times* had had nothing to say about me for the four preceding days. They had been working feverishly first to prepare their case, and figuratively and literally they had been burrowing through every foot of the ground.

They had dug up the grave in the garden.

It was a long article to which they treated the public and with its leaded headlines and its spaced paragraphs it occupied the whole of one middle page. It was a perfect orgy of sensation and never before, I suppose, had the public so had their fill of horror.

I could see the hand of Angas Forbes in it in every line. As I suspected then and learnt afterwards, he had practically taken charge of and conducted the whole affair.

When he realised on the Sunday evening that I was nowhere to be found, and that moreover the police were quite lukewarm in the matter and disposed, after a little display of energy, to treat the whole affair as one of very small importance, he went round to the *Times of Adelaide* office and there laid the whole matter before the editor-in-chief.

The *Times* people proved much more sympathetic and, as Angas Forbes stoutly and obstinately reitereated his suspicions, they were won over to his cause.

Angas Forbes was a rich man, and he could afford to take risks that a poor man would not have dared, so he had forcibly broken into and taken possession of the Tower House, and with a small army of private detective and newspaper men had pursued every avenue of investigation that suggested itself to their minds. There could be no denying that their investigation had been far-reaching and thorough, and as I read down the columns of the *Times* that morning, I gasped at the determination and shrewdness they had shown.

'It is a strange story,' began the *Times*, 'that we have this morning to unfold for our readers. A story that may seem almost incredible at first, for it is one as weird and fanciful as any in all the dark annals of baffling and mysterious crime.

'Dr Robert Carmichael, the one time celebrated surgeon of new South Wales, and later the eccentric recluse of North Adelaide, has been for dead for many months. The body was found yesterday, buried in the garden of his house.

'Exactly as to how he died has yet to be determined, but so far everything points to the absolute certainty of foul play.

'We say, Dr Carmichael died many months ago. The condition of his body proves that. But since his death, strange as it may seem to write it, his place has not been vacant either in his own house or in his many business transactions with the All Australian Bank. Incredible to relate, he has been successfully impersonated the whole time by an individual who, by forgery and fraud, has unhappily succeeded in laying hands upon the major portion of the estate.

'As we have said, it is a weird story, for the amazing part of it is this impersonator of the dead Dr Carmichael has, in another capacity, been well and glaringly before the public eye the whole time he has been perpetrating his frauds.

'He has been known to us as the Jockey Huggins.'

Then the *Times* related everything that had happened at the Tower House and explained how it had come about that Angas Forbes had appeared so inopportunely, at least for me, upon the scene.

Angas Forbes, also himself a medical man, it told its readers, had been a friend of Dr Carmichael, a lifelong friend, and during the last five years, every six months or so, he had spent at least a few days with him in his exile. This last time, his visit had been greatly overdue, but he had been away on business in America, and his return was nearly six months later than it should have been. A few days back he had written to Carmichael from Sydney, informing the doctor that he had returned at last to Australia but should not be coming Adelaide way for at least three weeks. A sudden change of plans, however, had enabled him unexpectedly to come right on, and last Saturday morning he had been nearing Adelaide on the Melbourne express, due in the city at half-past ten. Imagine his surprise then, on purchasing, at a hill station about twenty miles from Adelaide, a copy of that morning's *Times*, to see in it a photograph of a strange unknown man purporting to be that of his friend. But if he had been surprised at that, he had been surprised still more to read that his friend had become a noted jockey on the turf.

He knew at once it was impossible, for Dr Carmichael had never had anything to do with horses in all his life. Mr Forbes was quite sure of it.

Arriving at Adelaide and suspecting instinctively that something was wrong, he had jumped into a taxi and had been driven straight to the doctor's house.

There, it appeared, he had missed me, almost only by seconds. The man Hooker had been keeping watch and had just seen me go out. Hooker wanted to get into the sheds to fetch a coat he had left behind and, knowing he had offended me by talking to the reporters, he had been waiting until the coast was clear to go in. He had been just unlocking the entrance gates when Angas Forbes had driven up. Explanations had followed and Forbes had then driven instantly to the All Australian Bank. The bank had been shut, but the manager had been unearthed at his private address and, after much persuasion, had given Forbes the address of one of the clerks, who had been accustomed to wait upon me at the bank. Then Forbes had set off to catch me on the racecourse, and the *Times* went on to describe all that had happened there.

Next was set out in detail the suspicious nature of my sudden flight from the house and how that alone had at once convinced everyone that there was something very wrong.

It was patent to them all, however, directly an entrance had been effected into the house, that I had been preparing to leave, at latest, within a few days. Undoubtedly, the letter Angas Forbes had written to Dr Carmichael from Sydney had frightened me, for it was seen I had got things together as if for a long journey. But I had been packing carefully and methodically as if there had been plenty of time, and the trunk I had got ready contained nothing that had been thrown in in a hurry. There were books in it on poetry and travel, there was a silver-mounted riding whip. There was a box of carved ivory chessmen, and an oil painting of a horse's head. Evidently when these things had been collected, there had been no thought of immediate flight, but the very instant I had known Angas Forbes was about, I had apparently dropped everything precipitately, and no doubt had considered myself very fortunate to escape, even empty handed, by a trick. Or rather, they had thought I had escaped empty handed. They had thought so at first, but when the books and papers in the desk had come to be examined, they had unhappily seen it was very far from being the case.

The bank pass-book had been almost the first thing to catch their eye, and only a few seconds' investigation had shown I had secured a very rich haul.

During the last six months, or to be precise, from 18 February last, no less than forty-seven thousand pounds had been disposed of wholesale and bonds and stocks of all descriptions had been converted into cash.

What had become of the proceeds could only be guessed. At first the bank authorities had been most reticent and, not knowing how they stood, had refused point-blank to discuss any of Dr Carmichael's affairs. But presented with almost overwhelming evidence that the man they had lately had dealings with could not by any possibility have been the real Dr Carmichael who had first opened an account with them, they had at last changed their attitude and subsequently helped in the investigations in every possible way.

That all the cheques since 28 January were forgeries was now clear. The counterfoils of every one of them as shown in the heels of the used-up cheque books left behind in the desk at Tower House, were undisguisedly in a strange handwriting. Apparently thinking himself quite secure, the forger had made no attempt there to imitate Dr Carmichael's handwriting. But apart from that, other and even more conclusive evidence had been obtained.

Dr Carmichael's signature in the signature book of the bank had been photographed and enlarged. Some of the supposed later signatures had also undergone a similar process. Side by side they had been thrown on a screen. A startling difference in their characteristics had at once been observed and the bank officials could determine exactly when the forgeries had begun.

The first forged cheque had been drawn on 19 February, and it had been for the comparatively small amount of one hundred pounds. Then the *Times of Adelaide* seemed as if it paused to draw in a deep breath. It went on in a more solemn note.

'But has nothing yet struck our readers? Does imagination stop short when we have numerated these dates? Is there no blank that they want to fill in?'

Then came one line in leaded type all by itself:

WHAT HAPPENED BETWEEN 28 JANUARY AND 19 FEBRUARY?

It went on again:

'We will tell our readers. Somewhere between those dates, somewhere between 28 January and 19 February last, Dr Robert Carmichael met with death in a violent and a sudden form. Somewhere, in some way, perhaps we shall never know quite exactly how, he passed suddenly from the strength and joy of life into the silence of everlasting sleep. How do we know it? it may be asked, and we answer, we know it because he was buried in his clothes.'

Then it went on to relate the circumstances that had led up to the finding of the body and I saw there again how unkindly chance and fate had treated me. It was, as I had expected, that wretched photograph of the house that had given me away.

Angas Forbes, who apparently had had eyes for everything, had remarked, just as I had done, upon the different shading in the photograph in the ground under the tree, and, the moment they had started to dig, they had noticed a lightness in the density of the soil.

I felt the tears come into my eyes as I read on.

Six feet of digging and they had reached the body of a fully clothed man. It was known at once whose body it was. In a state of unusual preservation, due no doubt to the limestone nature of the soil in which it had been buried, Angas Forbes had been able to recognise the features of his friend.

The body had evidently been buried in great haste, for not only was it fully clothed but nothing apparently had been removed either from the pockets or the person of the dead man. His gold watch was there, the glass of it had been broken, there was money in his pockets, there were his eye-glasses in their case, and there was his signet ring upon his finger. The only preparation that had been made for burial had been to roll the body in a sheet, and another sheet rolled round the trunk had been employed to lower the body into the grave.

'Now,' said the *Times* in conclusion, 'let us face facts. Let us piece them all together as far as they go.

'Dr Robert Carmichael, a rich man living, so everyone believed, entirely by himself, has died and been buried secretly in his own garden. The man who buried him has disappeared, after having for six months lived on in the same house and usurped all his functions.

'But we know who that man is and we want him. He must be found, and there should surely be no difficulty at all about finding him.

'He is no unknown and obscure individual. For months he has been well in the public eye, and his features are familiar to thousands of our readers. Many photographs of him have appeared in the press and they can be broadcasted now with the greatest of ease.

'No man it would seem should be easier to lay hands upon, for it is almost certain that he is at present in hiding, somewhere within reach of the city. He was traced last on Saturday evening to the Torrens Road, just near to the Cheltenham Racecourse. He had had a spill from a bicycle there, and from the condition of the machine that he abandoned, it is not improbable that he received some injuries himself.

'It is true that a week has elapsed since then, but we confidently believe, in spite of that, he still has had no opportunity as yet to leave the State. Fortunately, thanks mainly to the initiative of Mr Angas Forbes, energetic precautions were taken from the very first.

'Long before the gravity of the matter was generally recognised, at the insistence of this gentleman, a complete cordon was drawn round the city and its environs.

'Ever since last Saturday, the railways have been quietly and unostentatiously kept under surveillance and all long-distance trains have been boarded by detectives, before being allowed to proceed.

'No overseas steamer has sailed since Saturday last, and all inter-state vessels have been carefully searched, before their departure, since that day.

'It is no secret either that all cars leaving South Australia by the great roads have been held up and examined at vital points.

'With all these precautions taken, surely it is not unreasonable to suppose that the ex-jockey is still in hiding close near, and in the interest of the community generally, it is incumbent on every one of us to assist in the best way we possibly can.

'It must not go forth that South Australia, and in the City of Adelaide particularly, malefactors can do all they will, and when discovered and brought to bay, just mock triumphantly at all authority and vanish like the proverbial thieves in the night.

'One thing, however, we must remember, the man Huggins may perhaps be no longer working alone. Unhappily he must be well supplied with funds, and it is more than possible that even now he is bribing a path to sanctuary by the disgorging of a potion of his ill-gotten wealth. He is almost certainly now encompassing a guilty silence by the money he has stolen from the dead.'

I read the article through three times, and each time I read it, it seemed worse. There was no ambiguity about it. It took it for granted straight away that I was a murderer.

I wondered what Dick Rainton would think of it, and with a dreadful pang I thought of the anxiety Margaret would be in too.

The whole affair looked so damning, and my sudden disappearance would seem to everyone to put the seal upon my guilt.

However popular I had been as a jockey, the supposed callous murder of Dr Carmichael would turn everyone against me and, in horror and exasperation at the cold-blooded nature of the crime, all sympathy would be alienated. To track me down would be the hope and aim of every decent-minded man.

No wonder Piper had looked uncomfortably at me when he had given me the paper. Of course he had read it all. I looked down through the railings of the grandstand. Piper was working just below me. He was rolling the lawn in front of the judges' box. I noticed he was alone. Scut was nowhere to be seen.

Seized with a sudden impulse, I leaned over the rails and whistled. Piper immediately stopped his work and looked up.

'Come up a moment, can't you? I want you,' I called out. Piper looked round and hesitated. Then slowly and reluctantly it seemed, he mounted on to the stand.

'Look here,' I said briskly, the moment he came within earshot, 'I'm not going to stand this.'

I held out the paper to him. 'You've read it, I suppose?'

He nodded without replying. His face looked very white and solemn. 'Well,' I went on, 'I'll tell you what I'm going to do. I'm going to write a letter to this beastly paper, telling them everything I've told you. It can't do any harm.'

'What do you mean?' he asked, very sharply. 'Are you going to give yourself up?'

'Not for all the world,' I said quickly. 'Unless you split on me, and then I'll shoot myself before they take me alive.'

'I'm not going to split on you,' he interrupted irritably. 'I'm in the soup now, as badly as you. I wish to blazes though I'd never seen you. I tell you that straight.'

Piper looked plainly frightened. There was no doubt about it, but strange to say, with his nervousness my own disappeared.

'Look here, Piper,' I said boldly, 'there's nothing in it. It's just like that other time when they were so cocksure I was Dr Carmichael. One word from me, and the whole thing will topple down like a stack of cards. I'm just going to write the *Times* a letter, and as I say, tell them all I told you. The explanation is so simple, that once they've got it the bottom will fall out of all their robbery and murder business, first shot. I'm sure they'll print the letter too, because of the sensation it'll make, whether they believe it or not. Now I want some notepaper and an envelope.'

In a few minutes I had talked Piper into quite a happy state of mind, and he was off home to get what I required. Scut, he told me, was ill. He had been on the drink again the previous evening, and was in bed as sick as a dog.

In half an hour Piper was back, and alone by myself again, I quickly made out my letter for the *Times*.

'To the Editor of the *Times of Adelaide*.

'Sir – this is a perfectly authentic letter, and when you have seen who writes it, you will understand why there is no exactness about the address.

'So much is disclosed in your columns this morning about my relations with the late Dr Robert Carmichael that it seems to me a pity that the whole truth should not be known, and so far as your investigations are concerned, the whole matter, once and for all, set at rest.

'Personally, I am in no way interested in the opinions you or your readers may hold of me, but I may perhaps still have a few friends left and for their sakes, at least, I am unwilling to remain under the undoubted stigma that your article in today's issue suggests.

'So I intend now to lay before you the real facts. I did not murder Dr Carmichael. He died as the result of an accident on the morning of Monday, 29 January. He fell from the top to the bottom of the turret stairs in his house, and broke his neck. He died in my arms a few minutes afterwards and I buried him, as you have described, in the grave in his own garden.

'I had been living with him since the first week of December. He gave me shelter and protection when I had to leave my first hiding-place, the house of Judge Cartright, next door.

'Dr Carmichael knew all of my past history, and to alter my appearance and enable me to escape ultimately from South Australia, he performed a surgical operation upon my face. He removed part of the bone and cartilage of my nose. To anaesthetise me he purchased six ounces of choloroform in the city from Mildred's on Thursday, 18 January, and he operated upon me the following Sunday.

'He had entire sympathy with my efforts to evade falling again into the hands of the law, and it was his many times expressed intention to arrange that I should make a new start in life under happier circumstances in some distant part of the world.

'When he died, by realising his estate as I did, I acted only within my rights, for with his last breath he gave everything to me. I cheated no one, and I robbed no one. I was only taking what was morally my own.

'If I am unwilling to again place myself within reach of the law, you, of all people, should easiest understand why. To what injustice I was treated last year, you yourself bore public testimony less even than a month ago. As you made clear, a perfectly innocent man, I was yet found guilty of a crime I had never committed, and placed under the brutal sentence of penal servitude for five years.

'Is it any wonder then that I fight shy of the authorities and prefer at all risks to keep out of their hands?

'One thing, I shall never be taken alive. I have no intention, if I can help it, of being taken at all, but if the worst comes to the worst, it will be a barren victory only that the authorities will obtain.

'I shall destroy myself rather than fall again into their hands.

'Certain facts that I have mentioned can be verified at once, and the autopsy will show that Dr Carmichael died as the result of a broken neck. That this is my handwriting too, can be made sure from an inspection of the ledgers of the Consolidated Bank.

'One thing more, I may add until Saturday afternoon last, Mr Rainton, the trainer, was never at any time aware that I was his old friend.

'Yours faithfully
'JOHN ARCHIBALD CUPS'

It was just before noon when I had finished, and Piper was ready to go home for his dinner.

I read the letter over to him and it did me good to see the relief on his face.

'That'll do them fine, Mr Cups,' he said. 'It takes all the juice, as you say, out of their murder business. Now, I tell you what I'll do. I won't post it, I'll deliver it at once by hand. Mark it 'urgent' and I'll go up and drop it straight away in the *Times* office box.'

Piper was back again about two and, finding the coast clear, came up at once into the grandstand. He had delivered the letter and was very excited.

'Everybody's talking about you in the city,' he said, 'and they're all looking out for the reward. I went into the Oriental bar, and they were all positive there that somehow you'd get here to the races tomorrow. One man even said that he shouldn't wonder if you didn't try and keep to your engagement to ride Eaton Boy in the Steeple. They say you would have nerve enough for anything.'

We discussed what I must do and, reluctantly, we agreed it would be impossible for me now to go away that night, as I had intended. Piper's cousin had told him every policeman in the city was out and that all leave had been cancelled for the weekend. It would be risky for me to move a yard even from my hiding-place, for the Cheltenham neighbourhood was of all places the most suspected. The police were positive somehow that I had been injured in the bicycle spill and could not be far away from where I had been hurt.

But what could I do? we argued. On the morrow there was a race-meeting on the course and a dozen or more people would be coming all the time, backwards and forwards, to the shed.

'As far as I can see,' said Piper at last, 'the only thing for you to do is to sit up in the corner here the whole afternoon. You must keep your head turned away and be using your glasses most of the time. After all, people only come out on to the roof here actually when the race is going on, so you won't be in danger the whole time, and if you are leaning over the rails, no one will be able to notice your face.'

It was the best thing we could think of and so we left it at that.

I slept very badly that night, and had an evil dream that Diana, the bitch, had got me cornered again in the kennels, only this time the face of Diana was the face of Angas Forbes. I woke up covered in a heavy sweat, and for hours and hours it seemed could not get off to sleep again.

Just as dawn was breaking, I was awakened by the hurried entrance of Piper. By the half light I saw he had a biggish parcel in his hands.

'Here, take these,' he said breathlessly, 'and put them on quick. They're Scut's clothes. He's still ill and can't get up, and it's lucky for us too. You'll have to be Scut today. My cousin says the police will be all over the place soon. They're certain, somehow, you'll turn up on the course this afternoon. They think you must be half mad because you risked being discovered by coming out as a jockey all these months. Your letter's in the paper, and it reads fine. I've got it here too.'

His startling proposal for the minute quite took my breath away. I was dazed and heavy with the sudden awakening from my broken sleep, and the bare idea of his suggestion made me sick with fear.

'I couldn't do it,' I muttered, 'I should be found out at once.'

'Nonsense,' he insisted stoutly, 'it's simply a wonderful chance of escape for you. From what my cousin told me, you wouldn't have an earthly if you were up in the stands. They'll be searching everywhere today, but who'd dream of looking for you right under their very eyes?'

A little thought and I saw the master-stroke of Piper's idea. Scut's red jersey and unkempt figure were known to everyone who went racing, and no one would give him a second glance. The very humour of it too, swept avalanche-like through my mind.

With a grin, almost of elation, I donned the filthy garments and pulled the greasy hat well down upon my head.

'That's right,' said Piper enthusiastically, 'now take the blighter's pipe and slouch your shoulders as if you'd got gripes in your back. Don't ever move quickly and do everything as if you knew you were being paid by the hour. There's only one thing,' he went on thoughtfully, 'you'll have to keep close to me all day, and I've got charge of the hurdles right bang in front of the grandstand. It can't be helped though.' He burst into a laugh. 'One thing, you needn't speak a word to anybody. Scut's always been a sullen brute. Now come on out, there'll be plenty of jobs to do this morning, there always are on racing days. I'll put you first to dust the judges' box and you'll be able to have a squint at the paper there.'

Two minutes later and safe in the security of the judges' box I unfolded the *Times*. I saw my letter at once. It was printed prominently on the middle page, and eagerly I looked down to see what comments they were making on it. They didn't say much, but what they did say was very much to the point.

'On this page we publish today,' ran their remarks, 'a letter that adds yet another chapter to the extraordinary story of the Dr Carmichael affair. Never perhaps in the whole history of journalism in our state has sensation so followed upon sensation, as it now is in this case. The letter is authentic and written, as it purports to be, by the convict John Archibald Cups. On its receipt, we immediately submitted it to the officials of the Consolidated Bank and, with our own eyes, we have been convinced it is a genuine communication. It is too early yet to comment upon it at length, but in bare fairness to the man who writes it, we will, in passing, mention two facts. For the first, although as our readers are aware, the inquest upon the body of the late Dr Carmichael has been adjourned until next week, it is an open secret in the city that the only cause of death so far discovered has been that of dislocation and fracture of the third vertebra of the neck; and the second fact, the turret staircase and walls in the Tower House were carefully examined last evening by an expert, and there are undoubted indications that a heavy fall has at some time occurred there. The wood of the top step is quite rotten and has been entirely broken away.'

I put down the paper with a great sigh of relief. At any rate now, I thought, the sting was taken out of the assumption that I had murdered Dr Carmichael. Everyone would see now there was another side to the matter, and that it was not to be taken for granted I was guilty of everything that was being so freely laid to my charge.

I was interrupted suddenly by the harsh voice of Piper.

'Now then, Scut,' he bawled loudly, 'Look alive, will you, I want you out here.'

I shuffled out slowly to find him talking to Sidney Oldway, the smart good-looking secretary of the Racing Club.

'Cut along now and look to those hurdles,' he went on. 'There's one there with a cracked rail. Take it away and change it with a spare.'

'All right,' I growled, and I moved off to do as I was bid. The immaculately dressed secretary eyed me openly with disgust. 'Does that man ever wash?' I heard him ask Piper, 'he always looks beastly to me.'

I don't know what reply Piper gave. I was too anxious to move away. I had no doubt too I did look beastly. I had a week's growth of beard on me and I had muddied over my face. My coat too was filthy to look at and had an abominable reek. My trousers were all bagged and greasy, and my flaming jersey was horrible enough to offend even the least fastidious eye. I had no wonder the secretary didn't admire me.

It was a thrilling day for me, that Saturday. I stood on the very brink of disaster the whole day long. I was right on the precipice side, and at any moment the slightest mischance would have precipitated me and all my hopes to an abyss from where there would have been no recovery.

But mischance never touched me. Through dangers that simply swarmed I passed unscathed, and had I only known it I need not really have worried at all. Haloed in the personality of the beast-like Scut, I was immune both to trouble and suspicion.

Not that there was not plenty of suspicion too. When the time for racing began, the course was alive with police and plain-clothes men. I learnt afterwards that, as Piper had said, everyone had somehow got the idea that I would try and come to the racecourse in disguise. The Chief Commissioner himself had been sure of it. He imagined he was an expert on the psychology of crime and he considered that mine was just such a case where the obsession of my master passion, which he considered to be racing, would drive out fear of everything else. He believed I would jump to take the risk and rejoice in the thrills of danger it would give me.

So, as I say, the police were everywhere. Big, burly, fine-looking fellows with the unmistakable policeman gait moved everywhere among the crowd. They eyed everyone inquisitively. They peered into people's faces and they stared hard at anyone whom they thought bore the very slightest resemblance to me.

But I was never among the crowd at all. Piper saw to that. I was always kept doing something on the racing track, and my flaming jersey and my baggy trousers were conspicuous features the whole afternoon long.

The hurdle race was the first item on the card, and along with Piper my station was right bang in front of the grandstand. We saw to it that the hurdles were properly staked and, with Scut's disreputable-looking pipe always between my teeth, I held on gloomily to the battens, while Piper drove them lustily into the ground. Then as soon as the horses had jumped over them the first time round, up we had to pull them and stack them out of the way.

Between the races we had to stamp down the turf where it had been turned up by the flying hoofs, and when the preliminary canters were going on we had to swing out the angle posts to prevent the jockeys bringing their horses over to the side of the course near the rails.

When I had got over my first nervousness, the interest of the racing gripped at me like it always had done, and I had to remind myself many times to keep my head down.

Rainton had a sweet little filly running in the youngsters' race, and with a pang I saw her just beaten, about two yards before she reached the judges' box.

Then the steeplechase was full of thrills, and Mulvaney came a dreadful cropper on the horse I was to have ridden, Eaton Boy. It didn't seem to be his fault either, at all. He was out in front by himself and free from all interference, but Eaton Boy took off badly at the fence opposite the stands and crashed heavily as he came over. For a few minutes the animal lay stunned where he fell, and the jockey was removed unconscious in the ambulance. I heard a man on the rails call out something about it being a lucky escape for Huggins, but I wasn't quite so sure about the luck. I had seen the press photographer snap the accident, and it came home to me with dismay that, standing just where I had been, I must have been directly in the line of his camera. I hoped to goodness I wouldn't come out in the picture.

I had one other distinct thrill of apprehension that afternoon. Of all the people in the world, I caught sight of Pepple, the vegetarian, among the crowd over by the rails. He had got his bruiser-looking assistant with him, and he was moving restlessly to and fro and peering about as inquisitively as any policeman or plain-clothes man. Three times during the afternoon I found him in my neighbourhood, although on each occasion I was in a different place on the course. The last time he was not ten yards from me, and I thanked my stars he was obviously near-sighted. He had got his eyes all screwed up in a puzzled sort of way, and he poked his nose in everyone's face as he came near. Looking for me, of course, the little beast! I thought, and keeping as close to the prize-fighting man as a baby to its nurse.

Just before the fifth race, I was in charge of the angle-post almost in front of the judges' box, and I suddenly caught sight of Angas Forbes and Dick Rainton talking together in the enclosure. I was a little too far away to exactly catch the expression on their faces, but from the way they stood their attitudes didn't seem very friendly. The Scotchman seemed to be doing most of the talking, and several times I saw Dick Rainton coldly shake his head. Presently I saw a third party join them, and it added greatly to my interest when I recognised him as Benson, the trainer, who had given me my first winning mount in Adelaide on Vixen Lady.

Apparently Benson asked Rainton to introduce him, and then began a pantomime that filled me with intense curiosity. Angas Forbes seemed more antagonistic than ever, but in Benson I knew he would more than meet his match. Whatever they were saying, the trainer was every bit as emphatic as was he, and I could see the rough decisive way in which he was pushing his points.

Much to my disappointment, however, the 'off' was suddenly shouted, and in the rush to the rails the trio were immediately blotted out.

The afternoon went very quickly, and almost before I could take it in, it was all over and the people were streaming from the course. Half an hour after the last race the whole place was quite deserted, and Piper came up to me gleefully rubbing his hands.

'Great, wasn't it?' he exclaimed, with a triumphant grin. 'See the police? They were everywhere, and the plain-clothes men too. You'd have been caught, sure as a gun, if you'd been up on the stands. They went through them time after time, and everyone left the course tonight through files and files of suspects. I told you they thought you were mad and that they were certain they'd have you today. I believe now that the worst is over, and you're sure to get away. The doctor says that beast Scut will have to be in bed at least a week, and at any rate, you're safe until then.'

The next day passed very quietly, and the Monday dawned with my hopes very high indeed.

Another week, I argued, and the whole thing would die down. I had thought of what I would do. Piper should buy a second-hand motor-bicycle and side car, and we would get away on it, to begin with, to the bungalow at Noarlunga. I had given Piper his five hundred pounds in twenty-pound notes, and he was going to throw up his present job at once, and, after getting me away, he was going to clear off to Queensland. He was now as anxious to get away as was I, and we both saw the great desirability of moving before the alcoholic Scut reappeared and awkward explanations might ensue.

Piper turned up very early that Monday. He brought with him some interesting, if rather disquieting news.

'The police are furious,' he said, 'now that they know you are Cups. They've never forgiven you for the way you put it across them last year, and your letter in the paper on Saturday has made them simply wild. The Chief Commissioner has put them all on their mettle and there's promotion for anyone who spots you. They think they're bound to get you, although they say they know now you've got hiding places prepared all over the place. My cousin says one of the Henley Beach men told him on the quiet that they've found a bathing hut crammed with tinned food and no one knows who the hut belongs to. They're certain you've got it ready, and they expect to catch you there, but he also says the Port Adelaide people have got a card up their sleeve too. He doesn't know quite what it is, but it's something to do with a motor-boat with a lot of food hidden in the same way. I tell you the police are awfully excited and as keen as mustard to catch you.'

His information made me feel pretty uncomfortable, but I thought with thankfulness that the bicycle accident had been, after all, a very lucky accident for me.

I opened the newspaper he had brought with him, and the first thing I saw was a letter from Pepple again. As I read through it, I confess it almost made my blood run cold. The man might be a consummate ass, but wrapped up in all his rot about psychic warnings and astral waves there were some clever guesses, which pretty well hit the truth. His letter was dated Sunday, and he wrote he was positive I had been on the racecourse the previous day. He had been there all the afternoon himself, he wrote, and many times he had felt his own subconscious waves vibrating in harmony to those of mine. He was sure I had been somewhere on the racecourse. He would stake his life upon it. Why I had not been found, however, although obscure to him at first, was at last clear to him. It had come to him as he lay awake in the night. A great mistake had been made. Everyone had been looking for me in the wrong place. I had not been among the crowd. I had been among the officials somewhere, and if only a moment's thought were given to the matter everyone would at once see why. The whole thing was quite plain. It was undeniable I was acting with confederates now, otherwise how could be explained my possession of the daily newspapers and the delivery to the *Times* office of my letter by hand. Well, given I had confederates, who were they most likely to be? Why, racing people, of course. I had been mixed up with the racing crowd, and no doubt to many I was still a hero in their eyes. Of course, it was they who were helping me. The morality of race-goers was notoriously lax and most of them wouldn't think twice of helping me to hide away. I had been last traced, a week ago, to just near the Cheltenham Racecourse, and probably I had been lying low all the time at the buildings on the course. He wouldn't be at all surprised if on the race-day I had been disguised as one of the ticket collectors, or had been taken on in the totalizator building as one of the clerks. Clearly, he concluded, it was the racing officials who were shielding me and they ought to be shown up.

I cursed the little wretch for his meddling. Although his rigmarole was sheer guess-work and spiteful at that, it might set some people thinking, and with the big reward offered, his ideas might be taken up and night prowlers might come around.

Piper laughed when I showed him the letter. He was in high spirits. He had hidden his five hundred pounds safely away, and was in no fear now as to anything that might happen.

'Don't you worry, Mr Cups, we shall get off all right now,' he said confidently, 'and if the worse comes to the worst, I'll borrow my cousin's helmet and cape. No one would think of stopping anyone with a policeman in the side-car. I reckon our troubles are almost over, and you'll soon be able to live a comfortable life again.'

But Piper was wrong, woefully wrong, and of all my escapes, the most perilous one was yet to come.

I was dozing off in the shed that evening, it could not have been much more than half-past six, when suddenly the sound of hurried footsteps came to me from outside. There was a sharp click of the key in the lock, the pant of laboured breathing, and Piper was bending over me and hissing breathlessly in my ear.

'Quick, quick, get up. Run for your life. The police are here, they're following me. They've found out all about Scut. Run! Run! Don't go on the Torrens Road, they're watching there. Get over the railway. Quick – be quick!'

Fortunately for me I was not undressed, and more fortunate still I had got my boots on. I was off the bed in a flash and, grabbing up my hat, was out into the night almost before Piper had finished his last words. I disappeared round one side of the shed and Piper the other. Only just in time. A big, tall figure loomed out of the blackness and struck fiercely at me as I rushed by. I felt a stinging blow on the side of the face, and someone grabbed hold of my arm. But I shook myself free and escaped by a hair's breadth from another outstretched hand. There was a quick sharp run with at least two people hot after me in pursuit. But I knew the ground better than they did and, dodging round the grandstand, I doubled back and gave them the slip. I heard a lot of shouting and there was a great flashing of electric torches near the stands, but two minutes later, the blackness of the night had swallowed me up, and I was plugging briskly along, right over on the other side of the racecourse.

For the moment, once again, I was safe.

CHAPTER 11

All that happened on that eventful Monday, so suddenly and unexpectedly to set the police upon my trail, was at the time a complete mystery to me, and I could hazard no guess then how it had come about that at a second's notice, almost, I was again flying hot-foot from my enemies.

But everything was in due course made clear to me, and weeks after, in Brisbane, in a copy of the Queensland *Picture Magazine* I came across a representation of the actual photograph that had so nearly led to my undoing. Reprinted from an Adelaide paper, it was a picture showing the fall of Eaton Boy in the Steeple at Cheltenham.

It was in every way an excellent production, but in a spirit surely of malignant chance, nothing in it had come out clearer than had I.

There was I standing hunched up in Scut's miserable attire, the battered hat, the flaming jersey and the awful baggy trousers, as I had feared I had been, right bang in the line of fire. My face was turned up straight towards the camera and every line and feature of it stood out as clear as day.

No wonder I had been spotted the moment the photograph had been printed. The miracle would have been if I had not!

It appeared, however, that the operator had been very busy that day and the photograph had not been developed until well on into the afternoon. Then a single print had been taken, and in a moment the fat was in the fire.

The photographer had rushed off like a scalded cat to the police station, the telephone bells had been set clanging in all directions, and shortly after six o'clock, much to the astonishment of the neighbours, a long black police car had avalanched up to the residence of the alcoholic Ebenezer Scut.

Scut had been still in bed when his peace had been so rudely disturbed, and, never at any time very bright in his intelligence, it had, happily for me, taken much longer than it should have done to obtain coherent replies to the police queries.

But he at last made it plain that he had been nowhere near the racecourse for four days, that he had not even left his bed since the previous Thursday, and that his mate Piper on the Saturday had borrowed his clothes, including the famous and filthy red jersey.

Asked to explain why he had lent Piper his garments, he had reluctantly admitted that he had thought the latter was doing him a good turn. He, Scut, had so often failed to report for work on the racecourse because of his drunken habits that the secretary had at last sworn he would sack him if it should happen again. So when Piper had burst in excitedly on the Saturday morning to announce he had found a temporary substitute, Scut had been ready to fall on his neck and hail him as a true friend.

This was the tale that Scut had told the detectives, and immediately suspicion was focused upon Piper and a move made towards the latter's house. But Piper had been actually coming round to see how Scut was at the very time the police were there, and the police car and the policemen lounging in front of the house had instantly enlightened him, and he had torn off to warn me of the danger I was in.

But he had been spotted taking a short cut over the fence and the police, reinforced by a contingent from Woodville, had as nearly as anything caught him before he had had time to reach me.

All this I learnt afterwards but, as I have said, at the time everything was a puzzle to me. All I knew was that I was fleeing once again into the darkness with a cordon of danger drawn round me on every side.

It was well for me I knew every yard of the course, for the pain in my ankle came back almost at once and in a straight out run I should have had no chance at all. But I picked my way stealthily along by the thick box hedge surrounding the course and, coming at length to a hole that I knew was there, crawled through it on to the railway and from thence got quickly on to the great Port Road.

I really don't think I had been at all frightened any part of the time. My chief feeling as far as I remember was one of anger, intense anger, that I was being so harassed again. I had everyone against me, I told myself, and it wasn't fair. The whole organisation of the state was out to crush me, and it was like a big giant fighting a little boy.

But I wouldn't give in, I swore. I would see them all in hell before they caught me. I would dodge them again. I turned up my coat collar and walked warily down the Port Road thinking desperately what I must do.

I knew I must act quickly. The Port Road wouldn't be safe for long. In a few minutes it would be alive with policemen, and already I guessed the telephones were buzzing energetically all over the city.

But I could think of nothing I could do. Every plan that suggested itself to me I had to turn down. There was nowhere that I knew of where I could hide, and every moment my foot began to warn me the more and more insistently that any prolonged exertion was entirely out of the question.

With my mind in dreadful turmoil, about three minutes' walking brought me to the railway crossing on the Port Road and then – without any premeditation on my part – my fate was decided for itself.

A train was about to go over the level crossing and the traffic was being held up. A big motor lorry there had been brought to a standstill, and I noticed that it was loaded well up with petrol tins. Suddenly I caught sight of a policeman in the distance and, panic-stricken and looking for anywhere to hide, I jumped on to the lorry and lay down among the tins. At the same instant the train thundered by. There were two sacks among the tins and frantically I pulled them over me. With a rough jerk the lorry started, quickly gathered pace, and in a few seconds it was rushing noisily towards the city.

For a minute or two I could hardly take in my good fortune. I lay under the dirty sacks scarce daring to breathe lest I should be seen as we passed by. Then gradually my confidence returned, and I laughed shakily that it had been so easy to get away. What a sell for the police again! I thought. Whatever was going to happen now, I was at least out of the immediate dangerous area, and my prospects were brighter with each yard the lorry drew away.

I wondered where the lorry was going to. It must have come straight from the Port, I knew, and loaded up as it was, its destination might be anywhere miles away from the city. In an hour or two even, I might find myself near some country town, and I should be able to slip away. I must be very careful, however, for once in the bush, if they had any idea where I was, they would put the black trackers on to me at once.

I waited anxiously to see which way the lorry would go.

In a few minutes we came to the confines of the city, and the lorry went straight on, as if it were going to pass right through. I was just rejoicing that, at any rate, somewhere in the country was evidently going to be its destination, when suddenly, just as we were right opposite The Grand Australasian Hotel, the lorry began to slow down.

I put my head out anxiously between the tins and, oh, horror! saw we were turning up the little lane into the garage of the hotel.

I had only an instant to make up my mind, but happily that instant was time enough. The entrance to the garage was narrow and ill-lighted, and the lorry had to slow down to a snail's pace. I slipped off the back without a sound, and then, as an afterthought, pulled one of the sacks off after me. When lying on the lorry I had felt a spot of rain.

For a minute or two I stood exactly where I had got off. I was in the shadows and I wanted time to think.

If ever I had been in a predicament, I was in one now. I was right in the very heart of the city and, whichever way I went, I should have to pass along well lighted and well-frequented streets. All the police-stations, I knew, would have been warned by now, and still in the disreputable attire of Scut, I should be an easy mark to pick out, even among a crowd.

For the first time that night I began to be afraid.

I heard a noise behind me. Someone was coming out of the garage. There was no help for it. I must take my fate into my hands and go out into the street.

I have often thought since, on going over matters again, that if in my wanderings, when feverishly pursued by the police, I had met with both bad and good fortune, the good fortune had certainly always preponderated over the bad, and it undoubtedly was so in the events of that night.

It had been rotten bad luck, of course, that the lorry should have plumped me down where it did for, on the face of it, the position could not possibly have been worse. But once that misfortune had been got over, nothing could really have been kinder than the way in which chance treated me.

As I walked boldly out into the street it began to drizzle, and I wrapped the sack over my head. The pavement was thronged with people and I saw several policemen about. Two, in fact, were not twenty yards from me, and another one was on point duty at the corner. Although I must have cut a queer figure, no one took the slightest notice of me. They all appeared to be interested in their own affairs or hurrying to get out of the rain.

On the other side of the street, and directly opposite The Grand Australasian Hotel, there was a small piece of enclosed ornamental garden, and I crossed over to it at once, almost automatically, so it seemed, but really probably because I must have noticed there were fewer people passing on that side of the road, and also because it was not nearly so well lighted. I leaned back against the low railings and contemplatively considered which way I should go. It certainly did want a bit of considering, for whichever way I looked I could see policeman, and with my wretched foot I knew I couldn't walk far. Whimsically I tried to imagine I was engaged in a game of chess, but for the life of me I couldn't determine my next move.

I must have stood there quite an hour watching the traffic, and at the end of it I was just as undecided as ever.

Everything seemed again quite hopeless, and the desperation of it suddenly got on my nerves. I went over all the worries I had been through lately, and asked myself irritably if they were really worth fighting against any longer. I felt sick of the whole business and dazed, like a man in a dream. All at once, it came to me I didn't mind what happened any longer.

I was tired of these continual excitements and just wanted to lie down and have a good rest.

I cocked my eye over the little bit of garden behind me. There was a high bed of flowers in the middle, with a low wall of rockery all round its sides. With half a chance, I told myself, I'd get over and have a sleep there.

And the chance came almost at the same moment as the idea entered my mind. There was a sudden noise of shouting at the street corner, a shriek from a woman somewhere, and I saw a car charging straight over the pavement in the direction of a big shop window. The steering gear had evidently gone wrong.

There was a fearful crash of breaking glass, a lot more shouting, and everyone rushed excitedly to see what was taking place.

Now was my chance, I thought. Whatever was happening was nothing to do with me. Every shop window in Adelaide might be broken for all I cared.

I scrambled desperately over the low railings and, stumbling across the strip of intervening lawn, in a few seconds was right in the middle of the bed of flowers.

To my surprise, there was a length of corrugated-iron there. It was being used to protect some seedlings from the night frosts and the ground was quite dry underneath. I tilted it up and, crawling under with my sack, quicker than it takes to tell it, was lying prone and once more at rest.

For the moment, I certainly couldn't have been in a better place. I was entirely surrounded by a wall of chrysanthemums about two feet high, and although actually within a few yards of the traffic of one of the busiest streets, I was nevertheless as secure and secluded as if I were miles and miles away from the city itself.

I made a sort of pillow of the sack and, in only a few minutes, I believe, I went to sleep. I was tired out.

It was just midnight when I awoke. I think it must have been the striking of the Town Hall clock that woke me, and for the moment I couldn't remember where I was. I was feeling rather cold and the pressure of the sheet of iron had made my shoulder ache.

There was a bright moon shining, and the city was wrapped in the silence of a grave. I leaned out from my hiding-place and peered cautiously between the stalks of the chrysanthemums. The streets were deserted and there was not a soul in sight. No, I was mistaken. There were two policemen standing by an electric standard at the intersection of the road. I watched them curiously. A car came purring up from the direction of the Port Road and immediately one of them stepped forward and held up his hand. The car pulled up, and I saw the policeman peer under the hood. Then there was some laughing, and a moment afterwards the car was driven away, and the policemen resumed their vigil by the electric standard.

Looking for me, I thought, and taking no chances I should be spirited away.

I don't remember that I went to sleep again at all. I started worrying what the next day would hold in store, and everything seemed black and hopeless to the deepest depths of despair. I realised that I was at the end of my tether at last, and I fingered my automatic thankfully and many times saw to it that the safety catch came easily to the release.

I shall never know perhaps why I lived through the next day. Long before dawn I had resolved to shoot myself and get it over. Deliberately I had condemned myself to death, and so miserable and weary was I that I waited gladly for the end to come. I had no fear at all of death. It would be peace and rest at last and, although I had been beaten in the fight, I should never yet hear the mocking of my enemies. I really wanted to die, but still, wretched as I was and with all hope gone, I clung unreasonably to life. Hour after hour I gave myself reprieve. The dawn rose high, and I still lived. The morning passed, and I had done nothing. Noon came, and I was still fingering the trigger. A dreadful thirst seized me, and I was faint with hunger. My body ached in every joint from my cramped position, and I was stiff and sore from lying on the cold hard ground. I was in acute pain from my injured foot, and every evil that I could think of seemed to possess me, and yet I dallied on the chance that some miracle might happen.

I really don't know what I expected, and how in any possible way it could happen now that I could get away. It was certain I could never pass again unchallenged along the streets. There was never anytime when there were not policemen in sight and, apart from that, it seemed to me as I lay watching that there was an air of actual inquisitiveness about each other apparent among the crowds that passed along the pavement near where I lay hidden. At the moment I thought it was only fancy, but if I had known the truth I need not have wondered about it at all.

It was actually expected by the police that I should be hiding somewhere in the vicinity of the place where I now was. I had been traced almost to the entrance of the garage of The Grand Australasian Hotel.

Although I flattered myself I had cleverly escaped unseen from the neighbourhood of the Cheltenham Racecourse, it appeared a signalman had seen me jump on to the lorry at the level crossing. He had thought nothing of it at the time, but later on when the cry was raised, he had communicated with the police and the destination of the load of petrol tins had been easily obtained. So when I thought I had puzzled everyone by my mysterious flitting away, the police were concentrating round the very place where I was hiding. They had actually gone so far as to search thoroughly through ever corner of The Grand Australiasian Hotel itself, although to the little strip of garden opposite they had never given a thought.

All day long, between my troubled broodings, I was interested in the hotel too. From where I lay I could see so plainly everything that was going on at the front entrance, and from time to time I recognised many of the people going in and out. Many notabilities of the city went up the steps, and many of the great lights of the racing world appeared there too. I saw Judge Cartright go in to his lunch, and Drivel Jones too with one of his inevitable long cigars. I saw Sir Joseph Carnworthy of the Consolidated Bank, and, later, my heart beat wildly as I caught sight of Angas Forbes.

For at least ten minutes the big Scotchman stood on the entrance steps talking to some friends, and for the first time in all my adventures I was enabled to have a good look at the man who had brought about my downfall.

The first sight of him filled me with the bitterest feelings of hate and revenge, and I cursed him deeply for the agonies he had brought me.

If only he had been a little bit nearer, I would have chanced it and tried to shoot him where he stood. But I measured the distance with my eye and saw it was hopeless. I would only be giving greater pleasure to them when they would stood round me when I was lying dead.

Angas Forbes disappeared in a while, but long after he had gone in I was thinking of him, and towards the latter part of the day he had become quite an obsession in my thoughts.

Strange to my own mind, when my first fierce burst of anger was over, I could not for the life of me think very badly of the man. He might be stern and uncompromising in his actions but, for all that, he had rather a kind face, and to me he had seemed to be looking very sad. Every line of him told of force and energy but, hasty and quick though he might be in his decisions, it struck me he would be always just in the end.

A very devil he had been to me I knew, but, after all, I remembered Dr Carmichael was his friend, and with everything he had done he had been acting always under the idea that I was a murderer and he was only avenging the dead man.

The long day waned and darkened, and with the fall of dusk there was all hell under the sheet of corrugated-iron, in the middle of the bed of chrysanthemums.

Every mental and physical suffering that could come to a man I thought then was mine, but my thirst, of all things, tormented me most.

I knew I was going to die, and the little automatic pistol, like a saviour, lay just beneath my head. I pressed my forehead on to its cool blue barrel, for my face was burning though my legs were icy cold. I was ready for death any moment, and yet I wanted a drink first.

I must get a drink somehow. The idea of water filled my thoughts, and I believed that, priest-like, it would give me physical absolution before I died. I must do something.

I raised myself on my elbow and then crawled out from under the sheet of iron.

The town hall clock struck seven.

Careless of who might see me, I sat upright among my bed of flowers, and then suddenly I happened to look up across to The Grand Australasian Hotel.

Angas Forbes was standing on the balcony of the first floor. For the moment he stood still, watching the stream of life that was flowing just below him in the street. Then he turned abruptly and went in. I saw the light go up in a room.

Mechanically I numbered off the room that he was occupying. It was the seventh from the direction of the entrance hall.

I was drunk with pain and suffering. Good, I would go and give him a call. The very least he could do was to give a drink of water.

I stood up and began weakly to rub my legs. Then I staggered across the strip of lawn, and at the second attempt succeeded in getting over the low railings. I crossed the road quite oblivious to how the traffic might deal with me, and the sudden grind of brakes and a hoarsely shouted curse from someone on the driving seat of a car were of no interest to me at all. I walked up the garage entrance of the hotel, turned up a little flight of stairs that I knew were there, passed through a small door and was in the luggage room of The Grand Australasian.

I knew the hotel well, and with no hesitation passed along a narrow corridor and reached the back service stairs used by the staff. In half a minute at most I had reached the first floor without having seen or been seen by a soul.

I sat down at the top of the stairs to have a rest. My hurried journey, short as it was, in my weak condition had taken away all my breath. It had also sobered me down a little, and with my mind much clearer I saw the perilous position I was in. Not that the danger worried me though; my only thought for the moment was that of getting something to drink.

I pulled myself to my legs and staggering shakily along, turned the handle of the first door I came to. It yielded at once and I walked in. There was a bright fire burning in the grate, but I looked for the light and switched it on.

I found myself in quite a fair-sized bedroom, and the first thing that caught my eyes was a bottle of whisky on the chest of drawers.

I believe I almost ran across the room to get that whisky and in a few seconds I had drawn an arm-chair up before the fire and was gloriously sipping a good stiff glass of the spirit.

Oh, the happy memory of those next ten minutes! The alcohol gave life and courage to me, and I no longer meant to die. It cheered all the senses in me and restored me at once to a sane, clear state of mind.

There should be still chances for me yet, I thought, and as evidencing the grip I had on myself again, although I would have dearly loved another drink of whisky, I resolutely put the idea away from me and to quench my thirst drank glass upon glass of water instead.

Then I remembered why I had come into the hotel, and a brain-wave surged through me that my salvation might lie there after all. I would get to speak to Angas Forbes, and drive into him that he was acting as an utterly wrong and mistaken man. In his persecution of me, he was doing everything his dead friend would have fought against and, by urging on the authorities as he was, he was nullifying all the efforts the latter would have surely made to save me from the law.

I got on to my feet at once but, as I stood up, I happened to look in the glass.

It was a dreadful face that looked back into mine. Ten days' growth of stubbly beard; grime, mud and the stains of blood; cheeks sunken and drawn in, eyes hollow, and hair all matted and fouled with earth. I looked like a man who had risen from the tomb.

There was a big wash basin in the bedroom with hot and cold water laid on, and in a twinkling I had taken off my coat and was rolling up my sleeves. There was a razor on the dressing table, and after a moment's hesitation I commandeered that too. Time after time I luxuriously bathed my face with the hot water and, when I had finally completed my ablutions, it was a very different person who was now reflected in the glass.

Scut's awful clothes I could not remedy, and I was in no mood now with so much at stake to run further risks by remaining any longer in the room. Already I told myself, I had stayed too long already, and any moment, I realised, the occupant of the room might come in. So hastily I obliterated as far as possible all traces of my visit and, switching off the light, I tiptoed softly out into the corridor.

There were ten rooms facing me and, with a quickly beating heart, I located the one, seventh from the entrance hall. It was occupied, I saw, for the lights were up. I knocked quietly on the door and a voice bade me to come in.

I turned the handle quickly and, stepping into the room, closed the door gently behind me.

Angas Forbes was writing at a small table, and he immediately looked up.

CHAPTER 12

For quite a long moment we looked silently at each other. I was taking in intently every line and feature of the big Scotchman's face, and he was regarding me with a cold and puzzled stare.

'Well,' he snapped sharply, at length, 'who are you and what do you want?'

'I'm Cups,' I replied drily, 'and you've been looking for me?'

'Ah!'

He said nothing more, but his blue eyes I saw grew bright and steely, and the big hand that rested on the table clenched itself up tightly as if it were about to strike a blow. He must have thought himself in danger, I knew, but to do the man justice he never flickered an eyelid or showed the slightest trace of fear.

'Yes,' I repeated slowly, 'I'm Cups, and I've come to have a word with you.'

He looked at me with contempt, as if I were some sort of animal.

'Ye dinna frighten me,' he said slowly, breaking into broad Scotch, 'I'm no afraid.'

'You've no need to be,' I replied quietly. 'I'm not here to do you any harm.'

'You've come to give yourself up then?' he asked sternly.

'Not at all. I've just come to speak to you, that's all.'

His eyes moved from my face and I could see he was taking in my clothes.

'Have the police tracked you here?' he asked abruptly.

'By no means,' I said. 'As usual, I've given them the slip.'

'Were you hiding in the hotel then when they searched for you?'

'Oh, no,' I said lightly, 'I was in the bed of chrysanthemums in the garden just across the street. There's no reason why you shouldn't know.'

He glanced down at my hands. 'But I've tidied myself up since then,' I went on carelessly. 'I've just had a shave and brush-up in one of the rooms opposite. And a drink of whisky. I badly wanted something to drink.'

He looked at me very thoughtfully, but just the ghost of a smile, I thought, for a moment played around the corners of his mouth. There was a quite a long silence, then he asked very quietly, 'What do you expect of me by coming here?'

I stifled a dreadful yawn. 'A couple of those biscuits, please, to begin with,' I replied, pointing to a biscuit box open on the table. 'I've had nothing at all to eat since yesterday, and for many days too, thanks to you, I've had only cheese and sandwiches. So there's no wonder I feel rather weak. May I have one?'

He made a rough gesture of denial. 'I don't care to offer hospitality,' he remarked grimly, 'to a man I am about to hand over to the police. But still' – and he shrugged his shoulders with indifference – 'I shan't stop you if you choose to take them, and from all I have learnt of your characteristics, over-squeamishness is not your weak point.'

I pulled a chair up to the table and, sitting down just opposite to him, helped myself to a biscuit and began to munch hungrily.

He watched me with a puzzled frown.

'Were you hiding on the racecourse all last week?' he asked suddenly.

'I haven't told you I was there at all yet, have I?' I said.

He ignored my query. 'How much did you pay Sam Piper?' he went on.

'Piper,' I said, innocently, 'who's he?'

'Oh, don't play the fool,' he snarled roughly. 'We know all about your relations with Piper, and he's been in the cells since last night.'

In spite of myself, I felt my face fall. I had given little thought to Piper in the last twenty-four hours but, still, at the back of my mind, I had hoped devoutly he was safe and, remembering what he had done for me, the news now that he was in prison made me wince.

Angas Forbes was watching me narrowly and something of what was in my mind must have come to him.

'Yes, you've got him into trouble right enough,' he said bitterly. 'The poor devil has lived to curse the day you ever came into his life, although all things considered,' he bent over the table and leant towards me, 'perhaps he's lucky to have his life at all.'

I looked him squarely in the face and thought the moment had now come to lay my cards on the table.

'Look here, Mr Forbes,' I said, curtly, 'I see it plainly enough now. I made a mistake in not telling you everything at the first, but you gave me no chance. You're a hasty self-opinionated man. You came here in absolute ignorance of everything, and you instantly formed your own opinion, knowing nothing whatever of anything that had taken place.' I felt my temper rising. 'You blundered into the whole business like a mad bull, and I tell you straight, you have just wrecked all that you friend Dr Carmichael built up. That's what you've done here.'

'Leave Carmichael's name alone please,' he burst out hotly. 'You murdered him, you black scoundrel!'

'Murdered him?' I exclaimed in a passion of temper. 'Murdered him, do you say?' I dropped my voice almost to a whisper. 'You big lumbering Scotch fool!' I hissed. 'Have you no more imagination than a Highland cow? What should I murder him for? Murder my only friend! Murder the one man that stood between me and five years in the stockade! Murder him just when I needed him most, with the stitches hardly out of my wounds, and with my face all swollen and cut about like a butchered sheep! Murdered him! I tell you, man, when Dr Carmichael died, and you have proved almost to a day when he did die, I was a sight for any man to see, and I was boxed in, in that house, like a rat in a trap. It was the most dreadful moment of my life, I tell you.'

I paused for a moment to get breath. Angas Forbes had taken his arms off the table and was leaning back in his chair. The expression of blind fury had left his face and he was regarding me, I saw, in a puzzled and rather surprised sort of way.

'Look here again,' I went on, but now more calmly. 'They say you were a doctor yourself once, and if so, you'll understand what was done to me. Look closely at my face. You can feel it, if you like.'

He hesitated just a moment and then he stood up. He came round the table and for a full two minutes, standing over me, he examined my face. I shut my eyes. I felt the great hands wandering over me, but his touch was very gentle, and I kept perfectly still. In a little while, to my astonishment, he heaved a great sigh, and then he returned slowly round the table and resumed his seat. I opened my eyes again.

'Now, sir,' I said quietly. 'You can tell what was done and you can estimate in exactly what condition my face would have been a fortnight after the operation.' I sniffed sarcastically. 'A nice state I should have been in to commit a murder, and my face would have looked pretty afterwards too if I had been obliged to show myself to anyone who had chanced to come to the house.'

Angas Forbes looked at me very thoughtfully and, with an idea in my mind, I suddenly stopped speaking. I would force him to some reply and, *seriatim*, he should answer to each point I made.

For quite a long moment the silence went on, and then the big Scotchman opened his lips.

'I'll hear what you've got to say,' he said, very slowly and with a sort of effort. 'Your version, I mean, of how my friend met his death.' His words became almost broken. 'Tell – me – exactly – how – he – died.' He stopped to draw a deep breath and then all suddenly his voice grew harsh and menacing. 'But look ye here, man, don't ye think ye'll deceive me.' He thumped the table heavily with his fist and glared at me with furious eyes. 'I'm a medical man, as you say, but I'm a barrister as well. I'm accustomed to weigh evidence, I tell you, and I'll trip ye, I'll trip ye, the first lie ye tell.'

The man's emotion was perfectly apparent. There was quite a sob in his voice, and the partial dropping into his mother tongue exposed the reality of the grief he was in.

I realised at once what had happened and a sudden feeling of great hope flashed through my mind. For the moment, at any rate, I knew I had broken down the absolute certainty he had had hitherto that I was a murderer. He was doubting for the first time. I had not misjudged the man. He would be just in the end.

I began to speak slowly and evenly, almost as if I were reciting a monologue.

'On Monday morning, 29 January, Dr Carmichael and I were in the garden. The question came up whether it was going to rain, and Dr Carmichael said he would go up into the tower and look at the barometer. He went into the house and about two minutes later, I heard him suddenly call out, and then the noise of him falling down the stairs. I ran into the house and found him lying all huddled in a heap in the hall. He was lying on his back. His right arm was twisted under him, and his head was at an angle to his body. He was dying. He couldn't get his breath and he could hardly speak. He whispered to me not to touch him. I wanted to fetch a doctor, but he said it was no good for his neck was broken. He said, "I'm finished." He spoke just a few words, he smiled at me, and then he was dead.'

I had not looked at Angas Forbes while I was speaking. I had kept my eyes down. When I had finished, however, glancing up at him, I found that he in turn was looking away. He was obviously controlling his emotions with an effort. He was staring fixedly into the fire, but by the firelight I could see his face was wet with tears.

He turned round and spoke at last, very quietly and with his voice unemotionless and well in hand.

'What time in the morning did this all happen?' he asked.

'I can't say for certain,' I replied, 'but I should think about half-past seven. We had just come out in the garden after breakfast.'

'How long elapsed, should you say, from the moment when you first found him, to when he was absolutely dead?'

'Two minutes, or less even than that.'

'Was he in pain, do you think?'

I hesitated. 'I don't think so – only he couldn't get his breath.'

'Did he struggle at all?'

'No, he never moved until his head fell sideways as he died.'

'Didn't he struggle much to get his breath?'

'No, he didn't struggle, he only gasped – his body never moved.'

'Where did the blood come from?'

'There was no blood at all.'

'Not from his nostrils?'

'No, not that I remember. I remember no blood at all.'

'Was he quite conscious?'

'Yes, perfectly so, for the moments that he lived.'

'Could he speak plainly?'

'Yes, quite plainly but very faintly. He could only whisper.'

'It was the right arm, you said, that was twisted under him – that was the one that was broken, wasn't it?'

I shook my head. 'I don't know. I never really touched him until I came to wrap him in the sheet, and then I was too agitated to notice anything at all. I had never touched a dead body before.'

'Now tell me exactly the words he said.'

'When I ran up I was going to move his head, but he said, "Don't touch me." Then when I wanted to get a doctor he just gasped, "No good – cervical vertebrae – neck broken." Then he said, "Good man, Cups – I give everything to you – don't be afraid – have courage, man – look out Angas Forbes – tell him." That was everything he said, and he died saying the last words.'

There was a long silence again in the room, and for several minutes the gentle crackling of the wood fire was the only sound that came up to our ears. If Angas Forbes was sorrowing over what I had told him of his dead friend, I too, was moved by the memories that my recital had called up. I saw in fancy again the dark and silent house, I saw the body lying by the stairs, I heard the great hounds whining in the garden, and I felt again something of that indescribable feeling of awe that even the most hardened feel in the presence of the dead.

My reverie was broken into by Angas Forbes. He had recovered first from the spell cast over us by the spirit of our thoughts.

'You say,' he asked very quietly, 'that Dr Carmichael died about half-past seven in the morning. When did you bury him then?'

'The same day,' I replied. 'About two hours after he died.'

He looked me very straight in the face.

'You're sure – quite sure of that?' he asked.

'Perfectly so,' I replied. 'The grave was filled in and smoothed over before the tradesman's bell rang, and he was always there by eleven o'clock.'

He spoke sharply and very sternly.

'And do you tell me – do you want me to believe that you dug a six foot grave in a couple of hours?' He bent over and put his face close to mine. 'Are you lying at last? Remember there had been no rain for nine weeks previous to 28 January, and the ground must have been hard as a rock.'

I didn't move a hair's breadth and his eyes, I know, were not one whit more hard and stony than were mine.

'The grave had been dug more than a week,' I said coldly. 'It was dug in the event of my not coming-to under the anaesthetic.'

He frowned puzzledly to me.

'Explain, please,' he said curtly.

'When Dr Carmichael first suggested that he could operate on my face and so alter me that no one would recognise me again, I jumped at the idea at once. He warned me, however, that under the circumstances we were in, the operation was likely to be a very dangerous one, because of his having to operate on me and give me the chloroform at the same time.

'I told him I didn't mind what happened either way, for if I did die, I shouldn't know anything about it, and in any case I should be out of all my trouble. He laughed, and said that would be all very well for me, but where would he come in? He would be saddled with a dead body in the height of an Australian summer, and it wouldn't be a pleasant thing. Then I suggested, half in joke and half in earnest, that I would prepare a grave in case anything should happen, and when he finally agreed to do the operation he kept me up to the idea. I think he really only wanted to make me realise the risk I was running. I dug the grave in the two days after he had bought the chloroform, and that is how it happens it was already there.'

Angas Forbes made no comment for a moment, then he jerked out rather brusquely, 'And if Dr Carmichael did not come to his end in the way you have told me, how are we to know that you didn't push him down those stairs and so cause the broken neck?'

I put as much contempt in my voice as I could. 'You can only assume my guilt by evidence that is wholly circumstantial.' I shrugged my shoulders. 'And, in the same way, you can only assume my innocence. As I have shown you, I had everything to lose by his death and nothing to gain.'

'Well, you've gained a good lot anyhow, haven't you?' he remarked drily. 'Forty-seven thousand pounds is surely a fair sum to have in any part of the world.'

'But how in common sense did I know I was going to get a penny?' I protested. 'It was all chance that I was able to realise his estate.'

'Explain again, please,' he said sarcastically. 'I don't follow you. I'm afraid I'm rather dense.'

'Look here, Mr Forbes,' I exclaimed hotly. 'You're not acting as a just man. You've been too prejudiced from first to last. Now just look at my position in that last week of January. With Dr Carmichael alive, everything was hopeful for me. I had got a strong friend and I had got a rich friend. I had got a protector who was interested in me, and who was so far interested in me that on my behalf he had brought himself within reach of the law by harbouring me, knowing me at the time to be an escaped convict, under sentence of five years. Also, we were bound together by a deeper tie. He had held my life in his hands and alone and unaided in that lonely house he had taken me down into the valley of the shadow and run risks that might easily, as none better than yourself can estimate, have landed him very much in the position I am now, with a secretly buried body and a hidden grave to account for. There was another thing, too. Dr Carmichael, in the last weeks of his life, had made up his mind to return into the world again, and I was to have gone with him. I tell you, with him living, prospects could not have been brighter for me.'

I paused for a moment. I began to feel rather faint and shaky. The duel between us was being so long drawn out that in my weak condition it was becoming too much for me.

'Go on, pray, Mr Cups,' said Angas Forbes drily. 'I will go so far as to admit that you are quite a plausible advocate.

I swallowed down a lump in my throat and went on.

'But where was I with Dr Carmichael dead, ask yourself? A fortnight out of a disfiguring operation and with a face I could show to no one, without arousing instant curiosity how I had come by it, and who I was. Practically with only a few shillings to go on with, and with no certain prospects of getting a farthing more, what chance had I of escaping anywhere without money? What chance at all? I tell you I was hemmed in in that house like a rat in a trap, and the very remembrance of the horror of it makes me feel sick even now. Think of it yourself. It was a grilling summer day. There were the rooms all darkened with the blinds down. There was the body lying on the floor. There were the great hounds whining round the house outside, and there was I, weak from my operation, hesitating and irresolute, cowering in a corner, in a perfect frenzy of fear that at any moment the gate bell might ring, and someone want to come in. And I had to do something too; that was the hell of it. I had to make up my mind at once.'

I paused from sheer exhaustion here, but Angas Forbes was eyeing me, I thought stonily and without pity.

'You had a signed cheque of Dr Carmichael's in the house,' he said, 'one for fifty pounds, and you cashed it on 18 February. Was that having no prospects at all of getting more money?'

'No certain prospects, I told you. How did I know I was going to live on undisturbed in that house until my face got well? How did I know chance was going to favour me as it did? It was chance favoured me all along. When I went to the bank to cash that fifty pound cheque they took it for granted I was Dr Carmichael himself. Chance helped me there. Then I heard the manager was away ill. Chance again! He was the only one who knew Dr Carmichael. Then the manager died. More chance! How could I have known he was going to die? If he had lived it would have been a hundred times more difficult for me to do any business at the bank at all. It would have been a dreadful risk at every turn, and certainly impossible for me to have got my signature verified when I was disposing of any shares. I tell you the manager's death made the difference of everything to me – and it was a thing I could not possibly have foreseen.'

'When did you first up your mind to forge Dr Carmichael's signature?' broke in Angas Forbes abruptly.

I hesitated for a moment. 'I think I first made up my mind,' I replied slowly, 'to try and adopt his signature' – I laid significant stress on the word 'adopt' – 'the day after he died. The possibilities of it came to me suddenly as I was going through his papers. I saw he was a very rich man, and you may believe it or not' – here in spite of myself I could not prevent my voice taking on a covert sneer – 'the chief pleasure I have all along derived from my successful "forgeries" has lain in the belief that in so acting I have been only doing exactly what he would have wished.' I shrugged my shoulders. 'He bade me have courage and I have just interpreted it that way, that's all.'

'Then you say,' said Angas Forbes, 'that within twenty-four hours of his death you were devising a plan of campaign to obtain the whole of his estate?'

'No, I don't say that at all,' I replied sharply. 'You are trying to trap me. My first idea of using his signature was only to obtain the money lying to his current account and, with any good luck, the money he had on deposit there. My intentions to begin with were quite modest, but they expanded, as I have explained to you, when I realised how easy things were being made for me at the bank.'

He looked at me very thoughtfully.

'And you have obtained altogether about forty-seven thousand pounds, haven't you?'

'Somewhere about that,' I said. 'Rather more than less, I should think.'

He smiled rather drily. 'And you have come to me,' he went on, speaking very slowly and as if carefully weighing his words, 'with the idea, you say, that I could help you to escape and carry all this money out of the state?'

Again a horrible feeing of faintness had come over me, but with a great effort I pulled myself together. 'Look here, Mr Forbes,' I said wearily, 'I'm so tired of the whole business that I don't seem to care what happens to me now. Many times today I was going to shoot myself in the bed of chrysanthemums over there, but tonight I was so thirsty, I wanted a drink of water first. I caught sight of you standing on the verandah and an impulse made me come to you here.'

My voice all at once seemed to gather strength, and I went on. 'You say you were a friend of Dr Carmichael. So was I. I come to you now for that very reason. He found me once, as you find me now, haunted, friendless, and flying from the law. A criminal, though I had done no wrong. He helped me and he gave me shelter. He gave me back to decent life again. Now, if you have any loyalty to his memory, if you have any affection for the man that died, for his sake you will help me now as he helped me then.' I leant forward and thrust my face up close to his. 'You know I didn't kill him, and if you won't admit it, it's only because your damned pride holds you back. You're as obstinate as a mule, I tell you, you're a big, blundering' – I shook my fist in his face – 'you're a – you're a – ' A dreadful buzzing came into my ears, my voice went very far away. My eyes grew dim and misty, and with a crash that I just heard, I fell across the table and everything was blotted out.

I knew very little of what went on in the next ten days. I realised somehow that I was being nursed, for I was conscious of often being fed and of cold bandages being laid upon my head. I remember, too, the prick of needles in my arm and of someone continually saying 'Hush!' and stroking my face. I know I talked a lot, too, for the sound of my own voice kept coming up to me and breaking through my dreams.

I thought Margaret Price was often near me and that Angas Forbes kept looking at me with his great big eyes.

I remember funnily that I was afraid of Angas Forbes no longer. He seemed to be guarding me, and I thought Dr Carmichael used to come in, too, and bring Diana to keep watch over me while I slept.

I had long talks with Dr Carmichael, and I told him everything that had happened since he died. He used to laugh a lot and ask me how I liked being in the stockade. Then he said he was tired of being in his grave and thought it was about time someone came and gave him a leg out.

One night I woke up and found the room very quiet. I felt quite different, and my mind was quite clear. I couldn't hear the clock ticking and was able to notice that the electric light had a dark shade over it. I tried to lift my head but found I was too weak. I think I must have moaned, for immediately I heard the noise of a chair being moved and a second later a woman glided up to the bed.

I could feel my heart stop beating for I saw she was Margaret Price.

She knelt by the bed and stroked my face. 'Hush, dear,' she whispered, 'don't worry, you're quite safe.'

Then the dreadful memory of everything came back to me and I could feel my eyes fill suddenly with tears.

In an instant Margaret had put her arms about me and was holding me close to her. 'It's all over, sweetheart,' she said, 'and you've nothing to worry about now. You're quite safe, and Mr Forbes is our friend.'

I was too weak to understand it, but her voice reassured me, and I sank again restfully to sleep.

A little over a week later, and one bright afternoon I was reclining on a long wicker chair, well wrapped up and with a hat low down over my eyes, basking in the gentle glow of the warm winter sunshine.

Angas Forbes was sitting just beside me, but he was quite a different Angas Forbes from the one the reader has so far been introduced to. It was a kind, good-hearted and almost an affectionate friend that was near me now. A doctor who was in every way anxious and solicitous about his patient, and a man who was employing all that strength and shrewdness that had at one time been used against me, to protect and save me from my enemies.

'Keep your hat down, Cups,' he was saying in a half smile and a half frown. 'Remember, you're not out in the bush yet, and I don't want to do six months either, before we're clear of Adelaide, for hiding you from the police. You're much too reckless, man, and someone may recognise you yet from the street even in that beard.' He heaved a big sigh and shook his head at me. 'A nice thing I've been let in for at my time of life, haven't I?'

We were on the first-floor verandah of The Grand Australasian Hotel, and nearly three weeks had elapsed since that eventful night I had passed in the bed of chrysanthemums in the garden opposite. A lot had happened since then, and yet, in a way, a very little.

I had been in the hotel the whole time, and yet no one had come near me except Angas Forbes, and Margaret Price.

A complete change to all my fortunes had come, and it had taken me many days, even after I was comparatively all right again, to take it all in.

It appeared that when that evening I had collapsed so suddenly in front of Angas Forbes, the big Scotchman had been for a time in a dreadful quandary. He hadn't known what to do.

At first he had believed it to be his duty to hand me over at once to the police, but still he had hesitated to do it, for, in spite of his prejudice against me, I had half convinced him that all I had told him was true.

Unknown to myself, too, I had played a much stronger card than I had thought when I had pleaded for his protection because his dead friend would have had it so. He had almost a superstitious reverence for the man who had died.

A few years older than Dr Carmichael, he had been passionately devoted to him. They had been friends from early boyhood, and in the early struggles of their profession they had shared alike fortune and misfortune together. Their affection had been that of very loving brothers.

But of late years there had been a deeper reason still for his devotion to the dead man and, when he had told me of it, his voice had broken and shaken with all the intensity of tears that could never be completely shed.

The woman whom Dr Carmichael had protected, and who had been the cause of the great surgeon's disgrace, had been Angas Forbes's own sister and a sister he had dearly loved.

Angas Forbes had been abroad when it had all happened, but upon his immediate return his sister had confided everything to him. Stung one night to desperation by her husband's brutality, she had suddenly left her home at a minute's notice, and, believing that Dr Carmichael loved her, she had thrown herself on his protection. But Dr Carmichael, knowing at any rate the social ruin it would mean to her, had fought down his love and urged her resolutely to return.

She had refused, however, and in the end he had proudly become her lover and protector before all the world. When all the public scandal and disgrace had later eventuated, never by one world of explanation had he allowed the world to imagine that the fault was not wholly his.

But Angas Forbes had known it and, with the consequent ruin of his friend, his affection for him had become almost an obsession.

He had thought of all these things when that evening I had been lying unconscious on the sofa where he had placed me and, in the end, fearful that he would be wronging his dead friend if he acted otherwise, he had decided to give me the benefit of the doubt and save me.

Money can do most things in this world, and once he had made up his mind it was easy enough for Angas Forbes to make all the arrangements.

He himself had undressed me and put me to bed. Then he had informed the hotel people that a friend who had been visiting him had suddenly been taken ill, and it would be necessary the latter should remain in the hotel and also that a nurse should be got in to look after him.

Next – and he told me he had smiled grimly to himself as he did it – he had rung up the Raintons and had asked for Margaret Price to be sent to him at once.

Margaret Price was not unknown to him. The previous week he had been down to Dick Rainton to upbraid him for shielding me, and in the latter's absence it was the girl who had received him. They had had a fierce argument and, as Angas Forbes frankly admitted, the first real misgiving about my guilt had come to him then. Margaret had disclosed to him everything I had told her, and she had held up to scorn the very idea that I was by nature capable of such a murder.

He had not agreed with her, but he had seen enough of her to realise she was a woman he could trust, and so when he needed her he had unhesitatingly placed his secret in her hands.

She had agreed readily to nurse me, and so with no bond of sympathy between them, the two had started to try and lead me back to health, and at the same time prevent my identity from being discovered.

But the reserve between them had been suddenly broken down, and in a few hours there was no difference in the beliefs that they held about me.

I had become delirious, and in my delirium I had gone again over everything that had happened at the Tower House.

'Man,' said Angas Forbes to me afterwards, 'I saw your soul then, and I could never doubt you any more. It's not in nature for anyone in the delirium of a fever to be upon his guard.'

For a few days I had been very ill, and they had been terribly afraid my ravings would be heard, but Angas Forbes had drugged me heavily to quieten me, and in the end I had sunk to peace.

'I'll see you through, Cups,' had said the big Scotchman, the first day I was able coherently to take things in. 'We'll get you right away in a couple of weeks or so, if you only lie quiet.' He smiled kindly at me. 'And you shall marry Margaret here,' he went on, 'as a recompense for all the sufferings you have had.'

The short South Australian winter was over, and spring was everywhere in the air, when one fine morning Angas

Forbes and party were being almost devotionally bowed out of The Grand Australasian Hotel.

In no country in the world is there a greater adoration of hard cash than in Australia, and the fortunate possessor of money there can be assured always of a deeper reverence than was certainly ever accorded to any of the twelve Apostles.

The big Scotchman was at last going away and, true to his promise, he was seeing me clear from the perils of South Australia.

There were only three of us in the car and the owner was driving it himself. I was at the back, well muffled up, and beside me was Margaret Price.

The manager of the hotel bowed his head reverentially, Angas Forbes let in the clutch, and away the big car purred on its journey.

No word was spoken by anyone. I just drew in deep breaths and clutched hard to Margaret's hand.

About a mile from The Grand Australasian Hotel, the car pulled up suddenly at the corner of a side street. A man was waiting there. He was very quietly dressed and was carrying a small bag. He wore a big cap and the collar of his overcoat was turned up.

He made a sort of motion with his arm to Angas Forbes and, then, mounting quickly upon the car, he took his seat beside him. Immediately the car moved off and, gathering pace, went rapidly in the direction of the hills.

Sill none of us had said a word.

About a quarter of an hour later, the car was again stopped and Angas Forbes, turning round towards us, said solemnly, 'Now everyone, please, take your last look in this life upon the wonderful city of Adelaide.'

We were high up in the hills and close beside us reared the summit of Mount Lofty. A glorious panorama lay before our eyes. Far away below us stretched the city of the plains, and in the bright sunlight, every street and square and monument stood out sharply.

A great lump came into my throat, and I could feel the beatings of my heart. I thought of all that had happened there and the sorrow and the sweetness of life struck at me with twin hands.

'Now, friend Piper,' said Angas Forbes with a big laugh, 'what price a couple of years in the stockade? Rather be going to Brisbane, would you? Well, so would I.'

Sam Piper, for he was the stranger sitting on the front seat, grinned sheepishly, but made no reply, and a moment later the car went on.

Margaret leant over and kissed me, and a tear from her cheek I could feel was wetting mine.

It may be wondered how it had come about that Piper was a passenger with us in the car, but the explanation is very simple. It was Angas Forbes again.

As I was getting better, directly he had heard of all Piper had done for me, he made up his mind on the quiet to try and get him released at once and immediately he set about it in his own characteristic determined way.

Piper, as he had told me, was in the cells under remand and was obstinately refusing, as the police put it, 'to make a clean breast of the whole matter'. He had pleaded ignorance of the identity of the man to whom he had given Scut's job, and stubbornly asked them to produce proof, when they insisted it was me he had been hiding all the week.

The police were in a dilemma. They were perfectly sure I was the man he had hidden but, as I had escaped, they couldn't prove it. So, hoping desperately I should be captured and then perhaps confess, they had got the magistrate to remand Piper twice.

That was how the case stood when Angas Forbes began to take a hand in the game, and then very quickly things began to hum.

Through a third party he arranged that the best legal aid in the city should be obtained, and finally it was, in consequence, Drivel Jones whom they picked upon to defend the prisoner.

Imagine then the interest when on Piper's third appearance before the magistrate, up got the mighty Drivel Jones and began to shout and bully and bluster in his usual way. The magistrate, the police, and the whole court were fairly taken aback, and a forty-eight hours' further remand was as much as the great man would assent to.

But two days later the police had been as unprepared as ever to complete their case, and Drivel Jones had thundered and hectored in his best high-court manner.

The magistrate had been undoubtedly inclined to side with the police, and a long acrimonious wrangle had ensued, but in the end the great counsel had been too many guns for them all and, reluctantly, Piper had been discharged.

The same night Angas Forbes had interviewed him in his home, and chiefly, I believe, to give me pleasure, it had been arranged that Piper should accompany us in the car.

Three weeks after leaving Adelaide, Margaret and I were married in Brisbane, and my quondam enemy bade us goodbye, with the tears welling from his eyes.

It is a long while since the happening of the events I have recorded took place, and I have only put pen to paper now, after all this time, to wipe from the memory of Angas Forbes the slur some evil-minded people would place there.

My friend and protector died suddenly last year in Singapore, and I have heard lately that scandal has been busy with his name.

Something of what took place in those last days of mine in Adelaide, seven years ago, has somehow leaked out, and it has been suggested that Angas Forbes was bribed by me to hide me and get me out of Adelaide. It is said that for reward I gave him one-half the money I had obtained from the estate of Dr Carmichael.

It is a base lie, and on the face of it absurd. Angas Forbes was worth more than a hundred thousand pounds when he died, and for twenty years and more he had been a very rich man.

Apart from that he was a man of stern integrity and incapable all his life long of any mean or dishonourable action. All who knew him will bear witness to that.

I have not disclosed, for obvious reasons, the place of origin of this narrative, but it may interest our Adelaide friends to know that both my wife and I are very well and very happy. We have three children and, in a part of the world where no one is likely ever to find us, there is no stigma upon them because of their father's supposed misdeeds. They will grow up, we hope, without ever knowing that their father is still an escaped convict under sentence of five years.

THE END

AFTERWORD

Arthur Cecil Gask was born in England in 1869 and was educated at the University of London, where he studied medicine for several years, but discontinued the course in favour of dentistry. He took out a licentiate in Dental Surgery of the Royal College of Surgeons in England.

He came to Australia with his family in November 1920, and settled in Adelaide where he wrote all of his novels between 1921 and 1951, the year of his death. His first, *The Secret of the Sandhills* (Rigby, 1921), was written in his surgery to relieve the tedium of waiting for patients. It was printed at his own expense in South Australia and the one thousand copy print-run sold out in three weeks. The now-defunct Herbert Jenkins Publishing House of London took him on and his fiction was published by them for the next thirty years. On his death Gask had published thirty-four mystery and crime novels, most with English settings.

During his lifetime he was a well known writer in these genres. In the 1930s his mystery-thrillers had large readerships in England and Australia and his publishers promoted him as a best seller in Germany and Denmark. Later in his career, and particularly as his detective-hero Gilbert LaRose developed a large following, editions were published in America and Czechoslovakia. We have found twenty-eight LaRose titles, all published between 1929 and 1939. Gask's gratitude to his fictional hero was shown by his naming his farming property purchased at Burra, South Australia, 'Gilrose'.

Gask's readers came from all social classes. Several of his novels were serialised in Adelaide's daily papers and many prominent people world-wide were amongst his fans. Two of them provide us with evidence of how much smaller and less competitive than today was the broad English-speaking cultural world half a century ago. H.G. Wells wrote to the Jenkins Office in London in 1939: 'Many thanks for *The Vengeance of LaRose*, I think it is by far the best piece of story-telling Gask has done. It kept me up till half-past one last night.' Bertrand Russell, then Earl Russell, in a letter replying to Gask's gift of one of his novels in 1951, said, 'I always enjoy your stories, particularly when the criminal escapes.'

Russell must have had some enthusiasm for Gask's work, because he made a point of visiting him when he was in Adelaide in 1951. According to 'Vox', the *Advertiser*'s gossip columnist of the time, Gask described Russell, when 'in thoughtful repose', as 'an eagle high up on some lofty mountain summit regarding with brooding troubled eyes the vision of the great world stretching away so far before him'. This is an example of Gask's high style, which occasionally crept into his fiction. Perhaps he believed that portentous words were expected by the newspaper's readers in interviews with celebrities. Certainly, such solemnity was not in Gask's nature. His family remembers him as a wicked practical joker with a decidedly odd sense of humour. Many patients left him because of his penchant for relating obscene jokes while they were captive in the chair, Gask poised above them holding his probes and drill.

Gask's rather sinister playfulness comes out in *The Secret of the Garden* (1924) in the actions of the main character, Cups. In him, however, there is a violent streak, which contributes to his ambiguous status in the story. Gask's pointed wit usually is used to deflate the pompous and the powerful. The law is a favourite target, and chapter one is full of unmistakable vitriol and subdued social criticism, which must have been daring in their time. Cups's sneering contempt for the judge is brilliantly conveyed: 'He was curled and scented and had beautiful white hands. He was a well- known fop in private life.' There is the wild violence of his attack on Drivel Jones, 'the bully of the Bar', unscrupulous and bitter, who 'juggled and cheated with his racehorses as he juggled and cheated in the law'.

In another chapter, Gask puts into Cups's mouth a piece which is so violent in its attack on Adelaide society and its amoral obsequiousness to both old and new money, that it suggests a reality and a private anger that Gask could not control. 'Anyone with money is a god, anywhere. Here, you may be the biggest, vilest, ugliest, most diseased blackguard in the state, but if there's cash behind you, you're respected.'

This is about Gask as much as about Cups, the outsider, lonely, undervalued – Gask had only been in South Australia for two years when the book was written. These outcries of frustration appear regularly in *The Secret of the Garden*, normally as bursts of physical violence or as aggressive feelings towards those who, temporarily, are Cups's adversaries. The preposterously named John Archibald Cups is a modern anti-hero long before his time. It is certainly too much to claim that *The Secret of the Garden* is a beacon of modernity in the popular thriller and crime genre, but it does represent a break with the pre-World War I convention of upright hero, falsely accused, who is tested in adversity and eventually restored to his place in the social norm.

Our hero is not upright. The first chapter provides plenty of warning that there is an unpredictability and wildness about him that could erupt into criminality at any moment. He contemplates 'bashing' the gardener on the head for the sake of his old clothes; he steals money from the judge's desk, forges his signature and goes through his private papers.

Gask forces us to speculate whether Cups might not in fact be guilty of the embezzlement charges that perpetrated the events. His life through the course of the novel is an imposture.

False face, false identity, a financial fortune whose legitimacy is barely credible, except in Cups's self-justifying subjectivity. By the end, he embarks on another shadowy adventure, in a new country with a wife and secret destiny. The book's final sentence makes the leap to the modern with its tantalising ambiguity.

During Cups's journey of contradictory impulses there is much to enjoy in this book, especially the countless small touches which place it in another historical time. Adelaide, for instance, had more newspapers in those days!

The horrors of the World War I still loomed large in the popular psyche. Gask refers to that instant in the garden when Cups is nearly discovered by the gardener as his escape from Sedan, that disastrous carnage.

In a more playful and deliberately artful mood, Gask makes Cups work a variation on the King's Gambit in his solitary chess playing, a prefiguring of his intentions. This move, seldom used these days, was very popular in the nineteenth and early twentieth centuries. It is an aggressive opening which sacrifices pieces in order to get control of the centre board. It was used by players not afraid to get involved in complicated situations, the stuff of Cups's future.

While in the judge's house Cups 'went twice very carefully through (Shelley's) *Prometheus Unbound*'. The book has some significance for Cups – he steals it and carries it around with him. Presumably Gask sees Cups, as Shelley did Prometheus, as champion of mankind, as the ideal type of man. A fanciful notion? Probably. Perhaps he is offering a hint of the novel's ending and to Shelley's main theme, the regenerative power of love.

Whatever, it is the playful, teasing, Gask; self-consciously literary, too, but serious in his plotting. And struggling to find a new form for the crime thriller, one which clings to some traditional realities in the face of a new and meretricious world.

PETER MOSS AND MICHAEL J. TOLLEY

WAKEFIELD CRIME CLASSICS

Peter Moss and Michael J. Tolley, general editors of the Wakefield Crime Classics series, are colleagues at the University of Adelaide. Late in 1988, they began assembling a series of Australian 'classic' crime fiction and soon realised that the problem was not going to be one of finding sufficient works of high quality, but of finding a bold enough publisher fired with the same vision.

This series revives forgotten or neglected gems of crime and mystery fiction by Australian authors. Many of the writers have established international reputations but are little known in Australia. In the wake of the excitement generated by the new wave of Australian crime fiction writers, we hope that the achievements of earlier days can be justly celebrated.

If you wish to be informed about new books as they are released in the Wakefield Crime Classics series, send your name and address to Wakefield Press, Box 2266, Kent Town, South Australia 5071, phone (08) 362 8800, fax (08) 362 7592.

Also available in

WAKEFIELD CRIME CLASSICS

LIGNY'S LAKE
by S.H. Courtier

A dead man alive at Melbourne's Festival Hall . . . a merino-shaped lake . . . a stolen copy of Thoreau's *Walden* . . . ASIO's wall of silence.

Sandy Carmichael can pick up the jigsaw pieces, but to fit them together, he needs to risk his life.

Ligny's Lake is a puzzling story of suspense that weirdly echoes the disappearance of Prime Minister Harold Holt.

'S.H. Courtier is unjustly neglected. His works show a good narrative style, ingenious plots, and integral settings that are powerfully atmospheric.'
Whodunit?

'An intriguing and ingenious novel'
Stan Barney, *Canberra Times*

Also available in

WAKEFIELD CRIME CLASSICS

A HANK OF HAIR
by Charlotte Jay

Gilbert Hand hasn't been the same since his wife died. He's moved to a dull but respectable hotel where silence seems to brood in the hall and stairway. In a secret drawer he discovers a long, thick hank of human hair, and his world narrows down to two people – himself and the murderer.

'Stark horror told as genteely as a bedtime story. Excellent nightmare reading.'
London *Evening Standard*

'Takes the reader in with the first sentence. All the succeeding sentences line up neatly, shudder to shudder.'
Duluth *News-Tribune*

'There *are* Draculas and there *are* Dracula victims.'
Charlotte Jay

Also available in

WAKEFIELD CRIME CLASSICS

THE MISPLACED CORPSE
by A.E. Martin

Introducing Rosie Bosanky, Australia's original female private eye, 'alarming, disarming and altogether charming'.

'*The Misplaced Corpse* is an excellent read, and fun in the bargain. Highly recommended.'
Lucy Sussex, *Body Dabbler*

'*The Misplaced Corpse* is a well-woven whodunit, but Rosie herself is the main drawcard. She's street-smart, resolute, sexy, Runyonesque and a laugh a minute.
John Carroll, *Australian Book Review*

'Bosanky is thoroughly engaging in the patois of either the Bronx or New York's East Side. She translates into the 90s as well as Danny Devito drives a cab. She is a delight and worth reading.
David Lawrence, *West Australian*

Also available in

WAKEFIELD CRIME CLASSICS

THE WHISPERING WALL
by Patricia Carlon

Laid out like a fish on a slab, Sarah listens as the walls whisper their deadly plans.

'A claustrophobic, edge-of-the seat thriller ... tight, tense, beautifully controlled writing.'
John Carroll, *Australian Book Review*

'With a doff of the hat to Patricia Highsmith, Carlon's brand of horror is all the more chilling for being so maddeningly matter-of-fact. Carlon has a cold fish eye for the faults and foibles of her characters which contribute to the claustrophobic suspense of this quite brilliant book.'
Simon Hughes, *Melbourne Times*

'A compelling suspense novel reminiscent of Ruth Rendell's psychological thrillers.'
Jeff Popple, *Canberra Times*

Also available in

WAKEFIELD CRIME CLASSICS

VANISHING POINT
by Pat Flower

'Cruel, egotistical Noel, a thistledown, a cheap balloon whisking willy-nilly away from the piercing, deflating needle of her fine judgement.'

Geraldine needs to keep her cool through the highs and the lows, but it's maddening when Noel keeps missing the point.

The trek up north was gruelling, yet every plant and bird she saw, every sweaty, purposeless mile she crossed, convinced her that they were made for each other.

Back home in Sydney, when there's still a gap between them, he has to be made to see.

'Miss Flower stands out as exceptional.'
Edmund Crispin *Sunday Times*